EVE IN EGYPT

CAIRO FROM THE CITADEL.

GYASSA LADEN WITH STRAW.

[*Frontispiece*

EVE IN EGYPT

by

STELLA TENNYSON JESSE

illustrated with photographs taken by the author

ADELAIDE
MICHAEL WALMER
2018

Eve in Egypt first published 1929
under the pseudonym Jane Starr

This edition published 2018

by

Michael Walmer
49 Second Street
Gawler South
South Australia 5118

ISBN 978-0-6480233-6-4 paperback

THIS BOOK IS DEDICATED TO

F. T. J. & H. M. H.

THE PARENTS OF EVE

IN MEMORY OF

A

£10 BET

LIST OF CHAPTERS

LIST OF ILLUSTRATIONS

EVE IN EGYPT

CHAPTER I

BREAKFAST

THE funny thing was that Eve woke up that morning rather depressed than otherwise. " If," as she said to herself afterwards, " I had had that wonderful feeling that something beautiful was going to happen, I could have understood it; but to think that everything lovely in life began that morning, and that I never guessed it ! I only woke up with that horrid feeling of there being something unpleasant in the background. That does really seem odd."

And, after all, the something unpleasant had not been so very bad. To be exact, it was two proposals; and though Eve, like all nice-minded young women, deprecated the idea of a proposal that she couldn't accept, nevertheless there remained in her mind, as in the mind of every woman similarly situated, a pleasant residue— a sort of nice sugary sediment, as it were. After all, every proposal is a tribute to one's charms, there's no getting away from that.

" All the same," said Eve to herself, " this is too much of a good thing. It isn't as though I wasn't quite fond both of Harold and Hubert, but ever since Serena's appendicitis everything has gone wrong—even the weather ! Fancy being proposed to by two men on the same afternoon ! That's because it was a Friday. It's all very well for people to laugh at superstition, but Friday always has been my unlucky day."

B

Here Eve paused, for the best thing about her was a certain faculty for honesty, and at the back of her mind she realised that a far worse thing than being proposed to too much would be not being proposed to at all. After all, it was very difficult to believe that the queer creatures really suffered anything—they all got over it. Still, it had been uncomfortable and it had been Friday—two facts that she could hang on to. Her thoughts ran on self-pityingly. " I wish I hadn't got rather tangled up with them both and told them both I would think it over. People oughtn't to be allowed to propose on a wet day. One's vitality is lowered, and that makes one weak and foolish. I wonder what would be the safest time for it ? Half-way between meals, I think. I wonder——"

But Eve never worked out the correct time, for at that moment the maid knocked at the door and came in with her tea. She was a new girl, just come up from Eve's old home in the country, and who, beneath her decorous exterior, was thrilled to her utmost capacity by the knowledge that she was in a situation in London, after having spent all her life in a quiet Wiltshire village. Eve gave her that peculiarly personal and sweet smile which she could never resist bestowing even upon a total stranger who held a door open for her; and Rose thought how pleased Miss Eve must be to have her to wait on her after all these London hussies whom she couldn't know or care about.

Just like a picture, Miss Eve looked—a picture in that odd fashion paper that Rose had found yesterday—*Vogew*, or some such funny name. Only Miss Eve looked far, far lovelier, because she was so beautifully coloured, while the pictures in *Vogew* were only sort of greyish, like a photograph—only not as real.

When Rose drew the curtains Eve could see that the weather had changed, and for the better. The clear November sunshine, pale as wine, but as heady, shone in and filled the room with a dancing pallor that lit the white turn-over of the sheet to a luminous brightness and danced in a long shaft that touched Eve's yellow hair as though it loved it. Rose did love it, and loved also with an ungrudging generosity Eve's small leaf-shaped face that had the fine texture of a flower under the clear morning light. Rose, in her stiff blue dress, did not even grudge Miss Eve her soft, silky, lacy nightgown, nor any of the symbols of luxury that were scattered about the room. Rose did not have these things herself, but it was right and fitting that Miss Eve should, because she was so pretty and so kind.

And Eve, sitting up in bed and rubbing the sleep out of her eyes—which she liked to think of as green, but which other people called hazel—thought what a duck Rose was and how it was a shame that she couldn't have just as nice things as she, Eve, had. Which only shows that both Rose and Eve, although they both in their different spheres of life spread devastation around them, were what is called thoroughly nice girls.

" Oh, Rose," said Eve, " it's a nice morning, after all ! "

" It's been a lovely morning this hour past, Miss," said Rose, without any sarcastic intent.

Eve began to think she had been wrong to wake up with a feeling that all was not well. After all, what in life was as important as sunshine ? And there was no doubt about it, the sun was shining this morning. She took a few sips of her tea, while Rose moved quickly about the room, folding up everything that Eve had thrown on the floor the night before.

" Rose," said Eve with conviction, as she put down the cup, " I feel quite happy this morning."

" Do you, Miss ? " said Rose, with enthusiasm, as though Eve had said something marvellous.

" Yes. I don't know why. I suppose it's because the sun's shining."

" Oh, yes, Miss. And Archer says her ladyship feels so well that she's coming down to breakfast with you and Sir Hugh, Miss."

" Hooray ! Turn on my bath quickly, Rose—and I'll wear my new jumper suit to celebrate the occasion—the yellow Chanel that came home yesterday."

Rose had no idea what " Chanel " meant, but she did know that a new yellow jumper suit had arrived the day before; she had caressed it with reverent fingers. Now she flew about busily. She brushed Eve's short yellow hair until it shone, handed her the unnecessary but delightful powder and lip-stick, and both girls enjoyed equally the donning of the brief yellow skirt and jumper which made Eve look rather like an absurd but delicious flower-fairy in a pantomime—a sort of animated stage buttercup played by a small child so full of real enjoyment that it ceased to be artificial and really conveyed something of the tender dewiness of the field flower.

As she ran downstairs, Eve just remembered that she had been depressed when she first woke up—but then she hadn't known that the sun was shining and that it would be the sort of day on which she could, without being too much howled down by an irreverent family, wear her new frock. She found Serena and Hugh already at breakfast. How lovely to see her sister almost as rosy and almost as delightfully plump—and although it wasn't fashionable, somehow it did suit Serena !—as she had been before that wretched appendicitis. Even dear, quiet, dry old Hugh, who was so much the type of Army Officer and Empire-builder that he was almost too true to be real, seemed somehow different just because Serena was down again this morning.

Eve kissed them both, and then felt a slight return of her earlier feeling of depression as she saw two letters addressed to Miss Eve Wentworth, c/o Sir Hugh Erskine, awaiting her at her place; one in Hubert's carefully dashing handwriting, the other in Harold's meticulous and scholarly script. Eve felt sure that was how Harold always thought of his handwriting—as a scholarly script —and indeed she was quite right, as Eve often was when she didn't stop to argue things out with herself or with others.

"Fish or bacon?" inquired her brother-in-law, who was hovering over the dishes on the side-table.

"Fish *and* bacon," said Eve firmly, "and I shall probably want some kidney omelette afterwards," she added, as she opened the first letter. She put it down and opened the next. "Isn't there a thing called a 'prairie oyster'?" she asked as she put that one also aside. "It's something you have in wild-and-woolly-west novels when you've been playing poker the night before. It has Worcester sauce in it somewhere. It's quite likely I may want that, too."

Serena gave her attractive gurgly laugh. "I know exactly whom your letters are from, Eve," she said, "and on the whole I think Hugh's plan is an excellent one."

"Hugh's plan?" asked Eve, without paying very much attention, as she hunted through her herring to find whether or no it had a soft roe.

"Yes," said Hugh. "How would you like to spend the winter in Egypt?"

Eve dropped her knife and fork with a clatter and gazed first at Hugh and then at Serena.

"It's quite true, darling," said her sister. "At least, it may be. Of course there's a lot to settle first, but we've really been discussing it."

"But how?—Why?—When?" cried Eve.

"You tell her, Hugh," said lazy Serena, entrenching herself behind an egg.

"I've had a letter from Jeremy," said Hugh.

"From Jeremy? What on earth has he got to do with it?" cried Eve.

"He wants to hire a sailing dahabeah," Hugh explained, "and suggests that I go shares in it. A trip up the Nile would be just the thing for Serena; she could sleep all day in the sun, which is her idea of bliss. She'll get too fat, but it would certainly be good for her just now."

"I feel such a fraud," said Serena placidly. "I was never better in my life, and I'm sorry to say I've put on four and a half pounds."

"Still, you've got to go slow for a bit," said her husband. "There'll be no hunting for you this season, and you'll be out of temptation's way in Egypt. It fits in very conveniently with the end of my time at the War Office, and we might just as well spend my three months' leave abroad as in England."

"It would be too glorious for words!" cried Eve. "Of course we must go!"

"I may mention," observed Hugh, "that Jeremy doesn't know you're with us. The invitation doesn't include you, my dear Eve, as far as he's concerned. That's still got to be broken to him."

"Pooh!" Eve dismissed Jeremy with a careless wave of her fork. "What's the good of having known somebody more or less all your life if you can't descend on him unannounced?"

"You and Jeremy always quarrelled," Hugh pointed out.

"I was young then," observed Eve loftily. "It's quite two years since I've seen Jeremy. I've learned a lot about men since then."

It was Hugh's turn to put down his knife and fork and gaze at his young sister-in-law, which he did with rather a disconcerting twinkle in his small but pleasant green-grey eyes.

"Dear little Eve!" he murmured with disarming gentleness. "It will be great fun to watch you trying your arts on Jeremy. I suppose it's no good warning you that it will be about as much good as stroking the shell of the giant tortoise at the Zoo—or rather, I should say the shell of the snapping turtle."

"Jeremy doesn't snap," said Serena loyally, for she had a soft spot in her heart for Hugh's cousin.

Whether Jeremy snapped or not, Eve certainly did. Her little white teeth came together viciously as she glared at Hugh. "If Jeremy tries to snub me now like he used to do, I shall show him that everything's quite changed," she announced. "And anyway, it will be half your show, won't it, Hugh? So he won't be able to be very unpleasant.—Now, Serena, I know just what you're going to say. You're going to say that Jeremy was always very good to me and used to take me to matinées and give me boxes of chocolates. I know he did—but it was always with a 'pat-me-on-the-head,' and 'what-a-dear-silly-little-girl-you-are' sort of manner. That, as I say, is all changed."

But Serena was not listening. She had gone off on a train of thought of her own.

"If only it didn't mean leaving the children!" she sighed.

"My dear, they'll be perfectly happy at Wishford," said Hugh.

"Darling Serena!" cried Eve, her heart at once throbbing in sympathy with Serena's maternal feelings. "But it isn't as though Uncle Eric and Aunt Helen won't simply love having them. You know how beautifully they will look after them."

"Yes, I know," said Serena, "but I shall be terrified something may happen to them while we're out of England. Shan't you, Hugh?"

"Not in the least," said Hugh. "Why on earth do women always imagine something dreadful is going to happen? Your uncle and aunt made a very good job of bringing up you two orphans—and Heaven knows there was nothing of the 'angel child' about Eve!"

"Indeed!" said his sister-in-law coldly. "Well, let that pass. Tell me more about Egypt."

"Nothing more to tell you yet," said Hugh. "I shall fix it up to-night with Jeremy."

"To-night?" cried Eve.

"Yes. He's arriving from Paris this afternoon and coming to dinner. So put on your best bib and tucker, and try and look as though you knew how to behave."

" I certainly shall make no change either in costume or behaviour for Jeremy," said Eve with dignity. " Tell me, Serena, if you were me would you wear your new white, or the rose taffeta ? I think the taffeta is the prettier, really, but then the white is new."

Hugh pushed back his chair and moved towards the door.

" I'm glad you're not going to make any change for Jeremy," he remarked.

" I've been brought up in circles that are accustomed to dress for dinner," replied Eve. " As you're up, Hugh, you might take away this plate. What's the good of a herring without a soft roe ?—And as you're still up, would you give me an egg. No, no, not any one—see which is the brownest."

" It would do you all the good in the world, my child," said Hugh grimly, as he complied with both requests, " to have to rough it for a bit."

Eve gazed at him with enthusiasm, her lips parted in childlike excitement. " Do you mean that we shall really rough it in Egypt ? " she cried. " How perfectly thrilling ! "

Hugh, who was, above all things, the soul of honesty, gave a fleeting thought to the luxuries of Egyptian travel and tried to temporise.

" As to roughing it," he said in an oracular manner, " you'll have to ask Jeremy about that. He's the leader of this expedition."

But Eve paid no attention to him. She had produced a pencil from somewhere, and she and Serena, their heads together, had started to make out a list of clothes.

CHAPTER II

DINNER

EVE wore the rose taffeta, after having changed her mind at least six times while she dressed for dinner. As each change of mind necessitated also her one brief under-garment being changed, she was the last to arrive in the drawing-room—but, then, this was invariably the case. Punctuality was not one of Eve's virtues, and Hugh's soldierly mind could never accommodate itself to this simple fact.

" But what does she *do* ? " he would inquire of Serena regularly every day; and Serena would reply vaguely : " Oh, the usual things ! "

" If they're the usual things, I suppose they're what you do, too," Hugh argued; " and I know quite well what they are. It's exactly the same before breakfast or before dinner. You have your bath—you put an awful lot of stuff that you call cream and I call grease all over your face and take it off again—then you put on powder and lip-stick and do little twiddly things to your eyebrows—pull a comb through your hair—and there you are ! The whole blooming lot doesn't take you more than half an hour."

" I do put on clothes as well," Serena pointed out. " You've forgotten that."

" Oh, women's clothes nowadays ! " snorted Hugh. " Even Eve can't take long over that.—It's no good, Serena, I never shall be able to fathom what it is she does that takes all that time. I myself have seen her when she was absolutely ready to go out to dinner or a theatre, and then it's always twenty minutes more."

Hugh would subside grumbling, but the subject never lost its freshness and wonder for him, and half-way through breakfast every morning he would murmur : " I heard Eve's bath run out an hour ago. What, in Heaven's name, does she *do* ? "

Therefore neither Hugh nor Serena was surprised when Eve strolled into the drawing-room that evening five minutes after dinner had been announced. It was really for her excessively punctual. Hugh, whose one rule was that he waited dinner for nobody, had allowed Eve a little grace on this occasion because Serena had whispered to him urgently : " It won't be very nice for her if you don't, darling—because of Jeremy, you know."

" Jeremy will soon find out, if we go on this dahabeah, that meals must be quite regardless of Eve. However, I'll give her five minutes, and not a moment more."

Eve arrived without any undue hurry, cool and fresh, eyes shining with just the right amount of pretty excitement at the thought of meeting an old friend, and yet with no undue fluster. Serena, from whom the movements of Eve's mind were not hidden, could not but admire the perfect blend of feelings which Eve presented with such an air of *naïveté*.

Jeremy Vaughan, who was standing leaning against the mantelpiece, looked at Eve with a quizzical light in his deep-set eyes.

" Dear me, Eve," he said as he shook hands and then held her off at arm's length, surveying her, " you certainly do know how to do it ! " He beamed at her with his nice one-sided smile, and Eve's charming girlishness fell away from her, leaving her just a nice human Eve that twinkled back at him responsively.

" You always were a brute, Jeremy," she said. " Don't you know that's quite the wrong thing to say ? You ought to think that all this effect is got without any trouble at all. If you'd led a more innocent life you would think so."

" My life's been extremely innocent the last year in Thibet," said Jeremy. " I defy it to be anything else in a country where the chief drink is tea with rancid butter melted in it. But the charm of your sex, dear Eve, is that none of you change. There are ages in which you are more so, perhaps, although there probably have never been ages when you were less so. Lately I've been furbishing up my Egyptian reading, and to anyone who has really followed out in detail the toilette and attire and general habits of an ancient Egyptian lady there are no secrets, believe me."

" That's what's so nice about the present day," said Serena. " Twenty years ago women had to pretend their complexions were the work of Nature alone— which, Heaven help them, they generally were ! Now a properly regulated face is a sort of uniform. Everyone knows it, and the only indecent thing would be to be caught without it."

" It's very convenient for you especially," Hugh pointed out, " because you're so darned lazy that you can't bother to do it properly. Not that it matters a bit in your case, because anyone could say to you : ' By the way, do you know you've only put rouge on one cheek and you've covered your nose with it instead of powder ! ' and you'd change it without being in the least embarrassed. A man would be terribly upset if it were pointed out to him that by mistake he'd shaved his eyebrows instead of his chin."

" I am rather careless, I'm afraid," confessed Serena placidly. " Let's go down to dinner. It was ready ages ago, you know, Eve darling."

" I'm so sorry," said Eve. " I can't think what happened. I got all sort of muddled."

" You probably didn't have enough tirewomen, Eve," remarked Jeremy as they went downstairs. " Wait till you've seen them all on an Egyptian frieze. You'll be green with envy. A different handmaid with each pot and bottle, all lined up in a row, like cabs on a rank."

" Oh, how lovely ! " breathed Eve rapturously.   " I suppose they took hours over getting up and going to bed."

" For Heaven's sake," said Hugh in alarm, " don't encourage Eve to take any longer than she does at present.   What you *do*, Eve, I can't for the life of me imagine."

Eve looked mysterious and womanly and started to eat her soup.

" Jeremy's got it all planned, darling," said Serena. " He's even written about the dahabeah."

" Eve may despise the one I have in mind," said Jeremy.   " It's the least of the dahabeahs, and hardly meet to be called a dahabeah, as the apostle said.   None of your big, vulgar, steam contraptions."

" I shall adore it ! " cried Eve.   " And is it really all settled ?   When do we go ? "

" We're probably sailing by a Messageries Maritimes boat from Marseilles on the twenty-third of December," said Hugh.

" Oh, dear ! that gives us less than a month for clothes."

" You won't want any clothes," said Jeremy cheerfully.

" What nonsense ! " said Eve.   " I've always heard that you've to be dreadfully smart in Egypt.   Tea on the terrace at Shepheard's, you know, and all that sort of thing," she concluded vaguely.

" My good child," said Jeremy, " we shall get in and out of Cairo as quickly as possible, and on board of our dahabeah, where it won't matter in the least what you look like.   As to people being smart in Egypt nowadays, why, good Lord ! you never saw such a collection in all your life.   It was bad enough when I went there a couple of years after the War—and I believe it's far worse now.   Earnest, high-brow school-marms who've saved up for years to do the trip—they'll be your only competitors.   Hardly worth your powder and shot—or should I say your powder and lip-stick ? "

" Women—outside of Thibet—dress for their own self-respect," explained Eve loftily.

" I thought women dressed for men," said Hugh.

" In spite of Thibet," said Jeremy blandly, " even I know better than that. Women dress for each other."

" Not at all," was Serena's contribution. " You're both equally old-fashioned. Eve is quite right—we dress for ourselves, and if it weren't that I should love to wear nothing at all if I were on a desert island by myself, I should take just as much care over arranging my fringes of palm leaves and seaweed as I do here over my Paris frocks.—By the way, Eve darling, I went to that place I told you of this afternoon, and I find that they will let us have their summer models really absurdly cheap, as the season's over. If we have six inches taken off the hem they'll be perfect."

Hugh groaned and started to talk to Jeremy about Thibet; but Eve listened, her soul in her eyes, while Serena described the various beauties of the summer models.

Nevertheless, the greater part of Eve's attention was fixed upon Jeremy, and she was acutely aware of his thin, sensitive face, with its twisted smile. It was funny how Jeremy, although not above medium height, being a slight, wiry man, whose frame concealed rather than displayed strength, always looked what the Americans call " a person." You simply couldn't not notice Jeremy, although he talked so quietly. Perhaps it was partly because most people knew about him and the wonderful things he'd done in the Mespot campaign, living for weeks and months disguised as a native and getting the most marvellous information.

Rather nice to be a man—and a clever man—and able to do things like that to help your country in time of need. It was tiresome of Jeremy that he never would talk about himself, but she knew that there was no one living whom Hugh admired more than his quiet, apparently casual cousin. Eve admired him too, but she couldn't help wishing that he would be a little more human—" By which, I suppose," she said to herself, " I mean I wish he'd show more interest in me. And yet I shouldn't like him half as much if he did. After all, one doesn't have to pretend anything with Jeremy. It's nice to have someone like that round about you when you're rather overdone with Huberts and Harolds ! "

After dinner Jeremy came and sat beside Eve and demanded the history of her misspent life since he had last seen her. He said, " Splendid ! " when Eve confessed that she was in a slight difficulty at the moment with two of her young men, in fact, almost engaged to both of them at the same time.

" Perhaps we can find a Sheik for you in Egypt," he said, " à la Ethel M. Dell."

" Sheiks aren't Ethel M. Dell—they're E. M. Hull," corrected Eve, " and I should hate to be knocked about and thrown across Arab steeds and all that sort of thing."

" You never know whether you'll like a thing or not until you've tried it," said Jeremy philosophically. " I daresay Harold and Hubert would do a bit better if they tried the Sheik touch."

Eve felt a little annoyed. She didn't like the attitude of her lovers to her, or hers to them, treated with levity by other people, however casually she might take these things herself.

" I'm the chief sufferer," said Hugh, as he handed Jeremy a whisky and soda. " I'm always having to give Eve's young men lunch at my club and listen to their woes and give them good advice."

" And what is your advice ? " asked Jeremy.

" Treat her rough, I tell them," replied Hugh.   " But the poor devils can never do it. Most of the men she meets are too ready to run after her. What she wants is to be made to do the running herself for a change."

" I wonder," said Jeremy.

" I don't wonder," said Hugh.   " I know."

CHAPTER III

ALEXANDRIA

EVE stood at the carriage door waving a cheerful good-bye to the gloomy figures of Harold and Hubert, as the train glided out of Victoria Station.

"Poor things!" she said brightly, as she settled comfortably into her seat and opened the *Daily Mirror*, "I do feel sorry for them. Fancy having to stay behind in this awful climate and see other people off to Egypt! I'll send them a lot of picture post-cards."

And she really thought of them quite often during the journey down France, and sent each of them a picture post-card of Marseilles, posted on board the boat, and wrote just the same words on both of them, so as to be quite fair.

Serena, after one glance at a grey, heaving Gulf of Lions, shuddered with repulsion at Hugh's suggestion of lunch and went straight to her cabin.

"It's so much wiser to give in at once than to stay up till the last moment but one, and then have that ghastly, wobbly stagger down to your cabin," she said to Eve, as she snuggled down into bed. "And undressing is so awful, when you're feeling like death. Will you be an angel and open my dressing-case again, and in the back right-hand corner you will see a little, square, flat box? If you'll give me that and a glass of water, darling, I shan't want anything more, and you can go off to your revolting meal."

"What have you got in here?" inquired Eve. "Oh, I see—it says on the lid. 'Keepdown—the World-Famous Sea-sick Remedy. Two capsules, one green

15

and one purple, to be swallowed an hour before motion of train, steamer or airship is expected.'—My dear, where did you get it ?   Did Dr. Lamb give it you ? "

" No, I got it myself from the chemist's."

" But you must *never* take a strange medicine unless the doctor has ordered it.   It's most dangerous ! "

" Oh, but I know this is all right, because when I was playing bridge the other night at Mrs. Hamilton's, I happened to mention ' Keepdown,' and she said she knew a girl who had taken it going to India, and it was simply marvellous, and it didn't do her any harm.   She got a sore place on her lip, but that was from something quite different."

" How did she know ?   Anyway, I should never take anything on Mrs. Hamilton's recommendation."

" No, but that's because you don't like her.   But it wasn't only Mrs. Hamilton.   That tall, dark man at the chemist's—the one who did so well in the War, you know—assured me it was really splendid, and perfectly safe.   He spoke most enthusiastically about it."

" Well, that does make a difference.   He was so sympathetic when poor Mac had that eczema between his toes, and the ointment he made up for him did far more good than the vet's.—Oh, but what horrible-looking things !   I should think they *are* green and purple !   It's wise of them to warn you on the cover. Which do you take first ? "

" Do you think it matters ?   They'll so soon be one."

" It sounds like the Marriage Service, but I suppose they will.   Here's the glass of water.   I should take the green first, it looks slightly the less deadly of the two."

In spite of her faith in the tall, dark man Eve could not repress a slight shudder as she watched Serena close her eyes and reverently swallow first the green and then the purple dose, and her relief was considerable when she looked in after a very good lunch to find Serena sleeping peacefully.   This state of things continued

OLD MAN TURNING BREAD TO DRY.

WATER CARRIERS WITH GOATSKINS AT ESNA.

[To face page 16.

during the afternoon, but Eve and Hugh began to feel rather uneasy when it came to dressing for dinner and Serena's slumbers still continued. The boat was pitching and tossing a good deal by then, and she would normally have been much more actively employed.

" It isn't a healthy sleep," said Hugh, " and anyway it's time she had nourishment of some sort."

So they woke her up, as much as they could, and talked encouragingly to her of clear soup, cold chicken, fresh air, making an effort, and all the other horrible things good sailors urge upon bad ones. Serena remained quite unmoved.

" I'm sho happy, sho very, very happy," she murmured drunkenly, with the beatific smile of advanced intoxication. Then the heavy lids closed again, and again she slept. The capable Australian stewardess took in the situation at a glance.

" It takes some of them like that," she explained cheerfully, as she raised Serena's head and skilfully administered half a dozen spoonfuls of soup with a practised hand. Serena swallowed mechanically, her eyes still shut, and Hugh and Eve averted their own in shame as the limp head was replaced upon the pillow and the woolly voice murmured once more : " I'm sho happy—sho very, very happy."

The next day, when the stuff had had time to wear off a little, they tried to reason with her, to rouse her to a belated sense of shame. But Serena only smiled at them with her usual sweet placidity, and remarked complacently that at any rate she hadn't been sick.

" It would have been far better for you if you had," said Hugh severely.

" That's the sort of remark only a good sailor makes," observed Serena gently.

" It's very injurious to drug yourself like that."

" Still—I wasn't sick."

" But you looked so—so abandoned," said Eve.

" Like a drunk without the disorderly," said Hugh.

c

" Exactly," agreed Eve.   " We were ashamed for even
the stewardess to see you."

They waited in silence for an apology, for some slight
expression of contrition, but none came.   Serena was
asleep again.

On the last morning of the voyage, when the sun
shone brightly and a light breeze whipped the blue water
into little crests of foam, Eve lay in her deck-chair beside
Serena's and watched the pale coast of Africa slipping by.

" Wake up ! " she said firmly, giving her sister's arm
a gentle shake.   " In an hour or two we shall be in
Alexandria."

Serena blinked a few times and then sat up briskly.

" Alexandria ! " she exclaimed.   " That's where Cleopatra lived."   Serena took the intense interest in Cleopatra that the respectable woman invariably takes in the
free-lance.

" Quite right," said Eve encouragingly.   " In a marble
palace so huge that it was like a small town—Jeremy
says—with a wide flight of marble steps that led down
to the water, where her state galley was moored; it had
great purple sails and banks of rowers with silver oars,
and Cleopatra used to lie under an awning with festoons
of flowers hung around her while her players made music
for her as she sailed.   It must have been great fun to be
Cleopatra," added Eve, a little wistfully.

" Darling !   Not to have to end with a bite from a
nasty serpent," Serena shuddered.

" Well, no, but she had great fun for a long time
before that, what with Cæsar and Antony and everything.—And to think that all that happened in Alexandria
and that there isn't a trace of anything left !   It's too
bad."

" Yes, isn't it ? " agreed Serena.

" I didn't know much about Alexandria until Jeremy
told me about it last night," continued Eve, " except
that it was founded by Alexander the Great.   According
to Jeremy it was a most beautiful city, with wide streets

lined with white palaces and gardens full of flowers and magnificent theatres and the Temple of Serapis, and a marvellous museum—fancy there being anything old enough to put in a museum then !—and the Pharos, which must have been the most wonderful thing of all."

" I seem to have heard of that," murmured Serena.

" It was the first lighthouse ever built, you know, all of white marble from top to bottom. It was one of the Seven Wonders of the World. I always forget the others, except the Pyramids and the Hanging Gardens of Babylon; they always stick in my mind because they sound so thrilling. I'm going to struggle with Kingsley's ' Hypatia ' again, because she lived in Alexandria, and was murdered there, too, poor thing ! Hullo ! here are Hugh and Jeremy all dressed up ready for the shore. —How beautiful you both look ! "

" We are beautiful," agreed Jeremy. " Had a good sleep, Serena ? "

" Fairly good, thank you."

" Only fairly good ? Has Eve been chatting ? "

" I have been very intelligent," said Eve proudly. " Jeremy, what were the Seven Wonders of the World, not counting the Pyramids and the Hanging Gardens of Babylon and the Pharos ? "

" The Temple of Diana at Ephesus, the Colossus of Rhodes, the statue of Jupiter at Olympus and the Tomb of Mausolus. My poor Serena ! Has it been as bad as all that ? "

" And to think that the Pyramids are the only one left, and that we are actually going to see them ! " said Eve. " I can hardly believe it."

" We are going to see Alexandria, such as it is, in an hour or so," said Hugh, " so we'd better go down to lunch now, or Eve will never be ready. It would be a pity if she got carried on to Syria and never saw the Pyramids after all."

Early in the afternoon the big steamer sidled up to the quay, and Eve leant over the side with Jeremy, watching the busy scene in the crowded harbour, and the small boats, full of shouting, dusky porters who turned the place into pandemonium. When she eventually landed, she found, as Jeremy had warned her, an uninteresting modern, commercial town, the centre of whose religion was the Cotton Exchange instead of the Temple of Serapis. As the Cairo train was not due to leave until the evening, they spent the waiting time driving round the suburbs in an open car, in one of the iciest winds Eve and Serena had ever been out in, so that they snuggled into their fur coats and blessed Jeremy for having told them to bring warm clothes to Egypt. They drove through what Eve described as " a Hampstead Garden Suburb, built by a French architect." Ornate villas, closed for the winter, stood in bleak, uninteresting gardens, and several of the wealthiest-looking houses had untidy stretches of waste land beside them which did not add to their gaiety.

" I don't like Alexandria," announced Eve firmly.

" It has the most perfect summer climate in Egypt," said Hugh.

" It needs to have something decent," she retorted. " Personally, I think its winter climate has given me pneumonia."

The only spot that interested Serena was the Ras-el-Tin Hospital, built round a square garden shaded with palm trees, down by the sea; for it was here that Hugh had spent several weeks recovering from wounds got in the Allenby campaign. The hospital was shut up now, but Hugh was able to point through a window to where, in an empty ward, his bed had once stood. Serena flattened her nose against the window-pane, and was duly thrilled.

" Darling," Eve heard her say, " just fancy if you'd never come back ! " And she saw Serena's hand slip into Hugh's, which gave it a quick, responsive squeeze. Eve felt a little out of it, and oddly forlorn, standing there in the windy courtyard of the Ras-el-Tin, with the palms blowing above her with a dry, derisive noise.

This finished their two hours' sight-seeing, and every-one was thankful to get into the train out of the cold wind. Dusk was short, and night fell soon after they had started, so that Eve had to give up staring out at Africa, and was glad when it was time for dinner.

In the middle of the meal things took an unexpected turn. The lights in the dining-car were suddenly extinguished and a steward entered, impressively bearing aloft a flaming Christmas pudding.

"Why, it's Boxing Day!" cried Eve, "I'd quite forgotten. How perfectly sweet of them!"

"I shudder to think of the quality of the brandy, judging from the height of the flames," said Hugh.

"Don't be superior," commanded Eve.

"Women and children first," murmured Jeremy, fighting the flames gallantly with a spoon and fork, as he helped the two girls.

Each member of the party took a mouthful. . . . A curious expression stole over every face.

"What on earth is it?" asked Hugh.

"I can't imagine," said Jeremy.

"I know," said Serena with a look of surprise. "It's chocolate pudding."

"How horrible!" Hugh pushed his plate a little away from him.

"Pooh! That's only because you're so conservative," cried Eve scornfully, "and have never had chocolate pudding and hot brandy together before. *I* think it's perfectly heavenly," and she proceeded to eat every morsel. The others watched her with no small alarm; nor did they feel quite happy about her until, back in their own compartment again, she fell into a child-like slumber which lasted until Cairo was reached. Then she stumbled out of the train, blinking sleepily like a little owl, and only just able to notice that the station had a satisfyingly Eastern appearance before she started nodding again on the drive to the hotel.

The manager showed them to their suite high up on

the fourth floor, and flung open the French windows leading on to the balcony.

There, far below them, Eve saw the Nile, with the lights of the big hotel reflected in the dull gleam of the water. On the further bank a fringe of tall palm trees stood darkly against the night sky.

"In the morning, Mademoiselle," said the manager, "you will be able to see the Pyramids; over there," and he pointed to the left.

"Oh-h-h!" breathed Eve, on a long sigh of fatigue and rapture.

She went in again reluctantly, got quickly ready for bed, and fell asleep to the sound of a mournful Arab chant and the distant barking of many dogs.

CHAPTER IV

THE PYRAMIDS

WHEN Eve opened her eyes the next morning the words of the hotel manager swam up in her mind, and she jumped out of bed at once, slipped her feet into her little " mules," pulled on a silk wrapper and ran out on to the balcony. The sun was shining, though it was still too early for any warmth to be in its rays, and the Nile, which last night had looked so dark and mysterious, was now a pale greenish-brown, sparkling with a myriad little ripples in the bright light. The palm trees on the further bank now showed themselves to be a large plantation, and a tall minaret reared its graceful head from amid the plumy green. So great was Eve's sense of anticipation that it was almost with an effort she turned her eyes southward. She looked—and for a moment she caught her breath with the wonder of what she saw. There they were—three dark, mysterious peaks rising out of the thick cloud of mist that still floated over the land, with something remote, almost stark, about their definite shapes, so arrogant in their immutability.

Eve had never imagined her first sight of them would be like this. She had thought of them, as she had often seen them pictured : as great cones rising out of the golden sand, tawny in the sunlight or silvery-white under the light of the moon. Now, in their darkness, their mist-enshrouded isolation, they were utterly strange, but very wonderful, and however she was to see them in the future, she knew this first impression would always be the most intense.

23

" People must feel like this who see the sea for the first time," she thought, and shivered a little with excitement in the cold morning air. But she had, besides her excitement, a curious sensation of insignificance, and as Eve was not used to feeling insignificant, perhaps this was rather good for her. She had a moment of wonder that she, such a small atom in a vast world, should find herself in this particular spot, looking at these unchanging shapes. Though built by man, the vast age of the Pyramids, and the fact that from earliest childhood they were a part of nearly every mind, even of the half-educated, made them appear symbols of Eternity. The last remaining of the Seven Wonders of the World! However long the earth were to last, they surely would remain, till conscious life itself had perished.

A footstep on the adjoining balcony made Eve look round, to see Jeremy emerge in a decidedly gaudy dressing-gown, smoking a cigarette.

" Well ? " he asked.

" Oh, Jeremy ! " she replied, and from the withdrawn look in her eyes he saw what this experience had meant to her.

" Of course you've seen them ever so often," she added, after a moment's silence.

" Yes, but with the same thrill every time."

" I don't wonder."

Eve's teeth were beginning to chatter with cold, and Jeremy looked at her with his most practical expression.

" You mustn't stay out here," he said—" not in that flimsy thing, at any rate. Run back to bed at once and get warm."

" Bed ! " cried Eve indignantly. " Do you think I'm going back to bed on my very first morning in Egypt ? "

" How would you like a walk before breakfast, then ? "

" I'd love it."

" How long will you take to dress ? "

" A quarter of an hour."

Jeremy raised his eyebrows.

" Indeed I will." And she was only another fifteen minutes longer than her word. When he knocked at her door exactly half an hour later—an act in itself an insult, as she would have pointed out if only she had been ready earlier—she came out looking as fresh as a rose. She was attractively garbed even to Jeremy's critical eyes, all in white, with a white felt hat pulled down over her yellow hair, where a few drops of water from her bath still glittered. How many women of his acquaintance, Jeremy wondered, could turn out like that at eight o'clock in the morning ?

He bought her a bunch of violets from the flower-seller outside the hotel, and she pinned them in her coat as they went along the shady walk by the river. Everything she saw was new and exciting to her. There were no women in the streets, but the men were delightfully strange in their long robes, which Eve thought of as nightgowns, with their dark faces under turban or fez. Halfway across the bridge Jeremy stopped for Eve to look at a fleet of gyassas coming up the Nile before the wind.

" How lovely ! " she cried. " They are just like swallows."

" That's the lateen rig," he told her, " the rig most like a swallow of any in the world, and thousands of years old. The earliest known sea-going vessels were built by the Egyptians."

" How funny ! You'd have thought it would have been us."

" Modest little thing ! "

" Well, if anyone talks of ships and sailors you do automatically think of us, don't you ? They're so important to people living on an island."

" And to people living on the Nile."

" I suppose they are. I remember reading somewhere, ' The Nile is Egypt—and Egypt is the Nile.' "

" Yes, and it's as true to-day as it always was. When

you sail up it you will see it for yourself.   There's desert
on the right hand and on the left; but in the strip of
land, the narrowest and most fertile in the world, on
either side of the river, you'll see the amazing richness
of the country to-day side by side with the remains of
the commerce and art and richness of the oldest of all
civilisations."

Eve's eyes turned from contemplation of the flowing
grey-green river to Jeremy's face.   He was not looking
at her; indeed, his intent and shining gaze was fixed
not so much on the actual pageant of the Nile spread
before him as on some inward vision of his mind.   It
was the first time Eve had caught sight of the dreamer
that lived within this man of action, and it came to her
with a little sense of shock that in Jeremy were whole
tracks of thought and knowledge of which she was
ignorant.   She thought rather wistfully that, to him,
she must seem a very futile little person.   But Jeremy,
suddenly bringing his gaze and his attention to bear
upon his companion, thought : " She seems different
somehow. . . . Of course, Eve couldn't *feel* humble,
but she looks it all of a sudden. . . . It would be rather
worth while if I could only make her feel and see Egypt
as it ought to be seen and felt. . . . I believe there is a
good deal more in Eve than people guess."

How thrilled Eve would have been could she have
known what was passing through the mind of Jeremy !
But, perhaps fortunately, this could not be, and so she
turned her whole attention to the subject of Egypt, and
Jeremy's new idea of her remained undisturbed.

" Jeremy," she asked meekly, as they crossed the road
into the public gardens, " how did it all begin—Egypt,
I mean ?   Why was the Egyptian civilisation so much
the earliest ? "

" It can't be proved that it was," Jeremy began, " but
the first records of civilisation have been found here.
The country's climate and its geographical position were
its great assets.   In the rest of the world, prehistoric

man had to spend all his time fighting for the bare necessities of life—food and warmth—and when he'd got them he had to defend them from his enemies. But here in Egypt the sun always shone and the soil was so fertile that the people only had to scratch it and drop in their seeds. They had no fear of invasion either. They were protected on the north by the sea, which no one learned to cross for thousands of years, on the east and west by immense deserts, and on the south by huge tracts of savage, uninhabited country. Nor could enemies make their way up the Nile, for a natural barricade of hundreds of miles of rocks and foaming cataracts made it impossible. The Egyptians were able to build, to make laws and to develop a great art, because they had leisure and security, the two things essential for building up a civilisation."

By now Jeremy had forgotten all about Eve as an individuality, and was fairly launched on a subject near his heart. Eve listened entranced, and it seemed to her that she was beginning, very incompletely and faintly, to grasp what Egypt has meant to the world by seeing what it meant to Jeremy. Touch by touch, as they strolled back to the hotel in the freshness of the pearly morning, he built up for her the wonder of the most ancient of civilisations, its unsurpassed art and its strange religion, forerunner of all others. She had known in a vague sort of way that Egypt was called the " cradle of civilisation," but what before had been only a phrase to her, now became a real and intelligible fact.

Back once more at the hotel, they stopped for a moment at the foot of the steps. Jeremy noticed what a glowing pink the keen air had brought to Eve's cheeks.

" I say, I've talked an awful lot," he said apologetically.

" Oh, I loved it ! " Eve was enthusiastic. " I've always longed to come to Egypt, and now I'm actually here I'm going to learn all about it that I possibly can. There are lots of things I've always wanted to see, and I ought to find some of them here."

" What are they ? "

" One is a man on a camel in the desert, outlined against a sunset. I know it sounds awfully like a picture post-card, but I do want to see it. And the other thing is something to hear, not something to see—a muezzin calling the faithful to prayer from a minaret."

Jeremy laughed. " You'll come across plenty of both before we've done."

" How gorgeous ! There are lots of other things I want, but I really think those come first at the moment."

" Do they ? " Jeremy carefully selected three or four of her violets.

" I hope you will always get what you want as easily," he added, pulling the long stems of the flowers through his button-hole.

" Thank you. Is there anything you want that you haven't got ? "

His dark eyes met hers, and she remembered his old trick of smiling with them while his mouth was grave.

" No. But there's something that I have which I want very much to keep."

" Oh, what is it ? "

" I hope I'll never have to tell you."

Eve could have sworn at him, only she never swore before breakfast.

" Then it's no good asking what it is ? "

" None at all," replied Jeremy cheerfully.

CHAPTER V

MOUSSA

At breakfast the four of them made their plans for the day.

"What ought we to see first?" inquired Eve, her mouth rather full of roll and honey.

"The Sphinx is having her toilet done," said Hugh; "the manager told me so last night. I don't suppose you two girls want to see her done up in scaffolding, do you?"

"I should think not," said Eve. "It would be like letting strangers see us when our faces are covered with cold cream. What a blow!"

"We shall have to leave her for the return journey," said Jeremy, "and we ought to leave most of Cairo till then too, as it's a mediæval and modern town. You'll see it in the wrong order if you see it now."

"Isn't there a museum?" asked Serena.

"Don't!" groaned Hugh. "The mere idea always gives me a crick in my neck and makes my feet too big for my shoes. Can't we leave that for the return journey too?"

"Coward!" cried Eve.

"Let's take away his D.S.O.," suggested Jeremy. "All the same it would be better to give the museum a go-by for the present. Most people make the mistake of going there directly they arrive. If they waited till they'd been up and down the Nile they'd understand what they were looking at."

"It's never difficult to put any member of this family off a museum," said Serena; but Eve, who was eager not to miss anything, inquired anxiously:

" What are we going to do, then ? "

" Hugh and I have to interview Cook's representative this morning," said Jeremy. " He is coming here at ten o'clock, and after that we are all going to look at our dahabeah. It's nearly ten now."

A few minutes later a waiter announced Mr. Johnson, of Cook's.

Mr. Johnson proved to be an excessively clean-looking man, with a rosy face, bright blue eyes and very white teeth. He looked rather like a large baby perpetually in the state of having just been dressed after its bath. In spite, however, of this innocent, not to say infantine air, he had the whole of the business of the Nile at his finger-tips.—Their dahabeah was ready for them, and he produced their charter out of his pocket, and told them in a few brief sentences most of the things that they should and should not do, to ensure health and comfort.

" Don't eat salad," he said, " once you've left Cairo. It's never safe."

" Why not ? " asked Eve, who was a perfect rabbit for green food.

" It may be grown in germ-sodden earth, you never know," said Mr. Johnson. " It isn't that they don't wash it and make it quite clean, but they don't understand anything about microbes."

" Well, I don't know," observed Hugh. " They always said the same thing in Malta when I was stationed there. None of the Service people would touch salad until I arrived, but I ate it the whole time, and never had anything the matter with me."

" I always ate it in the East," said Jeremy, " when I was lucky enough to get it, which wasn't often. After all, what's the good of having typhoid injections if you can't eat oysters and salad ? The only other danger is drinking water, and speaking for myself and you, Hugh, I feel sure neither of us wants to do that."

" Oh, I think we must have salad," said Serena

placidly. "I have always brought the children up on salad."

"It's so good for the complexion," said Eve, and that, at least for the moment, seemed to settle the matter.

"You must do as you like about it, of course," said Mr. Johnson. "I dare say it's quite all right. The residents wouldn't care to do it, though, but I often notice tourists can do with impunity what residents cannot. Now I want to show you your dragoman—he is waiting in the corridor, as I thought you might like to have a look at him. He has been with us nearly thirty years, and we consider him one of our best men. In fact, in all those years we have only had one complaint of him, and that was from some Americans he was with last winter. They found him lacking in 'pep.'"

"That's our man," said Hugh firmly. "If there's one thing more than another which this party lacks it is 'pep.' He will suit us down to the ground."

Mr. Johnson smiled.

"I am sure you will find he will take the greatest care of you all, and he prefers a sailing dahabeah to a steam one. May I call him in, Lady Erskine?"

"Please do."

Mr. Johnson opened the door and called: "Moussa."

There entered an enormous man, attired in a simple costume of striped strawberry-and-white sateen. His long robe reached nearly to his ankles, where it was slit up a little on either side like a nightshirt, thus allowing a chaste view of patent leather boots with grey cloth uppers, green worsted socks held up by a striking pair of Boston velvet grips, and a modest inch or two of bare leg. On the upper part of his person he wore a short reefer jacket, such as a child wears over a sailor suit, with brass buttons, and "Dragoman" embroidered in red on the left arm. Round the outer curve of his stomach, which was a noble one, was a sash of white cords. The whole was crowned by a fez, under which his round, chocolate-coloured face beamed with smiles.

His under-lip was a caricature of the famous Hapsburg one, and his tongue appeared to be so much too large for his generous mouth that either Nature or a dentist had thoughtfully removed his lower teeth to make room for it. When he talked, his tongue worked its way through the orifice and waved about in an attractive, *négligé* manner, making his speech a little thick. Serena and Eve decided at once that he was the kindest man they had ever seen, as indeed he proved to be, though it was not long before they were to realise that he was a benevolent despot in whose hands they were as wax. Weeks later, looking back on their first meeting, they realised it had been the occasion of their one and only victory. It was on the question of supplies. Mr. Johnson having left the room to reply to a telephone call, Hugh, Jeremy and Moussa were left to discuss stores for the trip. The list rolled out by Moussa sounded highly promising.

" The cook he knows make one hundred cakes," said he with an outward wave of his dusky hands.

" Oh-h-h-h-h ! " from Eve.

Moussa beamed upon her.

" Yes, Mam'selle. The cook he buy four hundred eggs to-day."

" *Four hundred ?* "

" Yes, Mam'selle. The cook he make many, many puddings."

" How lovely ! "

Jeremy laughed. " You will get fat, Eve. I never read such a list; we shall all die of sclerosis of the liver before we reach the First Cataract."

" No, sir," said Moussa. " We take many, many bottles Hunyadi János."

" Whatever is that ? " asked Eve.

" A mineral water," explained Jeremy blandly, " containing valuable medicinal qualities."

" Oh ! "

" Yes, Mam'selle," said Moussa, and in the clearest

CLIMBING THE YARD TO FURL THE SAIL.

THE STEERSMAN AND THE ODD MAN STANDING
AMONG THE CREW'S BREAD.

[To face page 33

diction they were ever to hear from him he began to enumerate them.

" Oh ! " said Eve again.

" I don't think we shall need that," put in Serena hurriedly.

" Very, very good medicine, ma'am," protested Moussa, and began again to describe its properties with yet further details.

" Excellent stuff," said Hugh, " but—er—I don't think we will take any this trip."

" But, sir, very, very important, especially for . . ."

" Yes, yes, I know. All the same I think we'll do without it."

" But, sir, for the ladies . . ."

" No Hunyadi János," very firmly, from Hugh.

" Very well, sir," said Moussa mournfully, dropping his hands despondently to his sides.

Mercifully, the door opened at that moment and Mr. Johnson returned with the news that a car was waiting below. They descended and piled themselves into it. It was rather a tight fit, and Moussa filled up the whole of the seat beside the driver. They crossed the bridge that Jeremy and Eve had walked over before breakfast, for their dahabeah, the *Isis*, was anchored at the foot of a little garden on the further bank.

The boat was nearly a hundred feet long, and its great yard, several feet longer still, soared upwards at a lovely slant high above their heads. A plank had been thrown across from the lower deck to the shore and, urged by Mr. Johnson, Serena led the way on board. The moment she reached the other end of the plank her feet were violently and unexpectedly attacked by a young man with a large feather brush until every speck of dust was removed from her white shoes. Slightly dazed, she stepped on to the deck. Eve was thankful to have had a little warning before her turn came, and while the others were being done she and Serena looked about them.

D

The lower deck was small and seemed crowded with men varying in colour from café-au-lait to a negroid black.

Mr. Johnson presented the captain to them, a tall, slender man in a long white robe and an orange turban, with a very dark skin, liquid black eyes and a gentle and charming expression. He touched his forehead, his lips and his breast, in the beautiful Arab salutation. The butler and the cabin steward also wore white, with crimson fezzes. The majority of the crew had gowns of indigo linen, red sashes, and turbans of various colours.

After they had all been presented, which made quite a little ceremony, Mr. Johnson led the way into the saloon, a cheerful and attractive place with its white paint and its green carpet, cushions and curtains. At the further end a door opened on to a short passage, off which were the cabins, two large and two small, and a miniature bathroom, all, like the saloon, decorated in green and white.

While the men discussed further details of the stores and drinks, Serena and Eve examined every nook and corner. Nothing had been forgotten; it was all complete down to such details as uncut packs of cards, bridge-markers, stamped and addressed notepaper, an unopened bottle of fountain-pen ink, and boxes of rubber bands and paper clips.

It was arranged that the party should come on board at twelve o'clock the following day, and Serena and Eve were reluctantly dragged back to the hotel for lunch.

In the middle of a delicious *salmi* of pigeon, Jeremy noticed that Eve's attention had wandered. She was staring fixedly in front of her, lost in thought. Following the line of her abstracted gaze, he was amused to find that it had fixed itself upon a young man at the next table, and that, though Eve was quite unaware of it, the young man was not. He was an exquisite product, dressed in a subtle scheme of mauve; dark mauve suit, and paler mauve handkerchief, socks and tie to tone, and he obviously attributed Eve's earnest glance to a whole-hearted admiration. But when Hugh said, " A penny for your thoughts, Eve," she turned her eyes away as though the young man did not exist, as indeed, for her, he did not.

" I was thinking," she said, " what a comfort Mr. Johnson's complexion is."

" *What !* "

" I mean, it is such a great comfort that it should be such a lovely pink and white. I was afraid that if you lived here long enough your skin would get ruined."

" Do I gather from this that you are thinking of taking up your residence permanently in this country ? " asked her brother-in-law, screwing his eyeglass more firmly in as he surveyed her with interest.

" Of course not, but you never know. Anything might happen."

" Sheiks," said Jeremy.

" What do you mean ? "

" You've been reading about them."

" I haven't." Eve was indignant. " At least, not for ages. Are we likely to meet any ? " she added casually.

" My dear child," said Jeremy, " you don't *meet* sheiks. They sweep up from the desert on Arab steeds, toss you over their saddles and disappear into the unknown like an arrow from the bow. Of course they don't wash, but I believe you soon get used to that; far from the trammels of civilisation, close to the great heart of Nature, such trifles won't worry you."

" How silly you are ! "

" I believe I am speaking on the highest authority, and the life would appeal to you, Eve. You would get on so well with the other wives."

" You're quite wrong about it all. They don't have any other wives. They live in oasises with every luxury imaginable."

" Including Keating's ? "

" Of course not."

" They would send one of your ears or the best bit of your nose to me for a ransom," put in Hugh. " It would be very tiresome."

" You're out of date, Hugh," corrected Jeremy. " Haven't you read any of the great literature of the day ? Serena will storm the Khedive's Palace and implore him on her knees to rescue her little sister. Just as his heart is melted by the sight of this lovely Englishwoman in distress, Eve will dash up complete with wedding dress, in an outsize in Rolls, her sheik at her side in the most faultless outfit from Savile Row. He will turn out to be Count Hunyadi János in disguise, and the rest of Eve's life will be passed between his castle in Hungary, his house in Park Lane and his tent in the Sahara."

The young man in mauve at the next table caught the end of the withering glance Eve turned upon Jeremy, and choked so severely over his liqueur that when she left the dining-room he was still as mauve as his suit.

CHAPTER VI

CARRIAGE EXERCISE

THE afternoon was taken up by an excursion in a little
open carriage drawn by two horses, with Moussa seated
on the box-seat beside the Arab driver.

Hugh always maintained that Serena had only one
idea—whenever they arrived at a new place she hired a
carriage and went for a drive, at the end of which she
would heave a little sigh of relief and say : " Hasn't
that been nice ? Now we have ' done ' dear little
Rome——" or " dear little Madrid " or Vienna, or whatever the place might be. He vowed she had behaved
thus even in Manchester, and on a day rainier than
usual.

This afternoon no such trial of strength was demanded
of her, but she and Eve found themselves in some
difficulty, owing to the acute slope of the back
seat.

" If we lean back comfortably," Serena complained,
" we look intoxicated. We shall have to sit bolt upright
like the man who did the Grand Tour without touching
the back of his coach."

" But it looks so stiff and unnatural ! " complained
Eve—" as though we were unused to carriage exercise.
Personally, as I am rather a snob, I would sooner look
intoxicated."

However, when a closed car passed them, containing
three or four ladies in black Parisian frocks and tiny
yasmaks of white chiffon, she sat up quickly.

" How thrilling they look," she exclaimed, " with
only their dark eyes showing ! So much more mys-

terious and intriguing than if you saw all their faces. Really it's very becoming. Who started the idea?"

"I don't know," said Jeremy. "It's older than Islam. I have heard it had something to do with fear of the Evil Eye. It didn't save Mahomed from a little bit of trouble in his own family circle, though."

"There's a great deal to be said for the idea of shutting one's women up, and veiling them when you do let them out," observed Hugh.

"Rather!" agreed Jeremy. "The Koran says that if a man's wife looks at any other fellow he is to put her into a separate bed and scourge her."

"A fine religion," said Hugh thoughtfully.

"Is this the result," exclaimed Serena, "of bringing men to a Mahommedan country?"

"If you feel," cried Eve, "that you are coming all over Eastern, please say so at once, and Serena and I will go straight home."

"But it will be such a good preparation for your future life, Eve," said Jeremy soothingly. "Sheiks are notoriously handy fellows with a scourge," he added, as their carriage stopped abruptly at a narrow entrance to the bazaar. He jumped out, and turned to help Eve.

"Please don't trouble," said she, coldly indignant. "I prefer to get down alone."

Jeremy dropped back at once, and Eve stepped forward with her haughtiest air, caught her foot in the mat at the bottom of the carriage—which, in true Eastern fashion, had a hole in it—and landed violently head foremost into Jeremy's arms. For one moment he held her; then lowered her gently to the ground. Serena, knowing her sister well, looked at him anxiously. He was certainly smiling a little as he bent to pick up Eve's parasol, but when he straightened up again and handed it to her his face was inscrutable. Hugh opened his mouth to laugh, but, quick as lightning, Serena placed her high heel firmly on his toe with wifely thoroughness and cried: "Do look at that man with the bagpipes!"

" They're not bagpipes," said Jeremy, throwing her a grateful glance, " that's a water-carrier with his goat-skin."

" How disgusting ! " said Serena. " Do people really drink the water that comes out of that ? "

" Indeed they do," replied Jeremy. " That's one of the oldest ways of bringing water from the river into the town."

" Did they use them in Cleopatra's day ? "

" Cleopatra was a parvenue compared with the water-carrier, and infinitely less important. It's difficult for people who have never had more to do than turn a tap, to realise quite what water means to people in a country where every drop is more precious than gold. The oldest Egyptian prayers are full of it. ' May I drink the water at the edge of my lake every day '— ' May water be poured out from my cistern '—' A draught of water at the swirl of the stream '—and so on."

Moussa led them behind the water-carrier along a narrow alley, and down a lane to the left. Serena and Eve, to whom an Eastern bazaar was new, looked about them with delight. They found a maze of alleys, only a few feet wide, strange and fascinating. The tall houses seemed to shut them in on either side so closely that if they had stretched out their arms to their fullest extent they could almost have touched the walls. The sun found its way in in shreds and patches, and the loose slippers of the passers-by made a curious shuffling noise.

" We go in here," announced Moussa, ushering them into a tiny shop no bigger than a ship's cabin, full of the loveliest scents of which Eve had ever dreamed. The smiling shopkeeper made them all sit down on a divan, while his assistant produced cups of Turkish coffee and amber-scented cigarettes.

" What a lamb ! " cooed Eve. " Just fancy if Debenham and Freebody or Fortnum and Mason entertained one like this."

Their host produced one marvellous bottle after another of pure essence, a single drop enough for each person. He touched the backs of their hands with a little glass rod dipped in the various perfumes, until the choice became bewildering. Eventually they decided on jasmine and mimosa, and with a great deal of ceremony two long phials were filled, paid for and handed to them. Eve was sorry when it was over. The shadowy shop, the streaks of sunlight and the dusty lane outside, with the silent passing figures in their long robes and coloured turbans, was like a scene from the Arabian Nights. She wandered with the others through the Street of the Carpet-makers, the Street of the Jewellers, of the Slipper-makers and Saddlers. In each one the merchants squatted cross-legged before their shops, and all the purchasers, Eve noticed, were men. She watched two dignified Arabs fingering a bale of material as thoughtfully as any two women at a bargain sale in England. Close behind them some black-and-white goats, with long flapping ears like spaniels, were foraging in a dust-heap. A little further on, on a kind of raised platform, half a dozen men were sitting, some smoking hookahs, and others playing a game of draughts.

"Oh, must we go?" said Eve regretfully when, turning round another bend, she saw their carriage awaiting them.

"Yes, Mam'selle," said Moussa. "We go now to the English shops to buy veils."

"Veils?" inquired Eve suspiciously.

"Yes, Mam'selle. Veils to wear in the desert to shelter the skin."

"But we never wear veils!" protested Eve.

"Must wear a veil in the desert, please, Mam'selle, or the sun will spoil your face."

"Not if we use plenty of cream."

"Veils must be worn, Mam'selle," declared the adamantine Moussa.

Jeremy was amused to see with what unaccustomed

meekness Eve allowed herself to be put into the carriage and driven off to an English shop, where both girls were forced to buy squares of hemstitched white chiffon. These were, they complained, cheap and nasty, and would have cost two-and-eleven in Oxford Street, whereas here they had to pay the equivalent of eight-and-sixpence.

The drive ended up at a bookshop, where they were to lay in a sufficient store of literature to last, at any rate, as far as Luxor.

" We want really serious books about Egypt," declared Eve.

" Then you must begin with Breasted's History," said Jeremy, " and go on to Moret's ' Nile and Egyptian Civilisation.' "

" Of course we must," agreed Eve, but Serena sighed a little when she saw the size of the volumes. While Jeremy added Weigall, Flinders Petrie, and several more to the growing pile, she wandered away to the other side of the shop, and came back with a couple of novels in her hand.

" Let's have these, too," she pleaded. " I've always heard Robert Hichens writes so wonderfully about the desert."

" He does," agreed Jeremy, " but the two you've chosen happen to be about Algeria."

" Oh, well," said Serena placidly, " I expect the desert is much the same everywhere."

They came out of the shop to find dusk had fallen, and it had grown so chilly that they were glad of the coats Moussa had insisted on bringing for them.

" I'm beginning to adore that man," murmured Eve tenderly, gazing affectionately at the broad back in the blue pilot-jacket on the box-seat of the carriage, as they clattered off home through the lighted streets.

CHAPTER VII

WHEN the hour arrived for the party to leave the hotel and go into residence on board the dahabeah, Eve was nowhere to be found. Shouts for Moussa brought that personage, large, bland and smiling, into the hall of the hotel from the pavement where he had been spending his time lording it over the other and inferior dragomans.

" Mam'selle, she goes down to the shop to have her hair cleaned," he explained.

" What on earth did you let her do that for, Serena ? " demanded Hugh. " I suppose it means hours and hours."

" Oh, I don't think so," said Serena. " She went directly after breakfast. Moussa took her."

" What was she going to have done ? " demanded Hugh.

" Oh, the usual things," replied Serena vaguely.

" I ordered the carriage to fetch Mam'selle at twelve," said Moussa.

" It's half-past now," said Hugh. " How far away is the shop ? "

" Five minutes, sir."

" That's all right," said Serena. " You see, if Eve ordered the carriage for twelve, it means she should be able to get away by about five-and-twenty minutes past, so she may be here any moment now. She must be having quite a lot done—she's been gone over two hours."

" My hat ! " said Hugh. " Can you understand it,

43

Jeremy? Would you for anything on earth sit in a stuffy shop and let some beastly dago paw you about the head for two hours?"

At this moment, with a rattle and clatter, Eve's carriage drew up at the hotel steps, and Eve descended from it, calm and unruffled. It was impossible to see whether her hair was satisfactory or not, for she wore a tight-fitting little green hat like a helmet that covered it all up. Hugh was too glad to see her to say more than:

"Well, anyway, here you are at last. We may as well stick to that carriage, as you've got it. Pop in, Serena."

"Did they do it well, darling?" asked Serena, as they drove across the bridge.

"So, so," said Eve. "You'll see it presently."

"There's one comfort," said Hugh, who took no more interest in Eve's hair now that she was no longer delaying the start. "Our bill at the hotel was so fabulous that the dahabeah will be an actual saving of money."

"And when we first took it," said Serena, "it seemed so fearfully expensive."

"A first-class Cairo hotel beats any American one into a cocked hat as far as cost goes," observed Jeremy. "Personally I think they are killing the goose that lays the golden egg. By the by, Hugh, I see in our contract that Cook's have undertaken to provide our crew with sticks, drawers and musical instruments, and for our part, we have to provide an occasional sheep or its equivalent in baksheesh."

Mr. Johnson of the pink-and-white complexion so admired by Eve was waiting on board to receive them and send them off. He showed them an imposing array of bottles stacked in the corner of the saloon and two enormous ice-chests on deck, and explained that it was only necessary to let Moussa know whenever they wanted anything; he would either flag one of Cook's steamers or wire to the head office in Cairo for it. Then

Mr. Johnson took his leave and waved them a friendly good-bye from the gangway.

"Do you know," said Serena admiringly, "that we are actually carrying fresh Aylesbury milk in sealed bottles from England?"

"I can't say that interests me particularly," replied Hugh, "I'm going to mix a cocktail."

"I must go and tidy," said Eve in rather a mysterious sort of voice, and she departed to her cabin.

The cocktails were just ready and poured out when she came back into the saloon. Jeremy, who was raising his glass to his lips, gave a smothered exclamation and spilt some of the precious contents. The others looked round and remained for a moment speechless.

"Do you like it?" asked Eve a little nervously, hesitating in the doorway. "You see, I thought, Egypt being the land of henna, and all the women of the harem using henna—even on their fingers and toes, you know, but I haven't had mine done—I thought it would be a pity not to seize the opportunity of having my hair henna-ed. Besides, you know, the Prophet had a red beard, so red hair is considered a mark of great sanctity. Jeremy told me that, so it must be true. And I thought it would start us off well with the crew if they thought one of us was a holy person."

"I . . . I expect I shall get used to it," said Serena rather faintly. "But, oh, darling! your yellow hair was so pretty."

"If you ask me," said Hugh, "I think you've utterly spoiled yourself. Your hair was your chief beauty, and now it looks like nothing so much as a tomato salad."

Jeremy drank off his cocktail and walked round Eve, thoughtfully observing her.

"I rather like it," he announced. "I don't say I should like it for always, or even that it's an improvement, but I'm all for change and experiment. It's the sign of an intelligent mind. I congratulate you, Eve."

"Thank you, Jeremy," said Eve gratefully. " I must admit I was a little startled myself when I took my hat off; it didn't look so bright in the shop, somehow, and I'm afraid that they told me it would go on getting more and more orange for a day or two."

"Good Lord!" said Hugh. "You'll look like a scarlet tangerine floating on the Nile."

Moussa at this moment came in to announce that lunch was ready. He started violently at the sight of Eve's head, but controlled himself admirably.

"The worst of it is," said Eve, as they all sat down and the gloomy-looking butler, Mahomed, began to serve the soup, "that it was so frightfully expensive. I'm afraid I shall want some more money, Hugh."

"More?" said the startled Hugh. "I cashed you a cheque only yesterday evening after the shops had shut."

"Well, I'm afraid it cost three pounds," confessed Eve. "But of course I shall never have my hair done again the whole time I'm in Egypt. I never thought of asking the price. This sort of thing in England would cost twelve or fifteen shillings with a tip. I just said I wanted a henna application, shampoo and water wave, and while they were giving me a water wave I had a manicure. When I got my bill it was two pounds fifteen, and I was so horrified that I determined to appear as though a bill like that was nothing to me. I didn't turn a single one of my new red hairs. I just said: ' You may keep the change,' and handed over the three pound notes and walked out."

"What a country!" said Hugh.

"It's very lucky for you," observed Jeremy, "that you didn't come to Egypt five thousand years or so ago."

"Why?" asked Eve. "Because I should be dead now?"

"Because you would have been dead very soon after arriving. It was the custom at harvest-time to seize any red-haired stranger and sacrifice him in the fields to the

Corn God, Osiris. The red hair was supposed to represent the red-gold of the crops when ripe."

" How foolish of red-haired strangers to come to Egypt in those days ! " said Serena.

Towards the end of lunch Hugh opined that it was foolish to come at all if you had any respect for your figure.

" We shall only be like the Pharaoh," remarked Jeremy.

" He used to be called the ' Lord of Five Meals a Day ' ! "

" That's all very well," retorted Hugh, " but, judging from the illustrations in some of the books you've brought on board, the Pharaonic costume was no hindrance to a hearty appetite. I shall have to order a new lot of uniforms when I get back if we have many meals like this one."

" Pardon, ladies and gentlemen," said Moussa from the doorway, " the cook he wants to know did you enjoy your lunch ? "

" Far too well," replied Jeremy. " Tell him, Moussa, he mustn't give us so much."

The smile was wiped off Moussa's face in an instant.

" I mean," continued Jeremy, " that everything was so good and so well cooked that we have, to put it mildly, ' grossly exceeded.' In future, we shall be quite content with two or three courses instead of seven in the middle of the day."

" Sir, I tell him." Moussa departed sadly, only to return in a few minutes. " Pardon, ladies and gentlemen, but he cook, he cries. He thinks you are not pleased."

" Oh ! " exclaimed Serena and Eve with one voice. " Poor, poor man ! What can we do, Moussa ? "

" Ma'am, I think a little brandy will make him well."

Jeremy, with an inscrutable expression, poured some into a glass, and Moussa departed with it.

" I would rather eat till I burst," protested Eve, " than make the poor man cry," but Moussa, putting his head round the corner of the door again, assured them that the brandy had successfully soothed the cook's ruffled feelings, and that if they came on deck they would see the anchor weighed and the sail hoisted.

The great moment had arrived. The journey was to begin. All the sailors were running about, the hem of their long blue nightgowns—which Jeremy told Eve she must learn to call jibbahs—between their teeth. They sang a chantey in a plaintive minor key, while they hove in the anchor and cast off the moorings. As the enormous sail unfurled, someone threw a handful of salt on to the little fire burning on the lower deck; the crackling noise carried Eve back in a flash to the fire of sea logs in their drawing-room in London.

"What is that for?" she asked, turning to Moussa, who was watching all this activity like a benevolent god.

"Mam'selle, they throw the salt on the fire to prevent very bad evil on the voyage."

The next instant the north wind, which was blowing strongly, filled the big sail; the water rustled at the blunt bows and spread away from the stern in a widening fan of ripples—the journey had begun.

. . . . .

It was all very pretty, thought Eve, gazing round the upper deck, which was furnished like an outdoor sitting-room. There were small tables and long cane chairs comfortably cushioned in green, and palms in pots stood in the corners. At present the trunks and suit-cases standing about, waiting to be unpacked, rather spoilt the effect.

As Eve sipped her Turkish coffee she began to sort out the different members of the crew. She already knew the captain, or the reis, as Jeremy told her she must call him, so that she imagined it spelt R-I-C-E until she saw it in print. He stood now at the top of a short flight of steps that led down from the upper deck to the men's deck in the bows. From this central position he could direct both the sailors below and the steersman

SHADÛF.

SAKKIEH WITH OXEN.

[To face page 48.

who stood at the big tiller in the stern. This individual
—who was also the second in command—was a Nubian,
so dark that he was nearly black. One eyelid had a per-
petual droop which gave his large, soft eyes a sleepy
appearance, and his movements were so graceful that it
was a joy to watch him walk across the deck in his
jibbah of deep indigo and his brilliant orange turban.
He drooped languidly over the tiller, and occasionally he
sang, or rather hummed, a plaintive little air in an
exquisite, faint falsetto.

The butler and the cabin steward, Mahomed and
Said, she already knew, for both had waited at lunch.
Mahomed looked disagreeable, Eve thought, but
seemed very efficient. Said appeared to be a rather
hysterical, moth-eaten individual, the kind of person
likely to be put upon by everybody. There was also a
tall, slender, very handsome young man, with a pale
olive complexion who ought to have had a rose dangling
from the corner of his mouth like the youthful hero of a
poem of Hafiz. He appeared to be of somewhat higher
class than the sailors, and wore a fez, like the two cabin
servants, and a stiffly starched white overall. He was
the laundryman, Jeremy said, and his name was Ibrahim.

Coffee finished, it was agreed that unpacking was the
next thing to be done, and here Moussa took complete
command. Neither Serena nor Eve was allowed to
take a very active part; they might lift their frocks and
other belongings out of their trunks, but under no cir-
cumstances were they to carry them down to their
cabins; this was done by Ibrahim and Said, Moussa's
A.D.C.'s. Slightly embarrassed at first, the two girls
made futile efforts to deal personally with their more
intimate under-garments, but: " I don't wish that you
and Madam carry anything yourselves," said Moussa
firmly, taking a large armful from Eve as he spoke.
" Said . . .! "

Said rushed up, full of enthusiasm, seized the
embroidered, lacy pile, scuttled across the deck like a

E

frightened rabbit, fell headlong over a suit-case, and dropped all Eve's lingerie down the companion.   It was retrieved by Jeremy with a perfectly unmoved countenance.

At intervals there was a pause in the unpacking, while Moussa pointed out places of interest on the banks : the higgledy-piggledy town of old Cairo, which the ancients called New Babylon, and the island of Roda, where, he told them, Pharaoh's daughter had found Moses in the bulrushes.   The river was crowded with gyassas; those sailing before the wind flying along under their canvas; those coming down-stream laboriously towed or rowed.   Some were laden with biscuit-coloured vases of earthenware, marvellously packed so that they made a mound, smooth-sided and flat-topped; others were laden with straw, also packed into mounds so smooth and even that Eve thought they must have been done by machinery, until Moussa told her they were made by hand and were often the result of several days' labour.   Evening drew on, and they lay in their long chairs and watched the sun sinking in a sky of unbelievable beauty.   A vast, clear expanse of rose, orange, violet and palest eau-de-nil.

On the west bank of the river the land was built up to form a high dyke, along the top of which ran a road of sorts.   As the sun sank below the horizon everything passing along the dyke appeared in silhouette against the glowing background.   Men and women on camels or donkeys; children, bareheaded and barefooted; buffaloes, goats and dogs—all went by in a long procession, home to the evening meal after the day's work in the fields. Their footfalls made no sound in the soft dust, but their incessant chatter, the lowing of herds and the snarling of camels, rose like a chorus into the still air.

Eve felt it was all too Egyptian, too like an illustration in some Eastern story, to be true.   Even the sunset was a gaudy, gorgeous affair, far more like a highly coloured picture post-card or some impossible lithograph than anything in real life. The wind dropped with the sun, the air turned very cold, and Moussa muffled everybody up in thick coats and wraps with his most paternal air. The reis gave the order to furl the main-sail, the jib being already down.

" What on earth are they going to do ? " inquired Hugh, as seven or eight of the sailors began to climb the mast, their skirts between their teeth and kind Mr. Cook's baggy white drawers in full view. " Why don't they fit up a simple tackle ? "

" Because everything on board a dahabeah is done in exactly the same way to-day as it was five thousand years ago," Jeremy told him. " It has been a superhuman job teaching them to put out a kedge; goodness knows how long it will be before they adopt a modern method of lowering a sail."

Serena and Eve—and indeed all four of them—held their breath as they watched the giddy performance. The immense yard must have soared fully a hundred and twenty feet into the air. Up and up the men climbed, looking like a row of tiny brown monkeys on a long stick.

" That's a good boy," said Hugh, " the one right at the top."

" Yes, sir," agreed Moussa, " he very good boy; he always go first. He the cook, sir."

" What ? " shouted Hugh. " Do you mean to tell me they allow a fellow who can cook like that to risk his life and limb ? What madness ! "

Moussa shook with laughter, rather like a large wobbly jelly. " No, no, sir. He not your cook : he only the crew's cook. Your cook, he never climb, sir."

" Thank Heaven ! " sighed Hugh piously.

They all said it again when course succeeded course at dinner. The curry soup was a dream, the quails were perfection, the vegetables of the freshest, and the toast served with the foie gras was piping hot. The pièce de résistance turned out to be their old friend, the

Christmas pudding, which everyone, except Eve, eyed with misgiving; but this time it turned out to be the genuine article, and very good at that.

While they were drinking their coffee, sounds of music were heard.

"We have seen kind Mr. Cook's drawers," said Jeremy. "Now we're going to hear his musical instruments," and he got up and opened the saloon door so that they could see along the short alley-way to the lower deck, where all the men except Moussa lived. White awnings had been put up along the sides and overhead, so that the whole was snugly enclosed against the night air.

About a dozen of the sailors sat cross-legged facing one another in two lines, and in the narrow space between a couple of the Nubians were dancing, with a peculiar swaying movement of their bodies. The seated men played primitive, oddly effective music, tapping rapidly on tiny drums and plucking the strings of miniature guitars. A single lantern, slung from a pole overhead, cast curious lights and shadows down upon the twirling figures of the dancers, rigid from the waist upwards, swaying from the hips and stamping rapidly with their bare feet. The seated figures, too, swayed from side to side, clapping their hands to the rhythm of the music and occasionally singing a line in unison, ending each stave with a curious yowling shout. Faster and faster twirled the dancers, their fingers clicking like castanets.

In the light of the lantern Eve saw the sweat shining on their dark faces and caught the gleam of their white teeth. The insistent throbbing of the little drums stirred her blood to a quick response, and when she went to bed it seemed to her that she could still hear them. What was there about a drum that was so primitive, so different from any other instrument, she wondered, as she slipped off to sleep, as ever in Egypt, to the distant sound of the barking of innumerable dogs.

CHAPTER VIII

MENES

Eve was walking in a garden with Alice and Humpty-Dumpty. From somewhere out of sight came the sound of drums.

"They are drumming the lion and the unicorn out of town," said Alice.

"No, they're not," contradicted Humpty-Dumpty, rather rudely. "Those are Cook's drums."

Alice made some reply that Eve didn't catch, for the noise was getting louder and louder. Suddenly it grew so loud that it woke her up, and she found it was real. She sat up in bed and looked out of the window.

On the distant bank hundreds of Egyptian soldiers in khaki uniforms and shorts were marching with a briskness and precision that even Hugh would have approved. At the head of each company came the drummers, whose cheerful rat-tat-tat sounded startlingly clear in the still morning air.

Eve looked at her watch. Seven o'clock. She was too wide awake to stay in bed, so, collecting her sponge and towels, she went across to the bathroom and turned on the cold water.

The dahabeah was moored against a strip of flat sand, and, as Eve stepped into her icy bath, something darkened the window. Looking over her shoulder, she was considerably startled to find a large camel staring in at her with obvious loathing and contempt, and she pulled the wire screen hurriedly across the window, her teeth chattering. "For though it's exciting," she thought, " to see camels in the nude, so to speak, I don't

53

feel intimate enough with them yet to want to bathe with one."

She hurried into a short skirt, a sweater and a pair of flat-heeled shoes and, bareheaded, went up on to the deck. The first person she saw was Jeremy, also in a sweater and a shocking pair of old grey flannel trousers. He looked at her head and grinned.

" It has come up a bit redder during the night," he observed cheerfully. " Are you coming for a walk on shore ? "

" It has," laughed Eve, " and I'd love to."

She followed him across the gangway to where Moussa was walking along the sand, a rosary dangling from his plump hands, his lips bubbling with prayer. Eve opened her eyes in surprise.

" Is he a Catholic ? " she asked Jeremy.

" No. Mahommedans use rosaries too."

" Do they? You know, I'm sure Moussa is a eunuch. He's so exactly the pictures of them in the Arabian Nights—the people who guarded the harems, I mean."

" I'm sure he's *not*," said the startled Jeremy.

" Then he must be descended from a long line of eunuchs. Have you caught cold ? " she added anxiously.

" No, thanks," said Jeremy, clearing his throat loudly.

At that moment Moussa caught sight of them and pattered across the sand, his large feet flapping, but Jeremy heartlessly told him his escort was unnecessary, and left him a little sorrowful at this exhibition of independence.

It was chilly, in spite of the sun, and Jeremy and Eve walked briskly along the narrow track between the river and a field of beans in full flower.

" Smell them ! " cried Eve. " Aren't they divine ? Oh, Jeremy, what a heavenly morning ! I'm so happy I don't know what to do. Do you ever feel like that ? "

" Sometimes, though not in quite the same way, perhaps. I'm thirty-six, you know, not twenty-one."

" Two years younger than Hugh." Eve pondered this for a moment. " Well, I suppose it does make a difference. Thirty-six is a nice age for a man, though. Personally I don't think them worth considering before that."

Jeremy's eyes twinkled. " Considering as what ? "

Eve blushed.

" Oh—as anything serious, you know.—How wide the Nile is here," she added quickly. " I had no idea it was so wide or so swift."

" It's wider still higher up," said Jeremy.

" Is it ? How odd ! I thought rivers started narrow and got bigger as they got on."

" So they do as a rule. The Nile is unique, because it's the only river which has no tributaries ; all its length it gives life to the land it flows through, and takes nothing, so that by the time it reaches the sea it has dwindled down to a number of insignificant, muddy streams."

" I think that's tragic, when it has been so important up here.—Oh, dear, there's a donkey braying. That means it's going to be wet."

" Not in Egypt. Wind, or the lack of it, is much more likely to bother us than rain."

Eve cocked a nautical eye up at the cloudless sky.

" Um—there's certainly not much sign of any at present. Where do we sail to to-day, if it does blow satisfactorily ? "

" Bedrechen, the starting-place for the expedition for Memphis and Sakkhara."

" Are we going on an expedition ? How lovely ! What shall we see there ? "

" Almost the beginnings of Egyptian history ; after the pre-dynastic period."

Eve stopped dead in the middle of the path. " What, in Heaven's name, was the pre-dynastic period ? Jeremy, you simply must not hurl such awful things at me without any explanation. It's not fair, and it's thoroughly bad form. Start again—in words of one syllable, please."

"Sorry! It came after the pre-historic period and before the first dynasty."

"Pre-historic things bore me," declared Eve. "I can't work up any interest in axes and tools made of stone and copper."

"All the same, some of their jewellery and pottery is beautiful," said Jeremy. "But it was more remarkable still in the pre-dynastic age, when the gods ruled in Egypt. That was a great time. Look up, Eve, and you'll see the oldest of them all, flying overhead at this very moment."

Eve looked up obediently, and saw a big, brown falcon sailing by.

"He was called Horus the Elder," explained Jeremy —" the falcon god who lived in the sky. The lord of all the celestial universe. He ruled with Seth, the God of the barren desert, of storm, darkness and evil. Seth ruled over Upper, and Horus over Lower Egypt, the delta region."

"How confusing!" said Eve. "I should have thought it would have been just the other way round. That the upper would have been the delta, I mean. It's higher up on the map."

"You are thinking in terms of north and south. They went by the Nile. Everything for them was either up-stream or down-stream."

"Oh! Well, I shall have to remember that it's the exact opposite of what I think. The north is the lower and the south the upper."

"As the centuries went by other gods grew up," continued Jeremy. "Osiris, the God of the Nile and the corn, and his wife Isis, the Goddess of the fertilised earth, and their son Horus the Younger. The ' Darling Son ' he is called in the old records."

"How sweet! I've heard of Osiris and Isis, of course, but I don't know anything about them."

" It's one of the oldest stories in the world," said Jeremy. " The Story of the Family, father, mother and child, with Seth to play the part of the wicked uncle."

" If he was wicked why did people worship him ? "

" Through fear, I suppose. He was a very powerful magician, and therefore a person to be propitiated. He murdered his brother, Osiris, and cut his body in pieces and scattered them far and wide. Isis collected the fragments and joined them together again with the help of Anubis, the jackal god, the patron saint of the embalmers. Then she breathed new life into the mummy by her magic arts, and Osiris rose from the dead, and became the King of the Underworld."

" They sound a thoroughly nice family," said Eve. " What happened to Horus, the ' Darling Son ' ? "

" Oh, he had been brought up by his mother with one end in view, the avenging of his father's murder. He fought and defeated Seth and became King of Egypt. He was the last of the great gods to reign over the land. After him came a race of demi-gods ; kings who were half human, half divine ; Manetho, the famous Egyptian historian, called them ' The Servants of Horus.' "

" Was Horus the Younger a falcon too, like Horus the Elder ? "

" Yes. You'll soon learn to recognise him when you've been to a temple or two and seen him carved on the walls. It's extraordinarily attractive the way the Egyptians drew their gods and goddesses with the bodies of men and women and the heads of animals. You will see Horus with his square shoulders and his falcon's head hundreds of times before you've done."

" I like the sound of him awfully," said Eve.

" Perhaps it's only because we still know so little about it that the pre-dynastic period is so interesting," said Jeremy, " and what we do know has been pieced together scrap by scrap with such difficulty. We know there were two capitals, one in Upper and one in Lower Egypt, each with its own treasure house. The White

House in the south and the Red House in the north. The southern king wore a high white crown, while the northern king's crown was red."

" It's like a fairy story," cried Eve.

" It's like looking through the wrong end of a telescope. You see everything small and crowded and very far off. A stage—peopled with shadows—a group of names, and no more, until one man steps out from this crowded background of strange men and stranger gods. The first real personality in history—Menes."

" And to think I never even heard of him! How humiliating ! "

" I shouldn't let that worry you," said Jeremy consolingly; " nor did I, until I came out here and began to get interested in it all. Menes came up from the south, conquered the Delta kingdom and proclaimed himself ' Lord of the Two Lands.' The dynasties proper began with him, and the pre-dynastic period, which so alarmed you, came to an end."

" When ? "

" 3400 B.C.; more than five thousand years ago."

" Heavens ! when shall I begin to think in thousands instead of hundreds ? I'm hopeless at dates."

" Don't bother about them, unless you like to remember that the calendar which we use to-day was drawn up by the astronomers of the delta in 4241 B.C. Just get it into your head that Menes reigned, roughly speaking, nine hundred years before Cretan civilisation was at its height in Cnossos, and between two and three thousand years before Rome was built."

" I'll try," said Eve, who had hitherto cherished a touching belief that the building of Rome had been the starting point of the world's history.

. . . . .

Eve was now to discover that man might propose, but the wind would certainly dispose of his plans on the Nile. According to the guide-books the north wind could be relied upon to blow steadily for eight hours a day; but Moussa and the reis knew better. And when it began to blow from the right quarter at ten o'clock that morning they determined to take full advantage of it. To Eve's indignation, Hugh and Jeremy agreed with them, and decided not to stop at Bedrechen, but to sail as far as possible while the wind lasted.

" But I want to go to Sakkhara and Memphis on a dear little donkey," wailed Eve to Jeremy.

" You shall," he promised, " on the way down."

" I thought the whole idea of sailing instead of steaming was that you could be nice and leisurely. I didn't know we were going to dash ahead day after day without a pause."

" Your innocence is pathetic. You little know the Nile. In a week's time, when you've been becalmed, blown backwards and stuck on half-a-dozen sandbanks, you will be a sadder and a wiser woman."

" Too much sight-seeing is dreadfully exhausting," said Serena.

" It doesn't look as though we're going to be bothered with too much," retorted Eve. " So far, it's true, we've only failed to see the Citadel and the Museum, the Sphinx and the Pyramids, Sakkhara and Memphis. But, of course," she added sarcastically, " there's no knowing how much more we may miss if our luck holds."

CHAPTER IX

THE GOLDEN AGE

THE sun shone, the river sparkled, and the *Isis* flew
before the wind until the great pyramids of Gizeh
dropped behind and other stranger pyramids loomed up
ahead, scattered over the plain. These surprised Eve
very much, for she had not known there were what she
described as " extra ones."

" And they're so curious-looking, too," she remarked
to Jeremy. " Why are they such funny shapes ? "

" Because they're much older than those at Gizeh,"
explained Jeremy, " and the Egyptians built them before
they had learnt to make the sides smooth and the tops
pointed. That one all in steps is the oldest of them all
—the Step Pyramid of Sakkhara."

" Who built it ? " asked Eve. " And why did they
do it ? And what's that odd-looking, lumpy one near
it ? "

" You've got your work cut out for you, Jeremy,"
remarked Hugh. " Eve reminds me of a book none of
you will ever have heard of—not having been blest with
a Victorian grandparent—' Mrs. Markham's History of
England for the Use of Young Persons.' "

" Young persons ! " chuckled Eve. " How sweet ! "

" My grandmother used to read it to me when I was
a small boy."

" But why did I remind you of it ? " asked Eve.

" Because at the end of every chapter Mrs. Markham's
children used to bombard her with a stream of questions,
such as you fire at Jeremy. Beastly children they were,
too ! "

" Well, really ! " cried Eve indignantly.

" Richard was the one I disliked the most. He had such an unhealthy craving for knowledge. The second one, George, wasn't too bad; in fact, I had a sneaking liking for him, because he once begged his mother to speak of the fore and aft of a ship instead of talking of either end. There was a little girl too—Mary. Funny, the way I've remembered their names all these years."

" It's one of the signs of old age," remarked Eve; " you forget what you've had for breakfast this morning, but you remember the lessons learnt at your grandmother's knee. Did Mrs. Markham's children ask intelligent questions ? "

" Appallingly; and they prefaced each one with ' Pray, dear Mamma.' "

" I adore that," exclaimed Eve. " Jeremy, you shall be Mrs. Markham, and Serena, Hugh and I will be Richard, George and little Mary, and you shall answer all our questions. I'll begin. Pray, Mamma, who built the Step Pyramid ? "

" Zozer."

" Who on earth was he ? "

" A Pharaoh of the Third Dynasty. It's the oldest big stone building in the world, as far as we know. The ancestor of St. Paul's and the Woolworth Building."

" Good gracious ! " exclaimed Serena. " And was Tozer, or whatever his name was, responsible for that other clumsy-looking one with the lumpy bit on the top, too ? "

" No, that was Snefru's, another Third Dynasty king, the great hero of the Egyptian legends. Thousands of years later, if a Pharaoh won an important victory or did anything he was particularly pleased about, his proudest boast was ' Nothing like this has been known since the days of Snefru.' This pyramid of his is the first smooth-sided one. He built it in steps first, like Zozer's, and then filled them in "

" Live and learn," said Eve. " I never knew anybody had even thought of a pyramid before Cheops."

" I never knew till yesterday that the Pyramids were really tombs," confessed Serena. " I thought they were just monuments."

" They were the most stupendous tombs in the world," said Jeremy. " The Pharaoh dead was as important as the Pharaoh alive, to the Egyptians. He was a god on earth and another kind of god after death. He still went on being the protector of his people, besides being the intercessor between them and the gods of the other world."

" He seems to have been worked overtime," remarked Hugh.

" He does," agreed Jeremy, " but the Pharaohs were all great workers. The poorest man in Egypt had the right to appeal personally to them. There were high court officials, called the ' King's Eyes and Ears,' whose duty was to bring everything to his notice."

" How delicious ! " cried Serena. " I wish we had titles like that now."

" There's a man in London to-day, a member of my club, called ' the King's Remembrancer,' " said Hugh.

" None of the Pharaohs were as great as Cheops, were they, Jeremy ? " asked Eve.

" There were others as great, but probably none had quite such limitless wealth, nor such an inexhaustible supply of labour to draw upon. Cheops was certainly the greatest man in the Fourth Dynasty, and his reign was the top note of the Old Kingdom—the ' Golden Age ' of Egypt."

" I wonder why the Egyptians set such store on their tombs," said Serena.

" They believed in a future life," explained Jeremy, " and they enjoyed this one so much that they wanted the next to be as like it as possible. So they preserved their corpses in the same form as far as they could, and covered the walls of their tombs with pictures of all their possessions, and of their work and their pleasures. How would you like the story of your misspent life indelibly painted round the family vault, Eve ? "

" I'd adore it. Only I shouldn't like people to see me in the clothes I wore the year before last. Skirts go up and down so quickly now that you look all wrong in no time."

" It's so dreadful to think of the millions of men who were driven to work on the Pyramids with whips and overseers," complained Serena. " Even though it all happened so long ago, it's horrid to remember how brutally they were treated, isn't it ? "

" You needn't let that worry you too much nowadays," said Jeremy. " The latest idea is that the men were only employed during the months of inundation by the Nile, when agricultural work was impossible; and during this yearly labour they were housed and fed, and well looked after."

" Oh, dear," sighed Eve regretfully. " Of course it's very nice to think they were kindly treated and all that, but somehow it makes it much less romantic. As it's all been over such thousands of years, I'm not sure I wouldn't rather the Pyramids had been built with blood and tears than in such a matter-of-fact, hygienic sort of way."

" Sweet little thing," murmured Hugh. " Your tender heart does you the greatest credit."

SAKKIEH WITH CAMEL.

THE GATES OF THE DESERT.

[To face page 65.

CHAPTER X

" ARABIC WITHOUT A TEACHER "

THE following day not a breath of wind stirred the surface of the water, which looked more like a lagoon than a river, and in its shining depths the tall palm trees stood upon their tufted heads. It might have been a perfect English summer's day.

" Ideal for nearly everything except hunting or sailing," said Hugh, as he and Jeremy watched the reis and some of the sailors row off in the dinghy to put out a kedge. The men drew in the rope until they had pulled the *Isis* across to the further bank, where the shore was flat and sandy, and here eight of them got out and started to tow her.

Eve felt that she was back in the old days of slavery. To her Western mind it seemed a little shocking that eight of her fellow-creatures, no matter what their colour, should pull the rest of them along, like beasts of burden, their backs bent under the weight, their toes dug into the sand, as they swayed from side to side in unison. It reminded her of a picture of some slaves she had seen as a child, and it was a relief to her to find that the men themselves treated it as all in the day's work, chatting away cheerfully and laughing every now and then at some extra good joke.

Anyway it was certainly delightful to glide along without sound or vibration through the still, warm air. Behind her the steersman drooped gracefully over the tiller, his bare feet among the heaped-up slices of the crew's dark brown bread that a wizened old man, who seemed to do all the odd jobs on board, had cut up and put there to dry in the sun. There must have been several hundred pieces, and already if you picked one up and dropped it on the deck it sounded as hard as wood. When they got in the steersman's way he just pushed them aside with his bare feet. At meal-times the sailors used a slice of this hard bread instead of a spoon, dipping it in and out of the one large, open pan of savoury-smelling stew round which they squatted in a circle.

The reis and the steersman had their meals together in the stern, brought on a wooden tray by the cook-boy. Presumably Mahomed, Said and the fastidious-looking Ibrahim had theirs in the pantry. Moussa was fed from the saloon and ate in solitary state in his own cabin. At the present moment he was sitting in a little wooden chair on the lower deck, his large round spectacles on his nose, reading the Koran. He read as a child reads, following the lines with a stout finger and forming each word with his lips.

Meanwhile, as the midday hour of prayer approached, each of the men towing fell out in turn, walked a few yards away and, facing towards Mecca, said his prayers. Eve was never tired of seeing the Mahommedans pray. Their complete lack of self-consciousness; the way in which they prayed wherever they were, or whatever they were doing, always impressed her. Sometimes it would be a solitary figure standing in the prow of a boat, dark against the pearly waters, or prostrating itself on the sand, or in some corner of a tiny garden.

" How do they know where Mecca is ? " asked Eve. " I wonder if they feel it in their bones, as Barty Jocelyn felt the North ? Do Mahommedan women pray ? "

" Not as much as men, I believe," said Hugh.

" Just the opposite of Christianity," observed Jeremy, and was reproved by Eve for being cynical.

" The truth is always cynical," he protested. " The sailors' prayers are a bit prolonged this morning, small blame to them. I should put in an extra prayer or two myself if it meant a few minutes' rest from pulling this boat along."

" It does seem a shame they should work so hard," murmured Serena, " when we are being so gloriously lazy."

As usual, she was stretched out in one of the long chairs, a blue cushion under her brown head, her eyes more often closed than open.

" I do wish, Serena," said Hugh, looking at her a little anxiously, " that you would sit upright for a few minutes every day. I'm so afraid you may turn into one of those flat fish you see spread out on a marble slab."

" That would be awful," confessed Serena, snuggling down a little more comfortably into her cushions. " But Dr. Lamb said I was to lie in the sun all day and do nothing. I'm only doing as I was told."

" We're all being disgracefully lazy," said Eve, who loved the life as much as Serena did, and spent hours watching the people on the banks or dipping into all the books in turn.

This morning she had been reading of the Old Kingdom, the Golden Age, the first splendid epoch of the Egyptian pageant. Breasted and the others had made its Pharaohs real people to her as they strode through his pages. Zozer—the first great builder in stone. The mighty Snefru. And the richest and most powerful of them all, the author of the Great Pyramid, Cheops, whom it was *so* confusing to find was the same person as Khufu.

Eve did wish that people could agree about the names of the Pharaohs. What could be more different than Khufu and Cheops, unless it were Khafre and Chephren ? And Jeremy told her it was worse still when you came to the gods. . . .

But how wonderful to learn of this civilisation, more than four thousand years old, greater in many ways than that of the Middle Ages in Europe ! Eve read of wise laws made, and justly administered; of art and mechanics so highly developed that they were never surpassed even in the later days of Egypt's magnificent history; of money minted; of writing taught in the schools so that business records and accounts might be methodically kept, and of the study of medicine. It was a state of things almost bewildering in its richness, and what pleased Eve especially, was to find that in this world of order and prosperity women were the equals of men, free, important and respected.

Eve read this last piece of information aloud, looking defiantly at Jeremy from under her lashes.

Jeremy cocked an amused eyebrow at her. " I entirely agree."

" Oh, do you ? " grumbled Eve, in a flat little voice. " How very disappointing, when I was wanting to quarrel."

" What an extraordinary thing to want to do on a morning like this," said Hugh.

" I know what we'll do," cried Eve, " as I'm feeling full of energy and Jeremy won't quarrel with me. Look here "—she rummaged among the pile of books on the top of the cabin skylight and held up one in a paper cover—" we'll learn Arabic—all except Jeremy, of course, as he speaks it already. I bought this in Cairo on purpose."

Hugh took the book from her and read the title aloud : " Arabic without a Teacher."

Serena's eyes opened in alarm.

" Oh, Eve darling, please, please don't make me learn Arabic."

" You must. Nobody can take an intelligent interest in a foreign country unless they know a certain amount of the language."

" But I'm sure I never could. I've listened to the crew talking, and it sounds like a language without any edges in it to me, and I can always get what I want, because Hugh knows several words already."

" Several words ! "

" He talks three or four Indian dialects, too."

" So useful in Egypt ! " scoffed her heartless sister.
" No, Serena, it's no good struggling, we must all learn
Arabic. Let's begin now."

" It's only necessary to learn three words in any
language," said Hugh, " bed, tea and hot water."

" Nonsense ! You're lazy, that's what's the matter
with you. When we went to Spain you only learnt one
sentence from the book I bought there—'I refuse to
travel with so many parcels.' "

" And a darn good sentence too—under the circum-
stances. You, on the other hand," said Hugh, " travelled
through Italy with conspicuous success on the one word
' sympatica.' "

" I like your book, Eve," said Jeremy, who had been
studying it with much interest. " Evidently the author
knows the gorgeous East, for, under the heading
' Sentences and Phrases in Common Use,' he begins
with : ' You are a liar ' ! I have an idea ! Each of
you had better learn a different bit, just the sentences
that you yourself are likely to need."

" My wants are very few and very, very simple,"
urged Serena.

" Yes, I think you need only learn half a dozen expressions. I'll read you a selection : ' *Ana anam el sa-ahh
ashra,*' which means : ' I sleep at ten o'clock.' "

" That's as good as a sick headache to Serena,"
scoffed Hugh.

" It is, isn't it ? " agreed Jeremy. " I'll teach her the
Arabic for ' morning, noon and night ' instead. Then
she might press on to ' this sheet is dirty,' ' fleas,' and
' hot bath.' That ought to see you through, Serena.
Hugh is catered for by ' Words Pertaining to the Mili-
tary '; Eve had better learn those, too."

Eve reached out her hand for the book, but Jeremy
held it out of her reach. " No—wait ! A fair young
thing like you must be armed at every point in this hard,
cold world. Here you can learn to deal with a cabman,

a donkey-boy, a boatman and a money-changer. I advise you to pay particular attention to the last. Money-changers are a stony-hearted, callous race."

" Give me back my book ! "

" Half a minute. Here are some gems ! ' Miscellaneous Expressions in General Use. Students are advised not to study these until they feel that they are advancing in the intricacies of the language.' Listen to this : ' *Balash awanta* '—' Stop this deceit.' And there's a footnote telling you that this is to be said to a person who beats about the bush or who endeavours to deceive you, but that if humorously uttered to a respectable individual, it will not give offence. Here's another : ' *Bokra fil mishmish* '—' When the apricots appear.' This is to be said to a person when he gives an exaggerated or false statement, and you desire to let him know that it is not accepted."

" That's the most polite way of calling someone a liar I ever heard," observed Hugh.

" Isn't it ?　The book goes on, with admirable caution, to warn you against saying it to anyone of a higher social standing than yourself, or when the conversation is serious. Here's an even better effort : ' *Esh ! Esh !* ' That means ' How wonderful ! ' and is to be employed when you desire to express irony blended with humour. Example :

" ' John : " This watch cost me twenty pounds." "

" ' James : " Esh ! Esh ! " ' "

" Unfortunately, it doesn't give John's answer."

" This is the best book you've brought on board, Eve," said Hugh.

" But I really did want to learn a little Arabic," she wailed.

" So you can," Hugh reassured her. " Of course, those bits do sound rather comic picked out like that, but as a matter of fact it's a jolly good little book. I remember it now. Our men found it no end useful during the War."

" In spite of your insulting suggestions," said Serena, " I shall be quite content with Hugh's three words : ' tea,' ' bed,' and ' hot water.' I carry on the bulk of my conversation with Moussa in English."

" By the by," inquired Eve, " what were you and our ' Dear One ' having such a heart-to-heart talk about in the saloon this morning ? I came in once, but I felt so de trop I went out again."

Serena giggled. " It was about our laundry. He was so mysterious that it was a long time before I could make head or tail of what he was saying."

" What *was* he saying ? "

" He doesn't want Eve's and my under-garments, which he very delicately described as ' particular lady-clothes,' to be washed on the lower deck where the crew would see them. The sailors wash Hugh's and Jeremy's things, but only Ibrahim and Moussa himself may set eyes on ours. Ibrahim has been washing them all the morning in the bathroom."

At that moment Ibrahim, in his stiffly-starched white overall, appeared on the upper deck, carrying a clothes-basket. He smiled languidly and murmured ' Sayeeda ' as he walked by, and proceeded to rig up a line across the stern, behind the steersman's head. Then he began to shake out and peg up one fragile garment after another. Hugh, whose chair faced that way, reported progress.

" He's hanging up that set Serena and I bought you in Monte Carlo, Eve, the pale pink one. He has just hung up the chemise, and now he is putting up the——"

" Hugh," protested Serena, " must you be so indelicate ? Moussa would be horrified if he heard you."

" There goes the nightdress I like, Serena—that pale mauve one with the what-you-may-call-it lace on it. There's a shirt of mine. Do you think Moussa knows that ? I don't feel he would approve of mixed bathing among the underwear."

Eve turned her head to look. The whole row, beautifully washed, waved slightly in the faint air made by the movement of the boat. The steersman's orange turban and dark delicate face, drooping sidewise on his slender neck, rose in the midst. Dreamy, unperturbed and melancholy, he gazed ahead up the shining reach of the river. All the " particular lady-clothes " from the Rue de la Paix might flap round his head; his thoughts were hundreds of miles away—in a little mud hut in a Nubian village, where somebody in dusty black cotton with a ring through her nose was waiting for him.

CHAPTER XI

Eve was beginning to learn what sailing up the Nile really meant. Certainly it was an occupation only suited to people of a leisurely turn of mind; not one for the hustler or the frenzied sightseer. Day after day the sun rose and set in a blaze of glory. Day after day it shone down upon a world so still that not a palm leaf stirred.

When the dahabeah stopped at a larger village than usual, Moussa generally went on shore to buy fresh vegetables. As a rule, the rest of the party accompanied him, preceded by one sailor carrying one of the tall, stout sticks so kindly provided by Mr. Cook, while a second, also complete with stick, brought up the rear.

" So that now," Eve pointed out the first time this happened, " we have seen them all: the sticks, the drawers and the musical instruments."

What struck Serena most was the extraordinary number of Singer's sewing-machines to be seen or heard, whirring away for dear life, in every third or fourth decrepit little house opening on to the narrow, dusty streets.

Back on board the *Isis* they read, smoked, talked, slept and watched the life of Egypt slipping by on the banks. They saw the women coming down to the water's edge to fill their earthenware pots, moving with all the grace of the East, their vessels poised on their heads. They waded knee-deep into the river, chattering like magpies, their legs unashamedly bare, but were ready in an instant to draw their voluminous black draperies across their faces at the sight of a man.

" Just the opposite of the Victorian ideal," Jeremy
pointed out.

Black-headed little children ran about after shrilly-
braying donkeys. Men sat on the ground in groups,
talking among themselves, their blue-and-orange clothes
contrasting with the invariable black of the women,
who distressed Serena and Eve terribly by the way they
allowed their long garments to drag behind them
through the dust.

All up and down the Nile, from dawn to dusk, the
shadûfs lifted the water from the river to the thirsty
land above, as they had done for thousands of years in
Egypt. The shadûf men in their blue or white loin-
cloths dipped and rose, dipped and rose, with endless
monotony, the muscles of their backs rippling like the
parts of some beautiful, smooth-running machine under
their bronze skins.

The song they sang was thousands of years old, too—
older than the Pyramids, Jeremy said.

" Though how they have any breath left for singing,
I can't imagine," he added. " You have no idea what
gruelling work it is." He and Eve had stopped beside
a shadûf on one of their early morning walks.

" Is it ? It looks easy, and I'm sure a shadûf must
be the origin of a see-saw, it's so exactly like one. It's
only a long pole fastened on to a cross-beam, with a
leather bucket at one end and a big lump of clay at the
other, instead of a couple of children."

" It's not as easy as it looks, though," said Jeremy.

" This man doesn't seem to be making much effort,"
observed Eve, as she watched him draw the shallow
leather bucket down to the water at his feet, while the
chunk of dried clay at the other end of the pole rose up
into the air. The next moment the heavy clay weighed
the see-saw down; guided by the man, the dripping
bucket soared a full arm's length above his head, where,
with a skilful twist of his hands, he tilted the water out
into the narrow channel dug to receive it. Then he

pulled the empty bucket down again, and the whole business began afresh.

" Do let me try," begged Eve, but with all her efforts she found she could not even pull the bucket right down to the water, and she and Jeremy were a very wet couple before she had finished. From then onwards Eve had a very great respect for the shadûf workers.

Higher up the Nile, Jeremy told her, she would see fewer of them, for there they had a different kind of apparatus—a sakkieh. A long loop of rope hung with a number of earthenware pots that dipped into the river in turn, worked by one or two bullocks or a camel, which walked round and round in a circle, turning a flat wooden wheel with cogs in it.

" But we shan't get as far as the sakkiehs at this rate," said Eve sadly. " I don't believe there's ever going to be any wind again in Egypt."

. . . . .

At last, one morning, a strong wind did get up, but alas, it came from the south !

Now the towing was really hard work, especially when the *Isis* had to round a projection of land. Time and again she stuck on the sand, and then the men got long poles and leaned and pushed, uttering the most heart-rending groans, until they got her off again. They sang chanties as they worked, as old as the song of the shadûf. " Leave it to the Lord, leave it to the Lord," they chanted, hauling on the ropes instead of following their own good advice. " Now we are looking for Helisa," was another favourite. Helisa, Moussa told Eve, was a son of Noah, who had been drowned. The crew worked valiantly, but what with hidden sandbanks, the powerful current which often drove them ashore, and the strong head wind, they were not able to make more than a few miles a day.

The lazy, sunlit life developed a kind of mental and physical inertia in the four idle passengers on the dahabeah, so that it was a considerable shock when Moussa

came into the saloon one breakfast time and announced
that they were to go an excursion. Everyone gazed at
him in horror, Serena the most agitated of them all.

What !—they asked—were they to be disturbed from
the even tenor of their ways for anything so exhausting
as an excursion ? What a horrible idea ! But Moussa
reassured them. It was hardly to be called an excursion,
he said ; it was such a very little one.

Groaning, they consented, and reluctantly set off. A
short walk up a sandy slope brought them to a great
limestone rock, high, square and solid, with a huge
archway in it, like some rude Arc de Triomphe, but
hewn out of the living rock.

" The Gates of the Desert," said Moussa.

Behind the archway was a quarry of the Twelfth
Dynasty, where the scarped cliff face still showed the
marks of tools.

" When on earth was the Twelfth Dynasty ? " asked
Eve. " I haven't the least idea. Pray, dear Mamma,
who were its Pharaohs ? "

" The Amenemhets and the Sesostris," replied Jeremy.

" Let's lie in the sand," suggested Hugh, " if Eve is
going to ask intelligent questions."

Moussa withdrew to a discreet distance and they settled
themselves down in lounging attitudes that would
certainly not have been permitted by the original Mrs.
Markham. Hugh and Jeremy lay flat on their backs,
their hands behind their heads and their panamas pulled
well over their eyes. Serena curled herself up in the
warmth like a contented cat, and Eve was conscious of a
sensual enjoyment in the feel of the hot sand as she
said dreamily :

" I know why the Old Kingdom came to a bad end
with the Sixth Dynasty. It was because the nobles got
so powerful that the Pharaoh couldn't keep his end up
against them. But what happened after that, Jeremy ? "

" Three hundred years of confusion, when a string of
vague Pharaohs struggled along somehow or other

through four dynasties, the seventh to the tenth. Ra, the sun god, came to the fore then, and became the great State god of the country."

" What a shame ! " cried Eve. " I don't think they ought to have put anyone above my darling Horus."

" The Eleventh Dynasty began to bring order out of chaos. That was the start of the Middle Kingdom."

" I don't believe it can have been as fine as the old one," declared Eve.

" It was quite as fine in rather a different way," said Jeremy. " The nobles had come to stay, and the Pharaohs ruled over what had really become a great feudal state. A big middle class appeared, too, for the first time. Men learned in arts and crafts, business and agriculture, who worked under the king."

" But were the Pharaohs themselves as splendid as Cheops and Zozer ? "

" The Twelfth Dynasty men were superb," said Jeremy. " Sesostris III was one of Egypt's greatest warriors, and Amenemhet III her greatest administrator. He was the outstanding figure of the Classic Age, as it's called, as Cheops was of the Old Kingdom."

" The Old Kingdom was the ' Golden Age,' " murmured Eve, " when the gods still held communion with men."

" Those were the days when it was good to be Pharaoh," agreed Jeremy. " I think it's Moret who points out the difference between the portraits of the Third and Fourth Dynasty rulers and those of the Twelfth. In the first you see Majesty omnipotent, serene and imperturbable. But a thousand years later conditions were altered, and the Pharaohs of the Middle Kingdom, gods though they were, had to study their people and learn the art of government. The faces of the Amenemhets and the Sesostris are very different from those of Cheops and Khafra. Their brows are furrowed and their eyes are weary. Royalty was no light burden in Egypt then."

" Moussa said to me the other day," remarked Serena, " ' Mr. Vaughan—he knows as much as Moussa.' "

" That's praise indeed," said Hugh, " for our ' Dear One ' is not what you would call a modest flower."

" But he's such a lamb ! " protested Eve. " I do so want to know if he loves his wife and if he has a large family and all about them."

" For Heaven's sake don't ask him ! " exclaimed her brother-in-law. " It's contrary to all etiquette to question a Mahommedan about his family. Serena and Eve are never happy," he told Jeremy, " until they know the life story of everybody they meet. I have actually known them able to tell me the number, names and ages of a porter's children, when he has done no more than put their luggage into a railway carriage. How they do it, I don't know."

" I'm sure Moussa is very much a family man," said Serena. " I can tell it by the tender way he looks after Eve and me."

" My dear child, Cook's pay him a very good salary to treat you tenderly."

" What a sordid view to take ! " cried Eve. " Everyone knows that there's one kind of service that is paid for and quite another kind which is given for love."

" And you think Moussa loves us ? " asked Hugh.

" I know he loves Serena and me."

" He ought to love us," said Jeremy, " seeing we are as wax in his hands. We must be a welcome change after the people who complained of his lack of pep."

" All the same," declared Eve, " I shan't be happy until I know if he loves his wife, and the names of his children."

" Wife or wives ? " inquired Jeremy blandly. But Eve scorned to reply.

CHAPTER XII

SOUTH WIND

THE *Isis* had been stuck upon sand-banks or towed for so many days now that through the consciousness of everyone ran the thought and feeling of the Nile, like a symbol of Eternity, without beginning or end— sometimes a pale greenish colour, sometimes a steely blue, sometimes silvery under the moon, but always slipping past them between the green strips of fertile land that made modern Egypt what it was, or between low sandy banks that told of the stark, relentless desert which could never be entirely conquered.

Jeremy and Hugh began to get restless, but, as Eve said, though they might not be seeing any of the sights, they were at least absorbing the daily life of Egypt into their minds. A pastoral life, unchanged since the days of the Pharaohs. Along the tops of the banks there passed continually the silhouettes of camels, donkeys, flocks of sheep led by piping herdsmen, women with water-jars on their heads, all strung out on a long frieze with palm trees and a deep blue sky or a rose-coloured sunset behind them. It was the painfully facile beauty of a picture post-card, Eve thought, but beauty all the same, unchanged and unchanging. It was only her own sophistication, she knew, that spoiled it the least little bit in the world for her, although she loved it so much and never tired of it. She laughed every evening when she watched the ferry-boats packed so tightly with humans and animals. It always seemed impossible that the last half-dozen could ever be crowded on board, but they were, until the closely packed boats looked just like a Noah's Ark with the lid off. Eve grew to know the sounds of the Nile too—the creaking of the shadûfs, which always made her think of the cawing of the rooks at home in Wiltshire, the lowing of the herds, the cries of the sailors, and their mournful, minor chanties, the chattering of innumerable birds and people, and the easy laughter.

Every morning she and Jeremy had their walk before breakfast, and to Eve this was almost the best part of the day, although they sometimes came perilously near to quarrelling, and would have, had not Jeremy been so difficult to quarrel with. That was the annoying thing about him. Sometimes, Eve didn't know why, she felt a prickle of antagonism towards him, a desire to make him angry, or even to hurt him just a little, though of course she would never be able to. Why did she ever want to, she wondered?

It was true he often teased her, but then so did Hugh. She was quite used to that and, as Jeremy had once told her, she liked any attention better than none. Jeremy had such an exasperating way of knowing what you were thinking, and seeing through you when, for some very good reason or other, you wanted to pull the least little bit of cotton-wool over his eyes. On the whole, though, they were the best of friends, which was lucky. For, although Eve knew that Serena loved her very dearly and that Hugh was what she described as 'extremely attached' to her, he and Serena were still so much in love with one another after twelve years of married life that sometimes Eve might have felt the least bit lonely if it hadn't been for Jeremy. Hugh wasn't what you would call a demonstrative person, but it was obvious that he was entirely wrapped up in Serena, who, for her part, openly adored him in a manner which Eve scoffed at as sloppy, but which she secretly thought delightful. She said as much to Jeremy.

"Yes," he agreed, " it's astounding luck in a world of misfits to have chosen as well as those two, though any

KARNAK.

KARNAK.

[*To face page* 80.

man would be hard to please if he couldn't be happy with Serena."

" She's an angel," cried Eve warmly, " and I ought to know if anyone does."

" The best of it is," continued Jeremy, " they're so happy themselves they make everyone happy round them. There's an atmosphere about their house that makes it the pleasantest I know. I feel as much at home there as I do at my mother's, on Long Island."

" Do you know," said Eve, " I always forget you're half American. Perhaps it's because I've never seen your mother. What's she like, Jeremy ? "

" A charming person. She and I have always got on very well together, although I haven't seen as much of her as I should like. I was still quite a small boy when she married again and went back to America to live, and I had to stay at school in England; but I always went out to them for the summer holidays, and a very good time they gave me too."

" And what's your step-father like ? " asked Eve, who took a passionate interest in other people's relations. " Do you like him too ? "

" Rather ! He's a most amusing fellow, and Dan, my half-brother, is exactly like him. Very good-looking too."

" What does he do ? "

" He's with his father, who's one of the best-known lawyers in New York. Dan's coming on very well."

" What fun if he could have come to Egypt with us ! "

" Yes, I wish he could have. It would have been a particularly good thing for him just now—for more reasons than one."

" Oh ? " said Eve, immediately devoured by curiosity.

What could Jeremy mean ? Perhaps he had some idea of making a match between herself and Dan ? What a romantic idea ! She felt quite excited about it. It was always so easy to feel excited about a young man you had never seen.

Or perhaps Dan had got into a mess at home? Probably there was some woman twenty years older than himself, a widow, or something intriguing like that. Eve glanced at Jeremy out of the corner of her eye to see if there were any chance of getting it out of him. He looked at her and laughed:

"No, it's none of the things you're thinking."

Eve laughed back: "I don't know why I don't hate you, Jeremy; sometimes I think I do."

At lunch that day the *Isis*, for the fourth time since breakfast, ran into the bank, and a large piece of Egypt came crashing through the window to scatter itself all over the floor. It was always difficult towing round a bend, because the current of the river was so strong that it pulled the boat in.

Moussa came along from the lower deck and gazed at the debris of earth and grass more in sorrow than in anger, and Hugh and Jeremy went out to watch the sailors push off again. Always well in the forefront of the picture, Moussa seized a long pole and pushed too, or rather he would have pushed, but his pole always fell limply on to the top of the water, and he himself appeared to be in grave danger of falling in after it.

"I don't believe the north wind ever blows in this infernal country," grumbled Hugh, later in the afternoon, slapping wildly about him with a fly whisk.

"Darling," protested Serena, "you don't kill the flies quite dead with that weapon. Look, some of them are still wriggling on the deck. You must put your foot on them. Even flies must be killed kindly."

"Kindly!" ejaculated Hugh. "If I had my way I'd have them all boiled in oil. I should like to know, too, why these infernal sugar factories that Egypt seems so full of want to blow their whistles all day long. They're worse than ever to-day."

"Let's ask Moussa," suggested Eve. "He always has a reason for everything."

" And it's always a damned stupid one," said Jeremy
" How can you say such an unkind thing about our
' Dear One ' ? " protested Eve.

Now there was nothing Moussa loved more than
giving Eve information, and he bustled up delightedly
when she called him.

" Mam'selle," he explained, his tongue waggling
violently as he tried to smile and talk at the same time,
" they blow to tell the people they do not need them at
the mills to-day."

Eve was puzzled. " But at that rate," she demurred,
" the mills never want anybody to work at them, because
they're always blowing their whistles. And surely one
blow would be enough just to tell them that ? Why do
they go on doing it ? "

Moussa looked a little dashed; the hand he loved had
dealt him a blow below the belt. He waggled his head
distractedly from side to side, while his hands shot out,
palms upwards, in an expostulating gesture.

" Mam'selle," he began again, vainly searching for a
convincing answer—but Allah, more merciful than Eve,
ran the *Isis* at this critical moment with a hard thud on to
another sand-bank, and Moussa, caught unawares, sat
down abruptly on the sharp, metal-bound corner of a
steamer trunk. His reputation for infallibility was saved
at the expense of a few minutes' acute pain. It was well
worth it, and, hastily picking himself up, he flapped
thankfully down to the lower deck, where he proceeded
to get more in the way than usual.

It turned out to be a particularly obstinate sand-bank,
but that was no reason, Eve considered, for both Hugh
and Jeremy to grumble so much. Perhaps it was the
fault of the south wind that, Mr. Johnson had warned
them, had such an irritating effect on the temper.

Unfortunately the cook chose this particular evening
to make the sauce for the iced asparagus of paraffin
instead of vinegar. The result was ghastly. The cook
cried so much over the sweet that followed, that it was

salt from his tears, and it needed an extra strong dose of brandy to restore him.

This disturbance subsided, Jeremy announced that he should speak seriously to Moussa.

" He ought to get into touch with Cook's," he declared, " and wire for a tug or something. It's ridiculous to stay here and do nothing, and I shall tell him so."

" Whatever you do," urged Serena, " don't speak harshly to him. After all, it isn't his fault. Even Moussa can't make the north wind blow, and I'm sure he does his best."

" And he is so sensitive," put in Eve.

" Sensitive ! "

" He is—very. You won't bully him ? "

" I shan't bully him, but I may have to speak to him for his good," said Jeremy as he stalked out of the saloon.

In a few minutes he was back again. " I've galvanised him," he told them, " into flagging a tourist steamer of Cook's that is due to reach this stretch of river within the next hour. It will anchor for the night near Minia, and Moussa will give instructions to somebody in authority on board to telegraph from there to Cairo and find out what can be done."

It was dark by now, and, as usual, the wind had dropped with the sun, so that it was not too cold to sit on the deck, muffled up in coats, and keep a look-out for the steamer.

In the still night they heard the noise of her engines long before they saw her round the bend of the river, gleaming with lights from stem to stern, thrashing the black water into whiteness with her paddles.

Moussa and Said, the latter more like a fluttered hen than ever, went off with two or three sailors in the dinghy, a lighted lantern in the prow. The reis hoisted the signal light on board the *Isis*, and Serena and Eve felt terribly important as the big boat slowed down and came to a standstill, while all the tourists crowded to the rail to see what was happening. Moussa climbed on board and was met by a uniformed official, and the pair of them could be seen walking away down the lighted deck and disappearing into a state-room. In a few minutes the dinghy was pushed off again without Moussa, the steamer's engines were re-started, and she thrashed slowly past the *Isis*, while the passengers waved scarves and handkerchiefs in friendly farewell.

"But they've got Moussa," cried Eve.

"This is awful!" wailed Serena. "What *shall* we do?"

They were but little soothed when Mahomed translated the message brought back by the fluttered hen—that Moussa had gone on to Minia for the night, four miles up the river, where he would get into touch with Cairo and Cook's.

Hugh and Jeremy, once they felt proper steps were being taken, were perfectly cheerful. But not even the mail-bag that Said had brought from the steamer, full of letters from home, could do more than distract Serena and Eve for a few moments from their despair.

They refused to be comforted. They had lost their Moussa. Those tourists had him. Their kind, their faithful, their devoted Moussa. Feeling forlorn, helpless and unloved they went silently and very miserably to bed.

.   .   .   .   .

Eve was surprised that the *Isis* started at the usual hour the next morning, and to see the early cup of tea and breakfast appear in due order. She had thought that without Moussa none of the lesser lights on board would be able to function, but the only thing which did suffer from his absence was the bath-water, which was only tepid. But then the reis and Mohamed were capable people, while the filterman, who was responsible for the bath-water, was a poor creature, furtive and uncouth-looking. Jeremy called him the 'pariah,' because he always sat apart from the rest of the crew.

It was a divine morning and the river at its loveliest. Soon after breakfast the dahabeah was towed past a little village whose inhabitants were busy making bricks at the water's edge. They shaped them in little four-sided wooden boxes without top or bottom, and, unlike the Israelites, made them of mud, mixed with straw.

All the villages of Lower Egypt were dirty and dilapidated, and this one was no exception to the rule. The goats, with flapping ears like spaniels, walked about on the flat roofs of the mud houses, and the women climbed up there too, to watch the strangers pass. These mud buildings invariably looked so decrepit that Eve always expected women, goats and all to fall through them to the ground. The shadûfs were working busily. Water buffaloes and camels came down to the Nile to drink; and children played happily in dust that would have driven English mothers, full of ideas of hygiene and microbes, to despair.

The second village was exactly like the first, only here things began to happen. A market of sorts was being held and the beach was crowded with people and camels, the latter so laden with bundles of sugar-cane that they looked more like emus than anything else, for the long stalks and leaves cascaded over their hind-quarters to the ground in an immense, curving tail. When the camels walked, the leaves made a rustling sound like silk petticoats. One animal was being laden with piles of straw, until Eve fully expected to see the proverbial last one break his back. Suddenly, into the midst of this busy scene, with a great cracking of whips and clattering of hoofs, burst a carriage and pair, shabby but impressive. The vehicle was of the "barouche-landau" type, so admired by Mrs. Elton, and in the middle of it, surrounded by wicker crates of cabbages, cauliflowers, carrots, lettuces, loaves of bread, oranges and goodness knows what else, sat Moussa in all his glory—strawberry sateen, yellow elastic-sided boots and Boston velvet grips complete. Even Hugh and Jeremy condescended to show a slight degree of pleasure. Serena and Eve were frankly emotional.

The sailors ran out the gangway and trotted off to unpack Moussa, who then produced his purse and started an excited discussion with the driver, listened to with admiration by the watching crowd. Their two voices rose higher and higher, Moussa's gesticulations became ever wilder, while the driver appeared in imminent danger of falling off the box-seat in his excitement.

A climax of vituperation was reached. It seemed inevitable that the most horrible bloodshed must follow, when, with startling suddenness, the whole thing ended, apparently with perfect satisfaction on both sides. Moussa proceeded to hand out infinitesimal coins all round with the superb air of a Grand Vizier distributing *largesse*, and came on board so full of chat and bubble that for the first few minutes it appeared as if he must have done something really effective in Minia. Alas! when the froth was blown off the top of his talk there was nothing very encouraging left. No tug was to be had nearer than Asyut, still more than ninety miles away. There was nothing for it but to go slowly on.

However, with their 'Dear One' back once more in the family circle and the fresh supplies he had brought with him looking so good, everyone sat down to lunch in a state of cheerful resignation. No sooner had they started on the *hors d'œuvre* than something happened.

A tiny puff of wind blew in through one of the open windows, swept all the note-paper from the writing table to the floor, and went out of the window opposite. Forks suspended, everybody waited to see if there were more to follow. In sixty seconds the wind was blowing steadily, growing stronger every moment and, most wonderful of all, straight from the north.

The saloon door opened and Moussa filled the entrance, swelling with pride. He struck an attitude, threw out his right hand with a dramatic flourish and announced triumphantly : " I bring you no tug, but see—I bring you the north wind ! "

.   .   .   .   .

The north wind blew and blew, the sun shone, and the *Isis* sailed so fast that she reached Beni Hassan in the evening. Here she was to anchor for the night, and, the following morning, Moussa told her passengers, they were to make an expedition to the tombs—whose yawning holes they could see high up in the cliff some way inland.

His announcement was received with heavy gloom. No one had heard of these particular tombs except Jeremy, and even he had never seen them, and no one wanted to.

" Must we go, Moussa ? " asked Eve plaintively. " We'd so much rather get on to Luxor."

" Must see the tombs, Mam'selle. Very good ones."

" Look them up in Powers's, Eve," suggested Serena. " See if he says we must."

Eve opened a little volume called " Egypt "—one of the University Travel Series, which they had already found full of useful information. Unfortunately she gathered from it that, whatever else they did or did not see, they must at all costs visit the tombs of Beni Hassan. They were, Mr. Powers assured them, the greatest monument of the Middle Kingdom, and possessed columns of such staggering importance that he devoted page after page to them.

" But what," asked Eve, " is a ' polygonal pier,' and what is an ' abacus ' ? Don't you think, Moussa, these tombs are for more intelligent people than us ?—Architects, at the very least ? "

" Must see the tombs of Beni Hassan, Mam'selle," repeated Moussa firmly, " very, very wonderful tombs."

" Somehow I feel we could still go on sleeping and eating without seeing them," protested Eve, but even her pleading glances were of no avail. Nothing would turn Moussa from his high purpose, and he then and there set out to hire donkeys for the following morning.

"Why, oh why," wailed Serena, "did anyone complain of his lack of pep?"

"We have one chance, and one only," said Hugh with the calmness of despair, "and that is, another gale from the north. We should have to go on then."

So they all went to bed praying earnestly for help from the right quarter, but, as they had already discovered, not even prayer would make the north wind blow in Egypt if it didn't want to, and they woke to find a chilly breeze blowing determinedly from the south.

They set out in bright sunshine on the best donkeys obtainable—which was not saying much, for the donkeys of Beni Hassan were always a notoriously poor breed. These started off at a promising pace, but at the end of a spirited gallop of two hundred yards, Hugh's animal, who rejoiced in the name of Rameses-Telephone-Telegraph, threw one of the best riders to hounds in England neatly over its head into the sand by the simple process of falling on to its own nose.

"For the Lord's sake, don't tell this story at home," exclaimed Hugh, as he picked himself up, "or I shall never hear the last of it in the Mess."

Moussa nearly blew up with indignation, but Hugh refused to allow the poor little brute to be penalised, and set off again at a sober gait better suited to its powers. They rode through the deserted ruins of a large village and climbed up the last steep slope of sand on foot.

The tombs, wonderfully set high up in the cliff face, were great square rooms. Standing inside them, Eve looked out over a glorious view of the winding Nile and the strip of vivid green on either side of it, and, beyond, the rolling desert, incredibly golden until it was lost in the haze on the horizon. There were one hundred and fifty of these tombs, Moussa told them, but added, to their great relief, that they were only to see four. They dutifully studied the columns the architectural

importance of which had roused Mr. Powers to such
enthusiasm, but felt that to light-hearted travellers like
themselves the wall-paintings, defaced as they were, were
of greater interest—especially those scenes which Moussa
told them represented Joseph and his brethren, apparently doing physical jerks. There were wrestling
matches and hunting scenes, all amazingly full of spirit,
with the bodies, owing to the flat style of painting,
going two ways at once in the engaging Egyptian
manner, which Eve decided looked quite natural and
possible once you got used to it.

"Now, Eve," said Jeremy, as they mounted their
donkeys again, "don't let me hear you complain any
more that you haven't been taken sight-seeing. When
you get back to England, and people ask you what you
thought of the Sphinx and the Pyramids, and the temples
of Karnak and Abu Simbel, you'll only need to look
down your nose in a superior fashion and say : ' Oh !
Nobody bothers about them now, but I have seen the
tombs of Beni Hassan.' You'll find it'll go very well,
for, as nobody will have heard of them, everybody will
be enormously impressed."

That afternoon they ran into a sand-storm. It came
with startling suddenness. A donkey ran amok on the
shore. The palm trees bent over, their leaves streaming
like flags in the wind. The river was churned up into
short rough waves. In three or four minutes the air
was so thick with sand that it was as dense as a London
fog, and no one could see more than a few yards in
front of them. That was the first evening they saw no
sunset, and though the wind dropped at the usual hour,
the weather was cold and gloomy.

Fortunately the cook elected to give them an extra
good dinner, perhaps by way of consolation, and it was
very snug and comfortable in the cheerfully lighted saloon.

As Moussa had remarked to Eve when handing her
on board after the morning's expedition : " Home is
always sweet home, is it not, Mam'selle ? "

CHAPTER XIII

A GAME OF GOLF

THERE was no trace of yesterday's storm the next morning, which dawned calm and cloudless. But although the day began like a dozen others, looking back upon it, Serena and Eve realised that it had been the turning point in their lives on the *Isis*, for after that day neither Hugh nor Jeremy ever grumbled again at the fine weather.

It was a stroke of genius of Moussa's that changed the whole face of things.

He appeared on the upper deck just after breakfast, and, with his most dramatic air, held out an enormous hand, in the palm of which lay four curious-looking objects.

" What are they ? " inquired Eve, getting up to look.

" Golf balls, Mam'selle," announced Moussa proudly.

At the magic word ' golf,' Hugh and Jeremy also came to look. The balls appeared to be made out of somebody's cast-off socks of a ginger shade of worsted, marvellously compressed, so that they were quite tight and hard, and bound round with very fine string which divided them into quarters like an orange. In shape they were like the " elliptical billiard-balls " in the *Mikado*.

" Where on earth did you get them ? " asked Hugh.

Beaming triumphantly from ear to ear, Moussa proclaimed them the work of his own hands, and further produced three pieces of firewood, each with a scrap of torn shirt attached for a flag.

" You have the clubs, I know, sirs, for I see them. Now we go to play golf ! "

"But where?" asked Eve, looking round her rather wildly at the sand-bank into which the *Isis* had just bumped softly.

"On there, Mam'selle," he replied, waving his hand at the same wide stretch of sand. "Very good place, Mam'selle," and he led the way in his cheerful sports costume of gold and black-striped sateen and very yellow leather elastic-sided boots.

The others followed meekly, carrying an iron and two putters between them : real golf balls they dare not take, as Moussa had seen fit to provide them with substitutes.

Lazy Serena excused herself from playing on the grounds of her appendicitis, but she came with them, for they were all beginning to get quite worked-up by Moussa's enthusiasm. Besides, it was so lovely in the sun, and the sand was so soft to walk on, and the Nile looked even more wonderful than usual this morning.

The game was held up at the start by a fierce discussion as to who should have the one ball which was slightly smaller and harder than the other three—and very nearly round.

"Of course *I* must have it," cried Eve, "as I'm the only girl. I shall take it as part of my handicap, and you must both of you give me a stroke a hole as well. Besides, I'm sure Moussa meant me to have this dear little ball, didn't you, Moussa?"

Moussa, who adored Eve, gave her his whole-hearted support. "Mam'selle, I make that ball on purpose for you."

"There, you see? Now move out of the way, you two. I'm going to drive."

"But there's no hole to drive to," objected Jeremy. "It's easy enough to drive with nothing but a plain stretch of sand ahead of you."

"I go to make the hole," yelled the excited Moussa, and flapped off, bearing his three little bits of firewood with him.

Eve took a full swing with the iron. Her worsted

ball tottered off the tee, rolled two feet, and settled down in one of Moussa's enormous footprints.

" Rotten ! " scoffed Jeremy. " That's your stroke gone, Eve."

" Try it yourself," she replied, a trifle dashed, " it's a jolly sight harder than it looks."

Jeremy did try, and his ball shot off at right angles into a large bed of onions, missing the head of the amazed fellah at work among them by the skin of his teeth.

" Hurrah ! " cried Eve delightedly.

" The fact of the matter is, neither of you can play golf," said Hugh. " Just watch me, and see how it ought to be done." And, to the intense annoyance of the other two, he hit his own tangerine-shaped ball of worsted hard in the middle, and it sailed a good five yards straight down the course.

" I told you so," crowed he, with vulgar triumph.

" Conceited creature ! " said Eve. " It was the wildest fluke, and, anyway, I'm not at all sure that an oval-shaped ball isn't better than a round one on such soft sand."

" Ah, it's too late to change now ! You should have thought of that before. I'll tell you one thing— we could only play with these worsted balls here. A real golf ball would go into the Nile at every shot."

" What do I do next ? " inquired Eve. " Is our ' Dear One's ' footprint a bunker ? Do I send him back for a niblick, or may I lift it out and drop ? "

" Oh, you must have a fresh shot altogether, darling," said Serena, " that's such a horrid place. They can't be so unfair as to make you play out of it."

" Unfair be blowed ! " protested Jeremy. " She had the pick of the balls and a stroke a hole—a grossly unfair handicap on a strange course."

" It is," agreed Hugh, " but as she had the first shot with these peculiar balls we'll let her have it again just this once. For the future we'd better agree to pick out of a Moussa footprint when it's on the green. We

can't possibly putt through them, and in our long game
we must treat them as bunkers."

"All right," said Jeremy. "But it's all very well for
you—you aren't stuck in a lot of green food. If Eve
gets into my onion bed I'm damned if she shan't play
out properly."

Fortunately for Eve her second shot was luckier,
though still short of Hugh's magnificent effort. Jeremy
walked off full of determination, waved the goggle-eyed
fellah to one side, and took a tremendous whack at his
ball. It shot straight up into the air in a cloud of
uprooted onions, and fell to earth in exactly the same
spot it had started from. After this the fellah took to
his heels and ran for dear life while Jeremy took his
putter, and hit ball, sand and onions about with strict
impartiality.

"How many?" asked Hugh tactlessly, as he finally
got back to the course.

"Don't ask stupid questions," said Jeremy, using the
putter as a brassy, and gradually working his way
towards the hole that Moussa, sunk on one fat knee,
had scooped out of the sand and adorned with one of
his bits of firewood.

With diabolical cunning, he had elected to make it
on the top of an eleven-foot mound, and Hugh's and
Jeremy's language grew violent. Up to the top of the
mound each ginger ball would roll, only to roll swiftly
down the sloping sand again. Again and again it
happened, until Moussa's fat sides shook with laughter.
He was highly delighted when Hugh at last holed out
in seventeen.

By this time the players were thoroughly bitten with
the game, and, hot and happy, the two men drove off
from the next tee, but when it came to Eve's turn, and
Moussa produced a large cork from his pocket and teed
the ball up for her a good two yards in front of the
men's tee, they made indignant noises.

"Hi, Moussa, none of that!" protested Hugh.

" She may get away with the cork, but I'm hanged if she shall have a start as well."

Moussa only chuckled and waved them airily aside.

" Mam'selle," he declared, " she has the arms weaker."

Eve stuck her tongue out in a regrettably vulgar manner, and drove off. By a miracle her ball sailed through the air and dropped with a thud well beyond either of the other two.

" The arms weaker indeed ! " snorted Jeremy.

Eve won that hole, which was hardly surprising, and Hugh and Jeremy halved the third.

On the fourth tee Serena said she would walk on and make the hole.

" Wait till we've driven," said Hugh, " it's safer."

" Not always," observed Jeremy, flinching slightly as Hugh narrowly missed him with a hooked shot.

" Can you claim a stroke when your ball begins to come unwound ? " asked Hugh. " Mine has a little bit of string dangling out of it."

" Certainly not. It's a rub of the green that may happen to the best of us," said Jeremy.

He sliced his own drive and so did Eve. But what was their rage and indignation when Serena calmly walked off in the direction Hugh's ball had taken, and proceeded to dig the hole only a short approach shot beyond it !

" But truly I always meant to make it out here," she insisted, " long before any of you drove. I did indeed, Jeremy."

" We don't believe a word of it, do we, Eve ? Your parents got your name wrong, Serena—you ought to have been called Sapphira every time."

" It's marriage that does it," said Eve, " I've always noticed it makes women quite unscrupulous."

" Don't talk so much," said Hugh, " I can't play a decent game in such a spate of conversation. I'm in another of Moussa's footprints."

" Stick to your putter," advised Jeremy, " the secret

of this unusual game is to play with a flat-headed aluminium putter all through."

"I can't putt to-day, though," complained Hugh, lashing wildly about.

"But to dig you are not ashamed," observed Jeremy. "Do you mind knocking up the sand into your own eyes the next time instead of mine? As a matter of fact, you can stop your excavations, because Eve holed out half an hour ago."

"Oh, did she? Moussa probably pushed her ball in. Well, it's your honour, Eve, thanks to Moussa's gross favouritism."

Moussa bubbled with joy, and when, by the most outrageous fluke, Eve's ball fell plop into the hole at her third shot, from a ricochet out of one of his own footprints, which gave her the match, his triumph knew no bounds.

"Well," said Jeremy, "in spite of the flagrant cheating of one of the players and the unscrupulous behaviour of the wife of another, this is a damn good game of yours, Moussa. I'll play you again to-morrow for twenty piastres, Hugh."

"I'm on," said Hugh.

And Serena and Eve looked at one another with mysterious little womanly smiles that said: "What babies men are . . . we shan't hear so many complaints now——"

And Serena and Eve were right.

KARNAK.

KARNAK.

[To face page 97.

CHAPTER XIV

AKHNATON

ONE clear, still morning, when not a breath stirred upon land or water, the *Isis* reached Tel el Amarna—a great natural amphitheatre of desert; and in the distance a semi-circle of tawny cliffs that curved round its pale smoothness like a crescent moon whose horns reached down to the Nile. Eve, fresh from reading the life of Akhnaton, was all eagerness to see the place where he had built his city, for the strangest, most fascinating of all the Pharaohs had cast his spell over her. She opened the book again now and studied the pictures.

What a frail, misshapen body he had, and such a curiously long, elongated head, like a rugger ball. But how profoundly interesting the face was, with the high, narrow forehead of the religious fanatic, and the full, curved lips of the dreamer; and what large, mournful eyes, heavy-lidded and beautiful.

Eve turned the pages until she found the coloured reproduction of the famous painted limestone bust of Nefertiti, his queen—the 'Beautiful One,' with the small, fine bones of cheek and jaw, the pouting red lips, the long, dark eyes, and, loveliest of all, the exquisite poise of the head on the slender throat.

" All that rubbish you read," thought Eve, " about a neck like the stalk of a flower wouldn't seem a bit silly if it were written about Nefertiti. What a tragedy that the children didn't take after her instead of Akhnaton, especially as they were all girls. I wonder if they inherited his epilepsy too ? And I wonder why so many great religious leaders were epileptic ? St. Paul

H   97

and Mahomed, for instance ?   It must have been
terribly upsetting for their wives.   But public men—if
you could call them that—are generally a little difficult
to be married to."

The dahabeah was tied up at the foot of the steep
bank for the crew's midday meal, and Moussa led his
party up it, through an untidy village and out on to the
edge of the plain.   Eve looked round her with a puzzled
air.

" Where was the city of Aton ? " she asked.

" Here," replied Jeremy.

" But the palaces and the temples and the gardens ?
There must be something left."

" There's a bit of a wall over there," Hugh pointed
out.

" That's all that's left of Akhnaton's palace," said
Jeremy.   " There was a rather wonderful painted floor,
but they moved that down to Cairo."

" Oh, poor Akhnaton ! " cried Eve as they turned
into the pathetic little ruin.   " Just a few bits of wall
and some broken pillars ! "

" Akhnaton ?   He was the fellow they called the
' Heretic King,' wasn't he ? " asked Hugh.

" Yes, but it's a wicked shame to call him that," cried
Eve, " just because he founded a beautiful new religion
and said there was only one God."

" Did he do that ? " asked Serena, dropping gracefully
down on to the warm sand in a patch of shade.   " That
must have startled the Egyptians rather.   Or had they
shed a few hundred of their old gods by then ? "

" Heavens, no ! " replied Eve, as she and the two men
followed Serena's example.   " This was only the
eighteenth dynasty.   Egypt had given up being an
ordinary kingdom then and had turned into a great
Empire, and the old gods were on the very top of the
wave.   The priests, especially the ones at Karnak who
worshipped Amon Ra, ran the whole show.   Akhnaton's
name when he came to the throne wasn't Akhnaton at

all, but Amenhotep IV, which meant ' Amon is satisfied ' ! "

" I like that better than Akhnaton," said Serena, " it's stronger. Why did he change it ? "

" Because he . . ." Eve broke off. " No, that's beginning in the middle. The difficulty was that when his father Amenhotep the Magnificent died, the Empire had got a bit out of hand, and needed a very strong, hard-headed man to govern it properly, and Akhnaton was only a boy of fifteen."

" Poor child ! " murmured the tender-hearted Serena. " Hadn't he anyone to help him ? "

" Yes, but they weren't really the best kind of people for the job. One was his mother, Queen Tiy."

" Tiy ? That's a funny name, too."

" It is rather; but she wasn't at all a funny woman, she was a rather masterful person. Then there was Nefertiti, Akhnaton's wife, and a favourite priest of his mother's called Eye."

" Two women and a priest ! " snorted Hugh.

" They certainly weren't very wise advisers for Akhnaton, but I'm sure being women had nothing to do with it," declared Eve firmly.

" I doubt if anything would have made much difference in the long run," put in Jeremy. " Akhnaton was a religious fanatic, and they are notoriously difficult people to deal with. He was a dreamer. A revolutionary who lived a few thousand years before his time."

" What was Nefertiti like ? And were she and Akhnaton fond of one another ? " asked Serena, who always wanted to know the colour of people's hair and eyes, and whether husbands and wives loved each other.

" She was too exquisite for words," declared Eve. " Her name means ' The Beautiful One has Come,' and her husband adored her. They were fearfully pure and good too—like Charles I and Queen Henrietta, you know. Akhnaton was always being painted and sculptured with Nefertiti and his little girls all round him, which was very unusual then."

" How sweet ! "

Hugh grunted contemptuously.

" When you two have quite finished your idiotic conversation I'd like to hear something about his religion," he suggested. " So far I've only gathered he believed in one God and one wife."

" The God wasn't a real, solid one like the Egyptians were used to," Eve explained, " and no one was allowed to make pictures or statues of him. His name was Aton, and in a way he was founded on Ra. Only Akhnaton said it wasn't the actual, concrete Sun that people must worship, but the invisible power behind it, and the heat that came from it, and all that sort of thing."

" That must have been a bit difficult to explain to the Egyptians. They always picked out such very stout fellows for their gods."

" It was terribly difficult," said Eve.

" I expect it was rather like me with the children," said Serena. " I'm always trying to explain to Jack and Jill that the Spirit of God is everywhere and in everything, although they can't see it or touch it. But they are only really interested in what Jill calls ' the kind old gentleman with the white woolly beard ' in the family Bible."

" You certainly ought to have a fellow-feeling for Akhnaton," chuckled Jeremy, " that was just his trouble."

" He had all the powerful priesthood against him," explained Eve, " and there were thousands of them at Karnak alone."

" What did he do about it ? " asked Hugh.

" First of all he changed his name from Amenhotep to Akhnaton, which meant ' Glory of Aton.' Then he knocked down the statues of Amon and all the other gods and got into his state barge and sailed away from

Thebes down the Nile, looking for a place where he could build a new capital; one where the old gods had never been."

" Hope he didn't have a head wind," murmured Hugh.

" And this is where he built it," ended Eve, with a wave of her hand.

" Darling, what a lot you know," said Serena admiringly. " Did he bring Nefertiti and the children with him ? "

" Rather ! He built a palace for Queen Tiy too, as well as his own. He laid out a whole city. There were houses for his nobles, and temples and streets. And he planted trees everywhere and laid out gardens, and filled them with flowers. Then he set up boundary stones north, south, east and west, and wrote on each of them the account of what he had done; how he had fulfilled his oath to build a city in honour of the one true God. I can't think," added Eve, " why we never learnt about Akhnaton when we were children. Why weren't we taught about the Egyptians instead of those wailing, untruthful Hebrews ? "

" Why indeed," agreed Jeremy.

" If only poor Akhnaton hadn't ended up so tragically," sighed Eve.

" Why, what happened ? " asked Hugh. " Did he run off the rails at the finish ? "

" Of *course* not ! He was a saint. Religion was the passion of his life."

" Humph ! " grunted Hugh.

" He only lived to teach everybody to praise God and to love one another. He wrote hymns, too— beautiful ones. The odd thing is that parts of them are almost exactly like our own psalms."

" Perhaps the Jews picked them up when they were in Egypt," suggested Serena.

" There's one lovely one," continued Eve enthusiastically, " all about the cattle resting on the herbage, and the birds fluttering in the marshes and the sheep dancing upon their feet in the sunshine. I do think there's nothing more adorable in the world than a cheerful little lamb jumping up and down on all its four stiff little legs. There's the sweetest bit, too, about a baby chicken chirping with all his might as he pecks his way out of the egg."

" It sounds rather like St. Francis of Assisi with his little brothers and sisters the birds," said Serena. " I'd like Jack and Jill to learn that poem. It sounds much more attractive than the things Miss Benson teaches them."

" What sort of poetry do they inflict on the modern child ? " asked Jeremy. " Edith Sitwell's ? "

" I'm not quite sure whose it is, but it's quite mad. I never understand a word of it, and it never, never rhymes, which must make it dreadfully hard for the poor babies."

" Probably Akhnaton's children were just as bored when they had to learn their father's stuff," murmured Hugh, " and I expect they longed for a nice substantial statue of a ram to worship."

" Of course they didn't," cried Eve. " Aton's symbol was far more poetic. It was the sun's disc with long rays streaming from it, each ending in a hand, to show the people how the power behind the sun poured its warmth and heat out all over the world."

" It's awfully interesting the way the art of that period broke away from the old conventions as completely as the religion," said Jeremy. " The sculptors and painters threw all the old rules overboard and copied straight from Nature. Some of their stuff was lovely."

" Where does Eve's tragedy come in ? " asked Hugh.

" It came here, in the city of Aton," said Eve sadly. " While Akhnaton was writing his hymns and holding his services in the temple, his empire was crumbling to pieces all round him. The governors of his far-away provinces in Asia kept sending messages imploring him to come and help them. Their letters were dug up here not so very long ago—the Tel el Amarna letters they're called—written on baked clay. But Akhnaton refused to send his armies to fight for him, because he believed that war was wrong and wicked, and that everyone ought to love each other."

" A conscientious objector ! " exclaimed Hugh.

" Don't put it like that ! " cried Eve. " It sounds so horrid."

" It generally does."

" Akhnaton was a conscientious objector all right— a very genuine one," declared Jeremy, throwing away his cigarette as he spoke. " But you must always remember," he went on emphatically, " that the Pharaoh was a god. One must never lose sight of that. It's the most important thing to remember in Egyptian history. It marks the great difference between the Pharaoh and every other ruler in the world, except the Mikado. He wasn't just a crowned head ruling by divine right, or the representative of God on earth, or anything like that. He was an *actual god*, in the real sense of the word, and an object of devout worship to all his subjects.

" The idea that a monarch only held his country in trust for the benefit of his people had never occurred to anybody in those days. Egypt was as much Akhnaton's personal property as his bed or his table. It was his own, to do as he pleased with. Looking at it from that—the only fair—point of view, we must admit that he had a perfect right to throw it away if he wanted to. He had to choose between his principles and his empire, and he chose his principles, that was all."

" That's all very well," argued Hugh, " but what about the poor devils who were trying to save his empire for him ? It was damned hard luck on them. I see no excuse for a fellow who leaves his men in the lurch. It's an unpardonable crime."

" In a soldier's eyes—yes," agreed Jeremy. " In all our eyes, to a very large degree. But we are dealing in this case with an abnormal mind, and you can't judge abnormality by normal standards. Naturally enough, Akhnaton offended both the ruling classes, the priests and the army."

" I hold no brief for the priests—they probably deserved all they got—but I'm damned sorry for the army," grumbled Hugh. " How about the common people ? What did they think of it all ? "

" Very little, probably. The great mass of them would be out of reach of Akhnaton's teaching, anyway. Besides, they pinned their faith on their own local gods, whose job it was to protect them from famine and snake-bite and so on. They were easier for the un-educated mind to grasp than the vaguer, more magnificent state god, who could hardly be expected to bother him-self with their small affairs. It was probably a matter of perfect indifference to them whether he were Amon or Aton."

" Aton must have been more difficult for them to get hold of than the others, though," suggested Eve, " because he was only a spirit, not even the sun that they could see."

" That's where we come up against rather a difficulty," said Jeremy. " I share your enthusiasm for Akhnaton, but unfortunately you'll find a considerable difference of opinion about him among the authorities."

" Oh," exclaimed Eve, " I dare say there are a lot of people who can't think badly enough of him for desert-ing his officers and letting his empire fall to pieces. But he did invent a most beautiful religion. If every-body else had taken to it, too, everything would have been quite all right."

" As a matter of fact, he didn't invent the disc wor-ship, it was already in existence."

" Jeremy ! "

" Moreover, plenty of people will tell you that there

are no grounds for believing he ever taught that Aton meant the power behind the sun instead of the actual disc itself."

" Oh, Jeremy ! " cried Eve again.

" But," went on Jeremy, " the worship of the disc would never have become what it did without him. He chose it out of all the other cults in Egypt, and built up a great religion upon it. What's more, it was a religion open to all the world, instead of confined to one particular race. That had never been done before. Nor is there any doubt that he insisted on there being one God and one God only. That in itself was a tremendously big step in those days."

No one spoke for a minute or two. Then Jeremy broke the silence again.

" Just think," he said quietly, " what Akhnaton stands for in history. No other Pharaoh, not even the builders of the Pyramids, are so amazing. He set his face against all that had been taught and believed in Egypt since the dawn of civilisation; and the Egyptians were above all things a conservative race, bound up in their religion. He condemned anger and greed and cruelty in an age when they were taken as a matter of course by everyone. He was the first idealist in history, and the very first man to preach the gospel of Love to all the world, thirteen hundred years before Christ."

" And, like Him, Akhnaton had no honour in his own country," said Eve sadly. " He was never called anything but ' the Heretic King ' or ' the Criminal of Akhetaton ' ever after."

" What happened in the end ? " asked Hugh.

Jeremy shrugged his shoulders. " He died a broken-hearted man. Quite young. Probably Akhnaton would have been murdered, like Christ, if he hadn't been the Pharaoh. He left no heir, only daughters; and he died with his empire tumbling into ruins about his ears, knowing that all he had lived for would die with him. It's as though a bright lamp had been lighted in the world for a few moments, and then blown out for a thousand years."

"The queer thing is," said Hugh, "that we are talking more about him than all the rest of the Pharaohs put together. Yet apparently he was a hopeless failure."

"The Egyptians called him a failure," said Jeremy. "We call him a glorious failure—that's all."

"Yes," murmured Eve, "that's all," and her eyes wandered to the distant hills in whose loneliest valley the tragic young Pharaoh had been laid to rest. He had been a herald, she thought, the fore-runner of One greater than himself. A Voice crying in the wilderness, whose echo still came down the ages; whose pale, gentle ghost still haunted this curve of desert that, for so brief a while, he had made to blossom like the rose; who still walked hand in hand with his Beautiful One through the streets of his ghostly city, where the burning flame of his eager spirit would glow for ever in the fierce sunlight that flooded earth and sky.

Eve could almost fancy she heard the chanting of his hymns floating across the quiet air.

CHAPTER XV

ASYUT

THE *Isis* reached Asyut, the great stronghold of the Copts, on the following afternoon.

"How funny it will be to drive about a real town again," said Serena, as the dahabeah was pushed slowly towards her anchorage.

"You may not find it a very real one," Jeremy warned her.

"Oh, mayn't I? Eve and I were going to shop."

"What on earth for?" asked Hugh. "What can one hope to buy here?"

"Just things," replied Serena vaguely.

"I don't know what 'things' mean," said Jeremy, "but I very much doubt if you'll find any in Asyut."

"Still, it's always fun looking for them," said Eve.

"You aren't going ashore in that white get-up, are you?" asked Jeremy.

Eve looked surprised and pained.

"Why not? It's a perfectly simple little suit. I can't imagine anything simpler or more suitable for a town."

"For Cairo perhaps, but not for Asyut. You'll get those white shoes horribly dusty."

"Well, if I do, the fluttered hen can clean them. He adores cleaning shoes—the dustier the better. Don't you all like this suit?" she added plaintively. "It's the first time I've had it on, so I think you might say it's rather attractive, instead of grumbling about it."

"There's nothing the matter with the suit," said

Hugh, " but I thought you looked all right in that yellow thing you had on at lunch."

" My poor dear! That was hundreds of years old."

" She had it all last summer," Serena protested.

" I had these grey flannel bags three years ago," said Jeremy.

" I can quite believe it ! " retorted Eve.

" That white get-up is certainly very successful," added Jeremy, stepping back a pace or two and studying her with the air of a connoisseur. " Only honestly it's much too good for this dirty place."

However, Eve was far too pleased with her own appearance to want to change it. After living for three weeks in a short skirt and a sweater, or a washing-frock, she was going to wear something real in a real town, whatever Hugh or Jeremy might say, and that was *that*.

The moment they landed they were besieged by a small crowd of men selling the famous Coptic veils of Asyut—those spangled monstrosities without which no self-respecting traveller of Victorian days ever returned home.

The more sophisticated Serena and Eve turned from them in horror.

Across the road a game of football was going on between two boys' schools.

" I never knew Egyptians played football ! " exclaimed Eve.

" Everyone plays football," said Hugh.

" The flag that waves on the green is really the flag of Empire," said Jeremy, " and the referee's whistle is the Empire's clarion. A ball will certainly be the salvation of the world."

He and Hugh would have spent the rest of the afternoon watching the game, but, fortunately for the girls, it was just finishing. Moussa piled them all into a dilapidated little carriage, and after Serena had given strict orders that the driver was on no account to use his whip, they started off along an astonishingly bad road, thick with dust.

The ornate villas of the wealthy Copts were as ugly and tawdry-looking as they could well be, and Eve was soon obliged to admit that a Christian town was no cleaner than a Moslem; that, in fact, the only difference was in the number of pigs, the first she had seen in Egypt. Jeremy, who always maintained that the pig was the noblest work of God, hailed their appearance with enthusiasm, and held forth so eloquently on the joys of bacon, ham and pork that Eve stuck her fingers in her ears by way of protest.

She and Serena failed to find any of the " things " they had hoped to buy, and all that Eve saw to please her in the whole of Asyut was a painting over the doorway of an undertaker's establishment : a Lord Mayor's coach, drawn by prancing horses, and escorted by gaudily-dressed negroes, with below it the legend, " Entreprise des pompes funèbres."

In spite of their struggles, Moussa insisted on dragging them to a secondary school for boys, where they were shown round by an enthusiastic head master.

" I hope something is being done for the girls, too," asked Eve at the end of the tour, fixing the unfortunate gentleman with a stern glance.

" We have two schools for girls here," he told her proudly, " because this is a Christian town."

" And that's the only good thing to be said for Asyut," declared Eve when they were back in their carriage again, having firmly refused to visit the tombs or to climb up somewhere to look at a view that Moussa would talk about.

" Egypt is going to land herself in the same difficulty as India," said Jeremy. " Like all the East, she has taken to education with such enthusiasm that she is turning out far more educated young men than she has room for. They will all wear the tarboosh—which is much the same class-symbol here as the top-hat of the clerk used to be in England—and there won't be enough clerkly jobs to go round."

" Moussa says it will make the girls more fit to run their homes well and to be companions to their husbands," said Eve.

" Do you and Moussa discuss the woman question ? " asked Hugh, with an amused glance at his young sister-in-law. " I wish you would have these talks with our Dear One in public, instead of in this hole-and-corner fashion."

" I never shall, because you'd only laugh at me; and it isn't really a discussion. I only ask him for information."

" Like Rosa Dartle," remarked Jeremy.

" Who's she ? " asked Eve suspiciously.

" Eve ! Eve ! Remind me to buy you a complete edition of Dickens when we get back to England. But do tell us what conclusions you and Moussa have come to in your hours of *rapprochement*."

" Moussa holds very advanced views. Don't snort, Hugh ! He says women ought to be educated just as much as men, and I think, but I'm not perfectly certain, that he even approves of their having a vote. At all events, he says there's a society which is trying to get it for them in Cairo. Moussa feels most strongly about the equality of the sexes. He hasn't put it into so many words, but I know he does. And he's only one of many. Those Eastern ideas you and Jeremy were so full of in Cairo aren't going to last here much longer."

" A pity," observed Jeremy. " However, there's always the strong arm as a last resort.—Do be careful, Eve," he added anxiously, as the ramshackle wheels of the carriage bounded in and out of a larger hole than usual. " You'll fall out at the next bump if you will give way to your emotions in a victoria."

. . . . .

The next day was Sunday, with such a strong head wind blowing that, after towing the *Isis* a mile or so out of Asyut, the reis gave up the unequal contest and the dahabeah was moored to the bank. It was the first cloudy day they had had, and by six o'clock Eve had the real Sunday evening feeling, so depressingly familiar to the English race. She thought it might be because, suiting the deed to the day, she had struggled to get some idea of the ancient religion of Egypt into her head.

" But what are you to do," she complained to Jeremy, " when you find that the gods and goddesses had at least three names apiece, and apparently even different names for different times of the day ? Take Ra, for instance; he was Ra and Re, and when he was rising he was Khepri, and when he was setting he was Atum, and then he got tangled up with Amon, and you got Amon-Ra, not to mention the Aton of Akhnaton ! I don't see how the Egyptians themselves ever remembered half of them."

" If you go back to very early times, you'll find him mixed up with the cow and the falcon as well," said Jeremy.

" I shall have nothing to do with that," declared Eve firmly. " The cow is Hathor and the falcon Horus, as far as I'm concerned. Horus is one of the few people I am more or less clear about, so for pity's sake don't get me all muddled up again ! I'm particularly attached to him. I think he's by far the most exciting-looking god, with his lovely square shoulders and his falcon's head."

" To think," said Jeremy, turning over the pages of Eve's book, " that this gives the earliest of all the accounts of the celebrated Day of Judgment. Strange, isn't it ? "

" Awfully comic," said Eve.

" It's the first time, too, that it's suggested that a man's condition in his future life depends upon his behaviour in this one."

Eve sighed. " What a lot of wear and tear that idea started ! Still, I expect it was great fun for Osiris

dealing out all the rewards and punishments; like Pluto
or Cerberus, or whatever the man's name was."

Jeremy laughed. "You'd better stick to Egyptian
gods for the moment," he suggested.

"Perhaps I had. Goodness knows they're enough
for anybody. Here is Nut, who was the sky or something, getting muddled up with Hathor; and sometimes
she was a cat goddess and sometimes a lioness, and I'm
not sure she and Isis didn't turn up as the same person
occasionally. I sympathise with the Egyptians for
making Ra the most important of all the gods, being a
sun-worshipper myself."

"I like the clever way the priests always managed to
discover that the god of their own particular temple
was only Ra in some other shape," said Jeremy. "That's
how you get Amon-Ra and Sobk-Ra, the crocodile god.
Horus was a solar god too, from very early times."

"I should have found it awfully difficult to decide
which one to worship, if I'd lived in those days," said
Eve. "I should certainly have begun with Ra, but
sheer funk of the Day of Judgment would have made
me want to keep in with Osiris. And of course I should
have been terribly attracted by Horus. I wonder if I
could have taken him for my patron saint?"

"I should have plumped for Ptah," declared Jeremy,
"the patron of the artificers and artists in the old days
of Memphis. Thoth the Wise was a good fellow, too,
the god of knowledge and letters; he's the one with
the head of an ibis."

"I thought the ibis-headed person was the god of the
moon," objected Eve.

"He was that as well."

Eve raised her eyes to heaven in mute despair, and
Jeremy laughed again.

"No, it's really awful!" she cried. "If I'd been a
Pharaoh I should have imposed a heavy tax on every
extra form of each god. For instance, I'd have let
Thoth be the god of letters and knowledge free of

RAMESES AND NEFATARI.

COLOSSI.

[*To face page* 112.

charge, but I'd have taxed him heavily when he was the moon. Then Hathor might have been the cow goddess free, but she'd have to pay double when she was anything else. Only I'd have allowed Horus to be everything he wanted. He had such charm and personality. I'm sure he'd be the greatest film-star in the world if he were alive to-day. I'm going for a short walk," she added, shutting up her book with a bang. "I've absorbed all the gods and goddesses I can digest at one sitting."

"You'll be late for dinner," said Hugh, who had just come up on deck.

"Oh, I'll be ever such a little time; besides, it'll soon be dark."

They watched her cross the sand at a good four miles an hour, Moussa agitatedly trying to keep up with her, and a sailor bringing up the rear.

.   .   .   .   .

Half an hour later she burst triumphantly into the saloon, where the other three were soberly playing cut-throat, her cheeks flushed, her eyes dancing.

"I've found out all about everything," she cried.

"Good God!" exclaimed Hugh.

"Everything about what?" inquired the startled Serena.

Eve lowered her voice and glanced round at the closed door.

"About our Dear One!" she hissed.

"Have you really?" Serena glowed with sympathy.

"He has a wife—a very good one, he says—and they love each other devotedly."

"How sweet!"

"He has a 'good' family, too. Three daughters and two sons. I was so glad he put the daughters first, considering the inferior ideas some Mahommedans seem to have about women. His eldest son is twenty-one, and he hopes to be a grandfather in two or three months."

"At twenty-one?" exclaimed Jeremy.

"Idiot! Not the son—Moussa. The eldest daughter

I

was married when she was only sixteen, and of course that made everything begin very early. I congratulated him warmly."

Hugh laid down his cards and gazed at his sister-in-law as though she were some strange animal escaped from the Zoo.

" My dear Eve, what on earth are you talking about ? "

" Never mind, darling," said Serena. " I've got them all perfectly clear. Go on."

" Well, he has a daughter of twelve and a boy of nine and a baby girl of three. Aren't they cleverly spaced ? "

" Very," said Jeremy. " Did you congratulate him on that too ? "

" No, I didn't like to, but I told him I thought it was all awfully nice. He says his wife is a very jolly girl. She's twenty-nine."

" The usual age for a woman," said Hugh.

" Stop a moment," said Jeremy, " let's get this clear. His eldest child is twenty-one and his wife twenty-nine ? She must have created a record in early maternity."

" Eastern women mature very early," said Eve loftily. Hugh laughed.

" My dear child, you can't add, I know, but try subtraction. Twenty-one from twenty-nine leaves eight."

Eve's face fell.

" Oh, dear ! Then of course he must have married twice. But he never mentioned it."

" Perhaps his first marriage was unhappy," suggested Serena, " and he can't bear to talk about it."

" Oh, poor Moussa, perhaps it was."

" He must have been left a widower with two or three tiny children. How very sad ! "

" He needn't necessarily have been a widower," said Jeremy blandly, " he may have two wives."

Eve flushed with indignation.

" How can you suggest such a thing about Moussa ! "

" My dear child, it's no disgrace."

" No disgrace to have two wives ? "

" Not in a Mahommedan country."

" It's just the sort of thing I should expect you to approve of ! "

" I didn't say I approved or disapproved."

" Well, I'm absolutely certain, from the way Moussa talked, that he has only one wife alive, and I know he loves her very much because he carries her photograph in his pocket-book."

" Bigamists always carry the photograph of their last wife in their pocket-book," said Hugh.

" You and Jeremy are the most cynical people I have ever met," cried Eve hotly. " Nothing, absolutely nothing, is sacred to you."

" Not even Moussa," grinned her brother-in-law.

" I agree with Eve. I think it's sweet of Moussa to love his wife, and I'm sure he's a perfect father," said Serena.

" Oh, he is," Eve assured her earnestly, " and he's so proud of them all. He showed me the photograph of the youngest."

" What was she like ? " asked the ever-sympathetic Serena.

Eve hesitated.

" W . . . . well, of course Eastern children always look a little different from English ones, don't they ? But she's a very fine child," she added hurriedly, " fat and healthy-looking, with enormous dark eyes. They're the least little bit bulgy, perhaps, but I think that's the fault of the photographer. And what do you think Moussa said when he showed it to me ? I thought it so sweet of him. He said, ' Mam'selle, I love that little one too—too much.' "

" The lamb ! " cooed Serena.

" And he told me that he and his wife are like an English couple, because he approves very much of the way Englishmen treat their women, and he says in his job he has had such a lot of opportunities of studying them. So, you two," she added, turning to Jeremy and Hugh, " had better be careful how you behave, if from no higher motive than that of keeping up the reputation of your countrymen."

" Dear, dear Moussa," murmured Serena, absent-mindedly picking up her cards, " I always felt he was a really nice man."

CHAPTER XVI

THE day came when Eve discovered Miss Amelia B. Edwards—two little volumes called " A Thousand Miles up the Nile." Miss Amelia B. Edwards was a lady author who had travelled up the Nile in a sailing dahabeah fifty years before, and in her book described everything she saw and did and what she thought about it all. Eve began to read with the mild condescension of the post-war girl for anything so old-fashioned; and then she found that nothing had altered, not even the south wind, which had blown as sadly in the face of Amelia B. Edwards and her party as in their own. Their dahabeah, their reis, their crew, their servants, all were the same; only Moussa, as Eve saw, was different. Amelia B. might have a lot to say about her dragoman, but it was clear to Eve that he was but a poor creature compared with the Dear One. " Listen ! " said Eve excitedly as she dipped into the first volume, " this is what she says about being towed, or tracking as she calls it. ' . . . Came on deck, however, before breakfast, and found nine of our poor fellows harnessed to a rope like barge-horses, towing the huge boat against the current ! ' Um—um—um. ' The sight of the trackers jarred, somehow, with the placid beauty of the picture. We got used to it, as one gets used to everything in time; but it looked like slave's work, and shocked our English notions disagreeably.' Isn't that just what we felt the first time we saw it ? And now we are horribly used to it."

" It may have shocked you and Serena," said Jeremy

coolly, stretching out a hand and unceremoniously taking the book from Eve. " It never shocked us in the least. You forget we have come all over Eastern and take slaves in our stride."

" It was my book," protested Eve, but Jeremy was turning the pages and gave no heed to her.

" I have found something in which Amelia B. is different," he announced. " She seems to have known how to make ' a home from home ' all right, which neither of you girls has even attempted to do, and yet you have the same material to work upon. Your saloon, like hers, has a gay Brussels carpet adorning the floor, the dining-table in the centre of the room and all the gentlemen's guns and sticks in one corner."

" Gentlemen ! " snorted Eve.

" But after that, what a difference ! " went on Jeremy; " for ' it's wonderful,' says Amelia B., ' what a few books and roses, an open piano, and a sketch or two will do ! ' And to think that Hugh sacrificed the piano and told Cook's we would rather have a second ice-chest for the drinks instead ! A few pages further on she says that the drawers under the divans ' being fairly divided,' held their clothes, wine and books. Our books are all over the upper deck and all over the saloon, while our drinks occupy the sites of two grand pianos at least. As to yours and Serena's clothes, I can only say that I know Serena's overflow into Hugh's cabin and Eve's are met with everywhere. As to water-colour sketching, you, Eve, who as the young, unmarried girl should be the exponent of that art on board, paint nothing but your hair and—probably—your face. I don't say you don't do it very well, but it isn't the same thing as having water-colour sketches negligently lying about on the top of a piano."

" Pooh ! "

" Here's another nasty jar for you. Miss Amelia B. declares it to be of paramount importance that the sights of Egypt be visited in their historical order. She admits

the day. There had been no time to pull herself together. Now it was different. Besides, she had just had one of Jeremy's most potent cocktails. Pointing a trembling finger at the perspiring Said, she fixed her wretched sister with just such a glance of pure, high courage as a virgin saint might have worn on her way to the stake.

" Serena,"—why was her voice so high and shaky ?— " Serena. . . . Said . . ." Horrors ! it sounded as though she were introducing them to each other for the first time. She swallowed convulsively. " Serena . . . Said . . . Christiani ! "

Said threw Serena's foot with a crash on to the floor.

" Thank you, thank you ! Christiani ! Christiani ! " he yelled, crossing himself fast and furiously with the feather brush.

Both girls, their eyes fixed nervously upon him, horrible glassy smiles upon their faces, followed suit, Serena empty-handed, Eve unfairly fortified by the powder-puff she happened to be clasping.

Faster and faster went Said and his feather brush. Faster and faster went the trembling fingers of Eve and Serena.

The air was loud with " Christianis " and thick with crossings. They would in all probability be doing it still, Eve decided later, if Mahomed had not rung the luncheon bell loudly at the end of the sixth round.

CHAPTER XVII

ABYDOS

THE north wind blew, and for two days the *Isis* flew past the steam-driven vessels and poured scorn upon them. On the second evening she anchored at Baliana, the starting-place for Abydos.

The following morning Moussa secured three magnificent donkeys, and a large victoria whose more important parts were tied together with yards of string. Serena, Hugh and Moussa set off on the donkeys, Jeremy and Eve in the victoria; on the return journey they were to change places. The driver of the victoria was a chatty young man, who was determined to improve the shining hour by learning English, and he left the horse to find its own way along the raised causeway that ran for four or five miles through some of the most fertile and richly cultivated country in Egypt. The donkeys and their riders were soon out of sight, but the young man calmly turned round on the box-seat, his back to his elderly steed, his bare legs dangling down into the carriage, and requested Eve to tell him the English of every object which he pointed out with his whip. A fair-minded youth, believing in due payment for goods received, he obligingly taught Eve their equivalents in Arabic. Every now and then Jeremy was obliged to remind him that they wished to reach Abydos that day. Then the young man would swing his legs round to the front again and curse his unfortunate animal with such fluency and variety that Jeremy was devoutly thankful Eve's lesson did not include this branch of the language.

It was a glorious morning, and there was so much to look at that Eve did not mind how long the drive lasted. The creaking noise of countless shadûfs mingled with the chatter of the men, women and children at work in the fields.   All along the road the carriage met and passed a constant stream of camels loaded with bersein, the green cattle fodder; bundles of sugar-cane or bales of straw; men on swiftly-trotting donkeys, groups of women carrying bundles or vases on their heads, children, dogs, sheep and goats.   Eve was sorry when Abydos was reached, where Hugh and Serena were waiting for them.

Later, when Eve had seen many other temples, she always came back to the memory of Abydos as the most lovable of them all.   No sullen, towering pylons here terrified the puny beholder.   This was a temple where room after room led the mind and the eye gently on, where there were no dark corners, no obscene and squeaking clusters of bats, but where everything was open to the sunlight, which made every wall look as though its exquisite reliefs were carved in ivory.   Even " carved " seemed too harsh a word to use, for in this temple the reliefs were so delicate that they seemed as though breathed upon the golden-white fabric of the walls.   Nothing more delicate than these half-shades of actuality had ever been called into being by Donatello. Overhead the sky was of such an intense, vibrant blue that it seemed to sparkle, and the only colours in the whole world were the blue of the sky and the golden-ivory of the temple walls.

Delicate profiles of faces and forms, as perfect now as on the day that the sculptor had laid down his chisel, seemed to hold in this still, charmed place a quality of Eternity, for here there was no sign of age.   Any Gothic cathedral would have looked old and crumbled compared with these still, yet glowing transcripts from life.

Gods and goddesses, human beings who had preserved their egotism intact throughout the ages because of the genius of those who had commemorated them, paced delicately or sat in state along these unchanging walls.

" Oh, it's beautiful ! " cried Eve, as they wandered about the great open courts and in and out of the sanctuaries. " But I wonder why some of the reliefs are cut so much deeper than the rest ? They look very effective from a distance, certainly, but close to they aren't half as exquisite as the delicate shallow ones."

" They're the work of Rameses the Great, a gentleman of whom you'll see and hear a good deal the further you get up the Nile," said Jeremy—" the first great journalist in the world. The forerunner of Northcliffe and Beaverbrook."

" What on earth do you mean ? "

" Rameses had the real journalistic mind, although he lived nearly three thousand years ago. He realised that the way to reach the populace was not by gentle methods, but by glaring headlines, the more striking and obvious the better; so he set his workmen all over Egypt to dig round the lovely shallow reliefs until they showed up as though they had been outlined in charcoal."

" What a vandal ! He might at least have spared Abydos," grumbled Eve.

" That would be too much to expect," said Jeremy, " seeing that it's the headquarters of the Osiris cult and the holiest place in Egypt. All the old Pharaohs of the First and Second Dynasties were buried there, and later on the rest of the world used to bring their corpses to rest for a time in the sanctity of this temple before they were taken away to their own tombs. It's the Westminster Abbey of Egypt."

" Sounds like it," said Hugh. " Cradle of the race and all that sort of thing."

Serena was distressed by the long trestle tables that were kept in the temple for the steamer tourists to lunch on. Their incongruity, she said, amounted to blasphemy. But there was no doubt their first temple was a great success, and Eve began to long for more.

" When shall we reach Karnak ? " she asked Jeremy as they mounted their donkeys for the return journey.

" In a couple of days, with any luck. It depends on the wind."

" It always does," sighed Eve, " and I don't believe it's ever going to blow again."

. . . . .

She was wrong, however, for the next morning the *Isis* started before daylight and ran before a good breeze to Nag-Hamadi, which she reached at breakfast time. Here the reis had to tie up for two or three hours until the railway bridge across the Nile should open and allow the waiting boats to go through. Eve and Jeremy, escorted by Moussa and the usual sailors and sticks, filled in the time with a walk through the cheerful, prosperous-looking village, with its clean, sandy roads. Several new, well-built houses, a couple of dark red palaces and a little mosque with lawns of real green grass, bordered with flowers, gave a cheerful air to the river frontage.

" It's like one of our model villages at home," said Eve.

" It all belongs," explained Moussa, waving a fat arm around, " to one very great man, the Prince Yousef."

" The Prince must be a very good landlord."

" Yes, Mam'selle. That palace he built for his mother."

" How sweet of him ! He must be a nice man, too, then," declared Eve. Her opinion of him rose higher still when she was shown the brick-making factory, the polo and football grounds, and the acres of highly cultivated fields.

" It's a pity all the landlords in Egypt aren't like this Prince," she observed. " The whole place seems so full of life and everyone looks so busy and prosperous."

" Ah ! Mam'selle," Moussa wagged his head sadly, " the Prince—he is a bad man."

" A bad man ? How can he be, when he looks after

THE VALLEY OF THE QUEENS.

MEDINET ABOU.

his people so well and is such a good farmer, and built that dear little palace for his mother, and that sweet little mosque ? ”

Moussa wagged his head more sadly still. “ Mam'selle, he will not marry.”

“ But that doesn't make him bad.”

“ Oh yes, Mam'selle. It is very, very bad for a man not to marry.”

“ We don't think so in England,” Eve protested. “ Why, the Prince of Wales—the King's eldest son, you know, isn't married; and though the newspapers are always trying to push him into it, nobody really minds. We want him to do just as he likes about it.”

Moussa was shocked to his very soul.

“ Ah, Mam'selle,” he cried, “ that is a great pity, for if he does not marry he cannot be king.”

“ He can. It doesn't make the least difference.”

“ No, Mam'selle.” Moussa was firm. “ Cannot be king unless he have a wife. It is bad, very bad for a man not to marry.”

“ Do you call Mr. Vaughan bad, then ? He isn't married, you know. Of course he's awfully annoying in lots of ways, but I don't think being unmarried has anything to do with it.”

Moussa wagged his head at Jeremy in a roguish manner.

“ Mam'selle,” he chuckled, “ if you were not here I would have to call Mr. Vaughan very bad names.”

“ Don't let me stop you,” cried Eve. “ I'd love to hear them.”

“ How about yourself ? ” suggested Jeremy. “ You haven't done much in the marrying line yet.”

“ Do you think it wrong for a woman not to marry, Moussa ? ” asked Eve.

“ No, Mam'selle,” said Moussa decidedly. “ If a woman do not marry it is because no one ask her. She cannot help it, Mam'selle. So we have no blame for her.”

K

Jeremy guffawed rudely.

"We call her poor thing," continued Moussa magnanimously.

"Oh!" said Eve, rather taken aback. "Oh, well, it's just the opposite at home, or rather it used to be in Victorian days. We rather admire a bachelor, because he has a jolly good time, and it's really rather clever of him not to have got tied up. But even now the married women feel a little superior to the single ones."

"Marriage is good, Mam'selle. Mr. Vaughan, we must make him marry. We must tell him shame, Mam'selle."

Eve cocked her head on one side and eyed Jeremy thoughtfully for a moment.

"Do you know, Moussa, I don't think I want him to marry. You see, I've got so used to him as he is; and, anyway, he wouldn't be at all nice to marry, he likes his own way far too much."

"That wouldn't matter," said Jeremy calmly. "My wife, if I ever have one, will be one of the sweet, clinging kind. I like them soft and gentle. Whatever I say will be law in her eyes."

"Heavens! How bad for you! You'd be perfectly unbearable. No, Moussa, I think Mr. Vaughan will have to follow Prince Yousef's example and remain a bad man. After all, bachelors are very useful; they fetch and carry and do a lot of things like that. Perhaps the Prince wouldn't be such a good landlord if he had a wife to distract his attention."

Moussa wagged his head till it nearly fell off.

For miles that afternoon the *Isis* sailed between the richly cultivated, well-watered fields of Prince Yousef, and Eve's good opinion of him rose higher and higher. His enormous pigeon cotes pleased her most of all. They were like a young village, and the birds flew in great clouds over her head and filled the air with the noise of their wings.

CHAPTER XVIII

KARNAK

" We are like the Bastard of Orleans," said Eve
during the three days of dead calm that followed, " only
we cry ' North wind, north wind,' instead of west;
and answer comes there none, except an occasional
derisive puff from the south."

At last, one very hot afternoon, the *Isis* turned the
corner into the long, straight stretch of river below Luxor.
On the left the pylons and obelisks of Karnak rose above
the palm trees. Away to the right, the Theban hills,
beautiful, mysterious and golden, shimmered in the heat
haze. Which of their folds, Eve wondered, hid the
Valley of the Tombs of the Kings ?

The dahabeah glided along until the pillars of the
temple of Luxor stood up behind the river's edge on the
left bank, and Eve, who had read that this was the
loveliest temple in all Egypt, told herself that this first
glimpse should have been wonderful, instead of which it
was frankly disappointing. The next moment she could
see why this should be so—a modern iron railing stood
up black and spikey between the road and the temple,
and against this railing was drawn up a line of cabs.
Why, why were people so silly as to spoil things like
that ? There was nothing good to be said for the
modern world.

As soon as the *Isis* had been made fast beside two
large tourist steamers, a man arrived from Cook's office
with the mail-bag, and when the letters were read,
Moussa suggested a walk along the river front, which
had all the appearance of a fashionable promenade.
Young Egypt, in the shape of youths in lounge suits

and fezzes, promenaded up and down in parties of five or six, and eyed both the girls with bold familiarity. Elderly English spinsters in garments of staggering dowdiness moved primly about in couples, their thin arms crossed, each pointed elbow held in a bony hand. Loud-voiced Americans and aggressive Englishmen sported quite unnecessary sun-helmets, and a couple of cheerful-looking nuns went by in charge of a group of chattering girls from a neighbouring convent school. While Hugh and Jeremy interviewed Cook's agent, Eve and Serena made an appointment at the hairdresser's under the arcade and bought a pile of books and magazines. When they turned homewards again the sun was setting behind the Theban hills, flooding them with rose and violet and turning the river into a stream of gold.

.   .   .   .   .

The loud beating of a gong on board one of the steamers woke Eve the next morning. Life for the passengers on these boats was regulated by gongs, she discovered. They were gonged out of bed, gonged to meals and gonged on excursions. After breakfast she watched them, obedient to the call of the gong, pile themselves into little victorias en route for Karnak.

" Let's hope they'll have left by the time we get there," said Serena, " or the place will be crowded."

" Not it," Jeremy assured her, " it's far too big."

" It isn't just one temple," explained Eve, " it's dozens. All the Pharaohs kept on building them, and adding pylons and girdle walls and things. ' Powers ' is full of them."

" How confusing ! " sighed Serena; " and it's such a hot day."

" I forget how many hundreds of square feet the ruins cover," said Jeremy cruelly.

" Square feet," murmured Serena faintly, " are larger than the ordinary kind, aren't they ? "

" Much larger," replied Jeremy, with a heartless grin. Serena shuddered.

"The oldest temples of all have practically dis-appeared," said Eve. "I expect those mysterious Hyksos, the Shepherd Kings, destroyed them. They did any amount of damage in Egypt."

"They brought the first horses into the country," Jeremy reminded her. "You must give them credit for that."

"I give 'em full marks for it," declared Hugh. "Good Lord! fancy a country without horses. It's past belief."

"They had a charming name," said Serena. "There's such a peaceful, pastoral sound about Shepherd Kings."

"They weren't a bit like their name, though," argued Eve. "They only got called it because they wandered in in a vague sort of way from no one knows where, with their flocks and herds; like Abraham and those other old gentlemen. Otherwise they were barbarians."

"The first Amenhotep took very kindly to horses and chariots," remarked Jeremy. "He used whole regiments of them in his campaigns against the Syrians and Nubians—against the Hyksos themselves, for that matter."

"I do wish English history were as easy to learn as Egyptian," complained Eve. "Theirs is so full of big gaps that can only be filled in in the sketchiest manner.— Such as 'Dynasties XIII to XVII were a period of chaos and obscurity and included the Hyksos.' Fancy if we could have skimmed over Victoria and the Georges like that."

"It would have been lovely," agreed Serena. "My youth was blighted by awful things called Reform Bills."

"I remember them. They were something to do with Corn Laws."

"Roman Catholics, I *think*, darling," said Serena.

"Perhaps you're right. Anyway, there's nothing so confusing in Egyptian history—in the ancient part at any rate. The only muddling thing about it is that, just as you're beginning to get it all nicely fixed in your head, somebody goes and digs up a new tomb, and proves everything you'd learnt was entirely wrong. Then you have to begin all over again."

" I couldn't bear it," declared Serena. " I shall wait until there's nothing left to dig."

" Don't you wish Napoleon's gunner had never dug up the Rosetta Stone, Serena ? " asked Jeremy.

" I did when I was a child. I had a governess whose spiritual home was the British Museum, and the Rosetta Stone was her pet piece. The only nice thing about it was its name."

" How did it get such a pretty one ? " asked Eve.

" It's called after the place at the mouth of the Nile where it was found," said Jeremy.

" O—o—oh ! " cried Serena on a long-drawn note of astonishment, " then I was always all wrong ! "

" How do you mean, always all wrong ? " asked Hugh.

" Why," explained Serena ingenuously, " nobody ever told me why it was called the Rosetta Stone, so naturally I always thought it had something to do with Rossetti and the Pre-Raphaelite movement."

" Yet you were never at a Public School," murmured Jeremy.

" Why was it so terribly important ? " asked Eve.

" It gave the experts the key to the hieroglyphs," said Jeremy. " It was engraved with a decree in honour of Ptolemy Epiphanes and his wife, Cleopatra."

" Cleopatra ! " exclaimed Serena. " Now wasn't that like a governess ? She never even mentioned her ! "

" It wasn't your Cleopatra," explained Jeremy. " This was only a queen consort. But the decree was inscribed three times over. In ancient hieroglyphs, in the demotic characters of a later period, and in Greek. It was the Greek characters that gave the clue to the others, of course."

" Fancy confronting a child with all that ! " cried Serena.

" You're going to be confronted with Karnak now,"

said Hugh. "Here's Moussa arriving, complete with carriage and pair. Come along."

Serena sighed, but, seeing there was no help for it, she went.

.   .   .   .   .

The carriage drew up at the foot of the great Ptolemaic arch. Eve gazed up at the winged sun-disc of Horus, where traces of an exquisite turquoise blue could still be seen.

"I do hope I shall remember who built that," she murmured as they got out of the carriage. "But I shan't," she cried despairingly as the immensity of Karnak began to dawn upon her. "Oh, Jeremy! I feel just like I did the first time I went to Monte Carlo. I'd worked out the most wonderful system in the Blue train, and the moment I walked into the Casino my mind became a complete blank."

"Don't worry your head about it," said Jeremy consolingly—"not on your first visit, anyway. If you spent six weeks here you would still be finding new things every day."

Eve listened helplessly to Moussa as he rolled out the names of gods and Pharaohs. How, she wondered, was she even to recognise a girdle wall when she saw it—let alone know which Pharaoh built it? How sort into any kind of order those pylons and obelisks and wall reliefs of which Mr. Powers had written with such authority?

The famous avenue of Sphinxes went a little way towards restoring her self-respect. It was so familiar to her in photographs that she felt almost at home in it. She was even able to feel the least bit disappointed, for the Sphinxes were more mutilated in real life than they had looked in their pictures. How she wished she could see them as they had been in those far-off days that Jeremy now described, when the avenue had stretched right down to the Nile, and the Pharaoh and his court had passed up it in gorgeous procession, right up to the temple gate between the towering pylons. The walls and pylons and obelisks had all been rich with colour then, and the great flags of state had flown high above them.

The hypostyle hall left Eve breathless. She gazed up at the monster pillars in awe and wonder, and Jeremy watched their effect upon her. " I feel," she gasped, " like Alice when she drank the little bottle marked ' Poison,' and found herself growing smaller and smaller. I *have* got smaller, I believe. These aren't pillars. They're fabulous monsters in stone." She heard Moussa say they were 69 feet high and 33 feet in circumference, but the figures conveyed nothing to her. She only knew, as she craned her neck backwards and peered up at their mighty heads, that they soared incredibly far up into the hot, blue sky.

" It's like a forest of giant trees that some ogre has turned into stone," said Jeremy.

" It's terrifying," said Serena. " I feel as if they must fall and crush us. One can hardly breathe among them."

" I must say I think the Egyptians put their pillars far too close together," observed Hugh. " You can hardly see the wood for the trees, so to speak."

" They had to support a flat roof," explained Jeremy.

" How dark it must have been," said Eve, " especially when it was cloudy with incense."

" Did the Egyptians use incense ? " asked Serena.

" Rather ! " replied Jeremy. " It was an important part of their ritual. You'll find any number of pictures of the Pharaohs burning it before the gods. I don't know what religion of ancient origin hasn't used incense ? Egyptians, Babylonians, Buddhists, Hindoos, Mahommedans, Jews, Christians—all of them."

" I adore it," said Eve.

" Beastly stuff ! " grunted Hugh; " makes me sneeze."

" That's only your Presbyterian mucous membrane," said Serena placidly.

" Akhnaton has gone up in my estimation since I've

seen this place," Hugh admitted. " I suppose the priests were as thick as ground bait here. It must have taken some pluck to dig them out."

Eve was delighted at Hugh's belated praise of her hero. The iconoclast of Karnak appealed more to her heart than the men who had built it. Yet, as she walked by Jeremy's side and listened to his account of them, she could not fail to be impressed. He told her of Ahmes I, the founder of the seventeenth dynasty; of Thothmes I, and of his lawful heiress, Queen Hatshepsut, and the tangled question of her right, as a woman, to succeed to his throne; of her successful struggles with her half-brothers, sons of her father's concubines, struggles made all the more complicated to Eve by the fact that both were called Thothmes, and that both were married to their half-sister, after the peculiar custom of the Egyptian royal family; of how the younger succeeded his sister as Thothmes III, and became the mightiest of all the soldier Pharaohs of Egypt, the equal of Alexander and Napoleon.

" And all Thothmes won for Egypt," said Jeremy, " Akhnaton lost. But after his death his general, the strong, determined Horemheb, set Egypt's house in order again and himself upon the throne."

Eve's mind swam with gods and Pharaohs. Wherever she turned she saw them. Carved in stone they sat or stood among the fallen masonry. On the walls they greeted one another, fought, slaughtered their prisoners, offered sacrifices, drove their chariots and manned the sacred bark of Amon. Truly the gods and Pharaohs of ancient Egypt were not dead. They still lived and warred and triumphed on the walls of Karnak.

CHAPTER XIX

LUXOR

" The temple of Luxor will be visited after tea," read Hugh from the guide-book.

" How splendidly British," said Jeremy, " to see no bathos in the coupling of the temple of Luxor with a meal of stewed tannin, and buns and bread and butter ! "

" It's British," argued Hugh, " because it's a thoughtful and sensible arrangement. Who could cope with a temple unless they were already in a state of repletion ? I should never dream of attempting such a thing fasting."

" It's true—we have it on the highest authority—that an army marches on its stomach," admitted Jeremy. " Suppose we go one better than Cook's, then ? Let us postpone the temple of Luxor till after dinner. The moon is full to-night."

" Oh, do let's ! " cried Eve.

" Yes, let's," added Serena, not seeing further than the fact that in that case she would not have to move after tea. And the matter was settled.

.   .   .   .   .

The moon was high when they followed Moussa past the cab rank and the iron railings which had so offended Eve the day before, into the temple.

The tall papyrus columns round the court of Amenhotep the Magnificent cast sharply-cut, inky-black shadows along the sand, blanched by the moon. Standing in the middle of the courtyard, Eve looked down an avenue of still taller papyrus columns, so incredibly tall that nothing but the fabulous monsters of Karnak could have topped them. Those had been giants, symbols of

139

brute strength and force.   These, in spite of their height
and girth, had an indescribable grace and elegance.
The pillars of Karnak towered, these soared up into
the sky.

Eve stood, hushed and very small, at the bottom of a
pool of moonlight and shadows.   A man at the far end
of the stone avenue looked no bigger than a pigmy.

They walked down between the long rows, their footfalls making no sound in the soft sand, and came out
into another open court, flooded with moonlight.
Between the pillars stood colossal stone figures, all
exactly alike, each with one vast foot advanced as though
he were about to stride across the big, blanched court—
ghostly demi-gods who seemed about to speak; seemed
for a moment to be actually moving, as though they
were really striding out in Time even as in Space, from
their dynasty into the present.

Eve gave a little tug at Jeremy's coat sleeve.

" Who are they ? " she whispered.

" Rameses the Great."

" What ? *All* of them ? " asked Serena.

" Every one.   Come closer and you will see his
favourite wife, Nefertari, tucked discreetly away behind
his left leg."

They looked, and there they found her, a charming
little person, so tiny that she only reached to the huge
knee of her lord and master.   One small hand was laid
confidingly against his swelling calf.

Serena thought she was sweet, and said so.

Eve thought so too, but she considered it infra dig.
that a wife should be so minute, while her husband was
given the proportions of a god.   Still, she admitted to
herself that there was something very cosy in the idea.
Nor, she felt sure, did the little queen make any bones
about climbing up to her husband's shoulder and whis-
pering her commands into his great, stone ear whenever
it suited her.

Some of the colossi were very mutilated, others less

so. Some of their faces were gone entirely, and most of them were broken. But the moonlight covered up all their imperfections, and they seemed to regain their features, so that Eve really had the illusion that they were almost as they were on the day of their creation.

Even the little white mosque, perched high up in the ruins, did not look so incongruous in the light of the moon. And when they walked back down the avenue of pillars and saw, beyond the court of Amenhotep, the remains of a Christian church, this did not seem incongruous either on a night of such peace and beauty. Amon Ra, Allah and the God of the Christians, there was room for them all, Eve felt, in the loveliest of all the temples of Egypt.

CHAPTER XX

JEREMY and Moussa had decided that the expedition to the Valley of the Kings must start bright and early, before the heat of the day set in. This meant a lot of running about on board the dahabeah and a busy collecting of cameras, sunshades and riding-whips, and the fly-whisks that Moussa insisted everybody should carry. Fortunately for Serena and Eve, their complexions slipped his memory, and they were able to set out leaving their veils behind them.

The sailors rowed them across to the western bank, where they landed into the middle of a crowd of seventy or eighty donkeys. Pandemonium followed. Every donkey owner shouted the superior merits of his own beast at the top of his voice, and the noise was deafening. Moussa was in his element. Shouting louder than any of them, he unhesitatingly selected the pick of the animals, made the defeated owners roar with laughter at his sallies of wit, and had his party mounted and galloping away through the sand in no time.

Eve was delighted with everything. With the larks that filled the air with their song, with the bee-eaters that darted across the road with a flash of bright green wings, with the freshness of the morning, the sun, the crisp feeling in the air, the magenta trimmings and little jangling bells that decorated her donkey, and the ingenious way his coat had been clipped and brushed into an intricate pattern.

The wide plain where " hundred-gated Thebes " once stood was now pale green with the young crops. On their right hand was the deep cutting of a canal, dry at present and full of grass. A long string of camels, led by a small boy, ran grunting down one side of the steep bank and up the other. Long after they had passed out of sight their indignant voices could still be heard.

" I can't think how even a camel can feel bad-tempered on a morning like this," said Eve.

" A camel could feel bad-tempered in heaven," replied Jeremy.

" Still, I do like them : they're so gorgeously supercilious and disagreeable-looking. One can't help admiring them; they do the thing on such a grand scale. Oh, do tell this horrid boy not to hit my donkey ! "

Jeremy turned round in his saddle and issued a few short, sharp words in Arabic which caused both their boys to drop meekly behind. Here, they realised, was an effendi who knew what was what, so they joined their fellows who were pattering along at a steady trot behind Serena and Hugh. Moussa had chosen the smallest donkey for himself, with the result that his legs hung only two or three inches above the ground. His tussore skirts were tucked up and showed his green socks, bare legs, Boston velvet grips, yellow elastic-sided boots and all. Eve had the gravest doubts that he would reach the journey's end, but Jeremy assured her that Egyptian donkeys were a breed apart, and certainly this wiry little beast seemed to take his colossal rider as all in the day's work.

A short stop was made at the little temple of Kurna, which Eve liked because it was dedicated to Horus, and soon afterwards they entered the beginning of the Valley of the Kings. By this time the freshness of the morning had gone. The sun had grown very hot and the flies very troublesome, and Eve was glad of her flywhisk. The tall sandstone cliffs drew nearer on either hand; not a twig, not a blade of grass was to be seen anywhere. Eve wondered what the tiny birds which flitted round them could find to eat. She concluded it

LUXOR.

LUXOR.

[*To face page* 144.

must be insects, though what kept the insects alive, she could not imagine. The road twisted and turned, so that when she looked back she found they were hemmed in on all sides by the hills which towered above them in crags and battlements. Everything was yellow and gold and fire colour, except for the burning blue of the sky.

" Sun and heat and fiery rocks ! Jeremy, it's wonderful ! Look at that great golden boulder over there and the blue pool of shadow that it casts. Do you remember that line in the Bible ' The shadow of a great rock in a thirsty land ' ? One can appreciate that here. This is a thirsty land, isn't it ? This stony, barren road with its twists and turns seems to be leading us right into the heart of the world."

" That's what the old Pharaohs must have felt, I suppose. Good Lord ! What wouldn't you give to see one of their funerals winding its way along this valley now, Eve ? The ceremonies at Karnak, the procession down the avenue of Sphinxes, the passage across the Nile all over, then Thebes left behind, and these hills shutting them closer and closer in; and all in the vain hope that they would lie in peace for ever, in a place where thieves could not break in and steal."

The mountains grew higher and higher and the road narrower. The heat shivered and danced visibly before their eyes. Not a breath stirred the air; silence and desolation reigned in this burning, fiery furnace. The rocks began to take strange shapes, like grotesque animals and pyramids; there seemed no end to their fantasy as they towered above the little group of humans on their little steeds. The last short, steep hill brought them to the end of their journey, but Eve sat still until Jeremy came to help her dismount. Even then she seemed to be in no hurry, and he waited too, his hand on her donkey's neck.

" All this beginning has been so wonderful that I'm afraid to go on," she confessed. " I'm afraid the tombs may be an anti-climax."

L

" I don't think they will. Not if you remember that Karnak and the Sphinxes, the Nile and this valley itself have been leading up to them all the way. One of the tombs, at any rate, will make you feel it : the one where they have left the mummy."

" Which is that ? "

" The tomb of Amenhotep II."

" How many are we going to see ? "

" Only three : Tutankhamen's, Seti I's and Amenhotep's. And we will keep the last until all these tourists who are arriving have been in and come out again."

" Bother them," groaned Eve, glancing back at the advancing horde as she swung her leg over and slipped to the ground. Then she smiled up at Jeremy as he stood stroking the donkey's neck. " Let's start on tomb number one, then, as you say it won't be an anti-climax. I trust you completely, you know. When I come to think of it," she added thoughtfully, " I always do."

.   .   .   .   .

A short flight of steps led down into the outer chamber of Tutankhamen's tomb; bare now, swept and garnished, but full once of such piled treasure that their discovery had stirred the whole civilised world to its foundations. The inner chamber, at a lower level than the first, was separated from it by a little parapet. Almost filling the small space below, lay an open sarcophagus of pink granite. Inside it lay the gold mummy casing fashioned in the likeness of the young Pharaoh. The whole figure, the young, round face, the royal head-dress, the clasped hands, all gleamed with pure gold leaf; and the sarcophagus was a casket worthy of the treasure it held, with its lovely design of long, outstretched wings carved at the four corners. Eve had been afraid of finding disappointment in the tombs, and instead she had found pure beauty.

.   .   .   .   .

" Where are we going next, Jeremy ? " asked Serena when they were outside again.

" To the tomb of Seti."

" I've never heard of him," said Serena.

" Oh, darling, you have ! " protested Eve. " He built the temple at Abydos, and he governed the country so well that the people called him the Good Shepherd. He was very dignified, and wise and good. Breasted calls him the stateliest figure who ever sat upon a throne."

" I never heard of him," repeated Serena placidly.

" Not too fast, not too fast, Mam'selle," called the panting Moussa as Eve started to run down a flight of steps that looked as though they penetrated to the bowels of the earth. After the steps came a long, sloping passage, and the heat closed in upon them ; a dull, crushing, palpable heat, like nothing Eve had ever felt before. They passed along corridor after corridor, between walls covered with paintings, into the gorgeously decorated halls beyond.

" There are some ripping pictures here of people going to hell," said Hugh. " They're nearly as jolly as the paintings of the Last Judgment in an Italian church."

" Hugh always gloats over devils prodding people down into flames with toasting-forks," said Serena. " He's so horribly bloodthirsty."

" He's a brutal and licentious soldier," agreed Jeremy. " He's right about these paintings, though ; here is the dear old dividing of the sheep and the goats, the sheep in this case being those who have learned all the correct passwords in the Book of the Dead. You see they are being carried safely through the Judgment Hall of Osiris, while the goats are being borne away into the Egyptian hell, amidst the usual unavailing weeping, wailing and gnashing of teeth."

Over and over again came the figures of Seti and the gods—Osiris, Isis, Horus, with his falcon's head, Anubis the jackal, the cat-headed goddess, and the gentle Hathor the cow, strange prototype of Venus. Again and again Seti answered each test set him by the gods, until he finally passed triumphantly into the presence of Osiris himself and entered the realms of eternal bliss.

" If the tomb of an unimportant youth like Tutankhamen had such treasure in it, what must this have been before the robbers broke into it ! " said Eve, gazing admiringly up at the roof of the empty funeral chamber —a dark blue-black, powdered with golden stars.

The sun was fiercer than ever when they came out of the tomb, and Serena asked wistfully how many more they were to see.

" Only one," said Jeremy, " the best of them all. There are dozens more, of course, but they are only for the people who come day after day and do the job really seriously."

Down they went again into the bowels of the earth, into the same heavy, dull heat, across a narrow bridge that spanned a deep, dark well, past a little alcove where lay three tiny skeletons, whose matted hair gave them a horrible impression of humanity that their shrivelled bones seemed to deny, and came at last to a spacious ante-room and a great burial chamber. At the farther end, in a second, sunken room, stood a lidless sarcophagus. Within it lay the black, mummied figure of the Pharaoh, as he had lain in solitary splendour for more than three thousand years.

No one spoke. The thought darted into Eve's mind, We oughtn't to be here—nobody has any right to be here—we're intruders. Then, as she looked longer at that immobile form, so dignified, though so long dead, so stately, though so dark and shrivelled and dried up, she realised that it didn't really matter, after all. Such dignity, such aloofness were above and beyond anything that she or anyone could do.

The Pharaoh was silent, but it was the silence of one whose lightest word had been law to a million. He was still, but it was the stillness of one whose raised finger had meant life or death to his servants.   Both his silence and his stillness seemed to come rather from obedience to his own will than at the command of that pale king whose name is Death.

The Pharaoh had been dead for more than three thousand years, but his personality still lived in that shrivelled form.

Past, Present and Future suddenly telescoped themselves in Eve's mind, and three thousand years were swallowed up in a fraction of a second in Eternity.

CHAPTER XXI

ISOBEL PAGE

IT was a relief to come out into the sunshine again, and to gallop all the way back down the burning, golden valley; a perilous but exhilarating proceeding on a road inches deep in soft sand and full of loose stones. By the time the party reached Cook's rest-house at the foot of Queen Hatshepsut's temple at Der-el-Bahri, they were hot, hungry and gloriously thirsty. Mahomed was waiting for them on the verandah, beside a table laid with the lunch he had brought.

Eve pulled her donkey up behind some Americans who had just dismounted at the foot of the steps. Rather a nice-looking party, she decided, quite different from the general run of tourists. It consisted of an elderly man, a motherly-looking woman with grey hair, a charming-looking girl and a particularly clean-looking young man. The girl said something to their drago-man, and, to Eve's astonishment, Jeremy turned sharply round at the sound of her voice.

"Isobel," he exclaimed, and a moment later he was shaking the pretty American's hands warmly. In fact, for the next moment or two he was completely taken up by her and her party. Then he turned round, his face unwontedly lit up with pleasure, and began to introduce his friends to one another.

Eve found that the people she already thought of to herself as Jeremy's new friends were, in fact, among his oldest. They were a Mr. and Mrs. Page, their son Tony and their daughter Isobel. Before she quite realised it, they were all sitting together at one long table, for Mrs.

Page was one of those American women so full of the
social instinct that she would have welcomed anything
approaching a party in any place at any time; and within
five minutes she and Serena had discovered half a dozen
mutual acquaintances. Everyone except Eve seemed
delighted with the meeting; but although she had to
admit to herself that Jeremy's friends were very pleasant,
she felt a little lost and out of it all, in spite of the fact
that young Tony Page was a most personable young
man and seemed properly prepared to give her his
undivided attention.

Jeremy and Isobel were evidently very intimate
friends, and as for Hugh, after gazing entranced at the
American girl, he sat murmuring, " I say, some peach,
what ? "

And some peach Isobel Page undoubtedly was—a
dark, slim, graceful little creature with that indescribable air of exquisite finish of which only French and
American women seem to possess the secret. " I wish
I had velvety brown eyes and a dead white skin," thought
Eve. She had never seen Jeremy so interested in any
girl before : Eve herself might not exist. Well, if
Jeremy chose to be completely absorbed in another girl,
she would be equally absorbed in another man, and here,
ready to hand, was one only too ready to be led like a
lamb to the slaughter. Jeremy should see, if he troubled
to look, that she, too, could play at that game. Constant
practice had taught Eve how to deal with a young man
though her thoughts might be miles away, and she
proceeded to do so with all her usual effectiveness.

Jeremy looked across at her more than once. She
was behaving scandalously, he decided, and she should
have a good talking to before she was many hours older.
To those of the party unused to her methods, Eve seemed
the embodiment of youthful innocence and candour, for,
with the art that conceals art, she set to work, under
cover of an ingenuous simplicity that was utterly disarming. But to her family and to Jeremy she was as an

open book. By the time lunch was over she had the conquest of Tony Page well in hand, and had warmed to her task with all the added ardour of success. Jeremy made up his mind that she should hear what he thought of her the moment he got her alone. But apparently that was going to be none too easy. Lunch over, she appeared to take no interest in the temple. She only said, as they walked up the steep slope that led to it, that the apricot-coloured pillars reminded her of the front of a Tube station. The annoying thing was that Jeremy had to admit there was some truth in the description, for seen at close quarters the work of restoration certainly gave rather this effect. He knew that on any other occasion Eve would have been the first to realise the enchanting loveliness of the rest of the temple : to feel its joyousness and its femininity, qualities that seemed so peculiarly arresting after the masculine strength and stupendous grandeur of Karnak. To-day, however, she left it to Isobel Page to show her delight over the little white colonnades with their slender pillars. To exclaim over the little coloured niches, the bright blue ceilings powdered with golden stars and the tiny chapels, the pictures of the famous expedition sent by the queen to the mysterious land of Punt with the little huts built on piles, the fishes and the birds and the dear little myrtle trees in pots that looked as though they had come straight from Heal's. The walls were covered with paintings; soldiers marching along so cheerfully that you expected them to break into a dance at any moment if only the officer at their head had not turned his head to see what they were up to; the gentle cow, Hathor, so full of dignity and peaceful charm, nourishing with her milk the young queen who knelt on the ground beside her. Although Eve did not tell Jeremy so at the time, she loved every inch of the temple; its delicacy and its enchanting grace. She loved the way it lay at the foot of the tall golden cliffs, with its view over the plain and the distant Nile and, farther still, the pillars of Luxor and Karnak.   In the burning blue sky overhead, big brown falcons swept backwards and forwards in wild, free curves above the temple of Egypt's greatest queen.

.   .   .   .   .

The donkeys trotted homewards over the plain.   The dusty road ran between acres of young crops, past creaking sakkiehs worked by patient oxen or supercilious camels.   It was refreshing on such a hot day to see the streams of clear, sparkling water, trickling down into the little channels.   There were plenty of people in the plain : men, women and children were at work in the fields;   a party of Egyptian students rode by, twenty or thirty of them, shouting and calling out to one another as they whipped their unfortunate steeds on to further efforts.   Eve had never seen such weird costumes : lounge suits of unknown pattern and of a horrible description, dirty white flannel shirts and awful blazers.

But aloof from the human ants who toiled or played round their feet sat the colossi of Memnon, their backs turned to the mountains, their faces to the Nile, whose ebb and flow they had watched, unmoved, through the ages.

" There were no crops here when I first saw them," said Jeremy.   " They stood in a sandy waste that suited them better than all this greenness.   Domesticity has tamed them a little."

" But they're like Amenhotep," said Eve, " nothing or nobody could really touch them.   They are so calm and so immovable."

When she had ridden some way past, she looked back at them again, across the green of a clover field.   There they towered, their patient hands upon their knees, their battered faces staring steadfastly out across the river, the same, in spite of surface mutilation, as on the day they had been created, for no mere shattering of feature could obscure their arrogance.   Had they lain broken upon the ground Eve felt that that would have survived.

.   .   .   .   .

" I think your friends are awfully nice, Jeremy," said Serena, as they sat on deck having tea. " I hope we shall see a lot of them. What a pretty girl Isobel is ! I rather gathered from her mother that she's thinking of getting married, but that she can't quite make up her mind, and her parents seemed to think a trip abroad in the meantime would do her good. You should have a fellow-feeling for her, Eve."

But Eve appeared to be engrossed in an Egyptian youth who was smiling away at her from the bank and saying something over and over again very quickly.

" What does he want ? " she asked Jeremy.

" He's a conjuror. He wants to come on board and show us his tricks."

" Oh, do let him ! " cried Eve, and before there was time to say anything more about Isobel Page, the young Egyptian was squatting on the deck in front of them, producing baby chickens, tiny squeaking balls of yellow fluff, from Hugh's trousers pocket and Eve's hair with lightning rapidity. He was an engaging youth, with brown eyes which laughed as much as his wide mouth. His white teeth shone in his brown face as he kept up an amusing patter in very broken English. Shaking a piece of cloth in front of him he gabbled :

" No chickens—no snakes—no rabbits," while with a deft twist he shook out still more baby chickens one after another.

" No chickens—no snakes—no rabbits," he cried again as he waved his hands over Jeremy and produced still more from the lapels of Jeremy's coat.

" No chickens—no snakes—no rabbits. No chickens —no snakes—no rabbits," he gabbled faster and faster when he threw Serena's pearl ring into the river, followed by a hundred-piastre note of Hugh's which he had first torn into a dozen pieces.

" My ring, my ring ! " wailed Serena.

" No chickens—no snakes—no rabbits," cried the youth, seizing a chicken and drawing an envelope from under its wing which he handed to Eve. She opened it and shook out the ring and the note, intact, into her lap.

By the time the conjuror had gathered up all his chickens, touched his breast and his forehead in parting salutation and retired to the lower deck to receive his fee from Moussa, neither Eve nor Serena knew whether they were on their heads or their heels.

Eve was so unusually quiet that evening that Serena wondered if she were too tired to see Karnak by moonlight as Jeremy suggested. But Eve said she was not a bit tired and she would love to go, for they were to leave Luxor the next morning.

" I do think," she exclaimed to Jeremy as she saw the avenue of Sphinxes looking whole and perfect again in the moonlight, " that one ought to see all the temples like this for the first time. The moon covers up all the damage that you see by day. Yesterday I couldn't help being disappointed with the Sphinxes, and to-night they seem to have got their faces again, and they look wonderful."

The fabulous pillars in the hypostyle hall were now white and silver; the shadows they cast clear and black against the white sand. Eve would hardly have been surprised if the priests of Amon had appeared, and wound in long procession between the mighty columns.

She felt as though she were drowning in temples as she stood among the vast ruins. Silence reigned here now; but with what a mighty thunder the fall of those roofs and walls must have shaken the earth! Yet the stone gods and kings still gazed at one another with grave, impassive faces.

" I wonder what they're thinking of ? " said Eve. " Not of us, anyway. They stare over our heads as though little creatures like us couldn't exist in the same world as a Pharaoh."

"It would have been a new experience for you, wouldn't it ? " said Jeremy, " if you had lived in those days and the Pharaoh had passed you by without a glance. Probably, though, he'd have lifted his finger the twentieth part of an inch, and before you knew where you were you would have been added to his list of wives."

"Should I ? " Eve was delighted with the idea. " I never thought of being a female Pharaoh, though I've always known that I should never have been able to say no to Charles II. I shouldn't have tried. A Pharaoh is rather a jump from a Stuart, though, but I dare say they had their own particular attractions. They look wonderful at night, standing still, frozen in stone or striding across the walls in those wonderful reliefs. Look at them holding their enemies by their heads in a bunch in one hand and gesticulating dramatic- ally with the other. How splendid my dear Horus looks in the moonlight ! I do think he's much the handsomest of them all."

" Perhaps a lot of us would look handsomer if we had hawks' heads on our shoulders instead of men's. Now Moussa wants to take us somewhere, so come along."

" Where to ? "

" I won't tell you anything about it beforehand."

" That sounds exciting," said Eve as they followed the others along a sandy path into a tiny courtyard. In front of them rose a little building. Three tall figures, swathed in black from head to foot against the mild night air stood beside a flickering lantern. They were the night watchmen of the temple. Moussa, bursting with importance, bade his party follow him in single file. Creeping slowly behind him, they felt their way in the blackness, turned to the right, and passed through a narrow doorway into a tiny room hardly larger than a cell. Only a small, square opening in the roof showed a patch of the night sky.   Suddenly Moussa switched on his electric torch, and out of the blackness leapt a life-size statue of black granite.   Jeremy felt Eve's hand grip his tightly.

" Who is it ? " she gasped.

" The Goddess Sekhmet, the Mighty One, the devourer and the destroyer," said Jeremy.

Eve was grateful for the comforting pressure of his hand, as she gazed awe-struck at the goddess, with a woman's body and a head, half lion's, half cat's, and wholly evil.

There was something horrible in the contrast of the slender, feminine body, taller than a tall man, and the animal's head, with the grim smile and the cruel jaw. Eve almost expected to see her lick her lips, slowly and thoughtfully, as though she had just devoured a baby with an unholy joy.

CHAPTER XXII

ASSUAN

" This is Heaven," murmured Serena blissfully, settling herself comfortably in her deck chair as the *Isis* set off on her travels again.

" Poor Serena ! " said Jeremy, putting an extra cushion behind her head, " the last two days have been a great effort for you. Never mind, the worst is over for the time being. If we get a good wind, we shall have to sail past Edfu, and then you will really be in luck."

" I don't know who or what Edfu is, but if it's a tomb or a temple I shall pray for the wind. Karnak and the Tombs of the Kings were splendid, but they'll last me for a long time."

" The poor girl hasn't slept, except at night, for over forty-eight hours," said Hugh.

" The doctors said——" began Serena.

" We know all about what the doctors said," put in Eve severely, " and anyone pinker and weller—and I must say it, Serena, fatter than you are now, I never saw."

" Oh, darling, don't say fatter."

" Fatter," repeated Eve firmly.

" Well, it's no good worrying," sighed Serena, closing her eyes. " Life is full of these little troubles," she added gently, and fell asleep.

There was hardly enough wind to fill the sails, and the boat glided slowly along, past a charming garden with a well, and steps leading down to the water, and rather a dreadful house with pink stripes. The river soon grew very beautiful, and Serena woke up for a few minutes to remark that it reminded her of Windermere. Serena was always finding stretches of the Nile that reminded her of Windermere, and she maintained her theory with gentle persistence in the face of much opposition.

" Except that both are made of water, no two places could be more utterly different," argued Hugh.

" Very, very like Windermere," murmured Serena drowsily, and dropped off to sleep again.

The hot day ended with a particularly gorgeous sunset; the sky glowed with orange, crimson and violet. A boat came floating down the river with two great red eyes painted on either side of its blue prow—the eyes of Horus seeking for his father and his father's murderer—and the boat was dyed the same marvellous colours as the water and the sky. What little breeze there was still lasted after the sun had gone, and, dinner over, Hugh and Serena sat on the cushioned divan on one side of the deck, Jeremy and Eve on the other.

" Warm enough ? " asked Jeremy as he wrapped a soft rug round Eve in business-like fashion.

" Quite, thank you, and blissfully happy."

The moon was full. The shadûfs had stopped work, the villagers and their herds had gone home, and no sound disturbed the peace of the night, except the distant barking of dogs and the swish of the water against the sides of the dahabeah. It was a world of black and white and silver. In front of Eve the great lateen sail soared up into the air, curved and pearly tinted like the inner side of a mussel shell, against the deep indigo sky. On either bank were tall palms or shining desert. If Eve turned her head she could see the graceful figure of the steersman, drooping languidly over the tiller. Two sailors, their heads muffled up against the night air, squatted on the gunwale ready to trim the sails. The reis sat on the top step of the companion. Over his usual robe of white linen he wore the khaki overcoat of a Tommy in the British

DAM AT ASSUAN.

PLAYGROUND OF MUD TO KEEP CHILDREN SAFE FROM
SNAKES AND SCORPIONS.

[*To face page* 161.

Army, a relic of the time when he had served in one of the Egyptian Labour Battalions during the War. Two or three of the men wore the same overcoats, and it gave Eve a strange feeling of kinship with them. She felt she wanted to sail on like this for ever, her body and mind steeped in the still beauty that wrapped her round. Occasionally the cook-boy would pad softly up from the lower deck on bare feet carrying a tiny brass pot of fragrant Turkish coffee to the steersman. Eve felt far away from all she had been accustomed to, and the unusualness of her surroundings gave a keener edge to her enjoyment. Only the scent of the cigar that Jeremy was smoking drifted across to her every now and then, and added a fascinating touch of civilisation.

It was one of the rare, perfect moments which come occasionally to everyone. Eve gave a little sigh of regret when the *Isis* took up her berth for the night, within sound of the water that poured through the barrage at Esna. At eight o'clock the next morning the lock gates opened and the dahabeah passed through.

" But there's a temple here," protested Eve.

" It can't be helped," said Hugh. " We're going to have the wind of a lifetime to-day; it's blowing quite strongly already."

The result was a grand sail of more than fifty miles, and although Eve bleated again as they flew past Edfu, whose pylons they could see rising behind the palm trees on the western bank, she did not mind so much when she realised that both Edfu and Esna were temples of the Ptolemaic period; for she now scorned anything later than the first Empire.

At sunrise the next morning she was on deck with Jeremy, both with thick coats over their pyjamas, to watch the *Isis* carefully navigated through the tricky gorge of Silsila. Jeremy had tried to rouse Hugh as well, but he had only turned over and grunted, and of course Serena was always a non-starter at six in the morning. The river narrowed as they entered the

M

gorge, and the tall sandstone cliffs came right down to the water's edge, honeycombed with tombs on the western bank and quarries on the eastern. They watched the sun rise, while the moon was still shining sulkily, although, as Eve pointed out, it had no business to complain of the sun's being there at that hour of the morning.

A good wind was blowing, so poor Eve was not allowed to stop at Komombo. She could only admire its fine position—standing as it did high up on the left bank on a wide bend of the river—and the lovely patches of turquoise blue that still lingered in the design of vulture wings above the fluted pillars.

"And that," said Eve bitterly, " is the third temple we've passed since we left Luxor. We're doing pretty well."

But she fell so much in love with Assuan that she instantly decided it was better than all the temples in Egypt. Although it was late in the afternoon when they arrived, it was still very hot, and only the breeze prevented its being oppressive. They hired a little sailing-boat manned by a small boy with limpid dark eyes, lashes a yard long, and a lower lip that projected beyond his nose. Jeremy took the tiller and the sheet and sailed the boat in and out among the great black boulders which shone like wet seals emerging after a dive. The Nile was wide here, and divided in two by the Island of Elephantine; Assuan itself lay on the eastern bank of the mainland.

Eve exclaimed with rapture over the rocks. "Look!" she cried, " there's one like a crocodile, and another like a crouching grasshopper, and it's quite as big as the crocodile."

"I always think they're like a vast herd of ante-diluvian monsters," said Jeremy.

After the eternal palm groves between Cairo and Assuan the variety of trees up here was a welcome change. They were large and luxuriant, especially on

Kitchener's Island, which they covered down to the water's edge.

"I love Assuan, it's so cheerful," said Eve. "Have you noticed that all the rest of Egypt is a little sad? What are we going to do to-morrow, Jeremy? You won't forget you promised me a camel ride here, will you?"

"I haven't forgotten. Moussa's gone to make arrangements this evening; we'll all have camels and ride into the desert to-morrow."

"Oh, dear, shall I like a camel?" asked Serena.

"I shouldn't think so," said Hugh, "but it'll be fun seeing you try."

"Will it indeed? That's a nice way to talk to the mother of your children. Isn't it, Jeremy?"

"Brutal. Trust yourself to Moussa and me, Serena. We'll see you have an animal warranted to carry a lady."

He turned the boat round and slipped down-stream, winding in and out among the rocks. The sun set in a blaze of fire on a violet background and turned water, rocks and trees into a scene of indescribable beauty.

.   .   .   .   .

Moussa escorted Eve across the road to where their five camels lay in a group in the shade. Swelling with pride, he pointed out the one he had selected for her particular use. Eve's heart dropped into her riding-boots.

"It . . . it looks a very large one," she said feebly.

"Mam'selle, I chose you the biggest."

"But why? I'm the littlest of the party, you know."

"Mam'selle, you want camel ride. I chose for you the largest and the best."

"They all look as big as houses."

"Moussa's chosen you a very handsome one," said Jeremy.

"Oh, he has," agreed Eve. "Yours are only beige, and mine is white, and I love his rose-coloured saddle-cloth. But . . . well, don't you think, Jeremy, he has an unusually disagreeable expression even for a camel ? "

" He does look as though he had a permanently bad smell stuck under his nose," agreed Jeremy, so cheerfully that Eve privately thought him very heartless.

Serena was in a condition of mingled resignation and despair.

" It's a comfort," she remarked to Hugh when he and Moussa settled her on her camel, " to think that if . . . if anything happens to me, the children will have Aunt Helen to look after them."

Hugh was as lacking in feeling as Jeremy.

" You'll be all right as long as you don't go to sleep," he assured her. " If you do, the results will probably be disastrous."

" Sleep ? My next sleep will probably be the long, long one, from which there is no awakening. Are you frightened, Eve dear ? "

" Terrified," said her sister as Jeremy mounted her and Moussa rushed across to see that everything was all right for his beloved Mam'selle. She gripped the single strand of rope—all she was allowed in the way of reins—and longed for the stirrups to which she was accustomed.

" If it breathes I shall fall off," she declared, turning an anguished glance upon the two men.

" No, no, Mam'selle, you will be quite safe," Moussa assured her, waving his arms in the air.

" I shall fall off," repeated Eve firmly. " I think I'm going to begin now, before he gets up."

" No, you're not," said Jeremy, laughing. " All you've got to remember when he starts to rise is to lean forwards, then backwards, and then forwards again."

" Tell him, ' Get up,' " said Moussa to Eve's camel-boy.

The youth shouted something that sounded very rude. Eve felt as though the whole world were heaving under her. Heavens ! What had Jeremy said ? Was it forwards and backwards and then forwards again ?

Or was it just the other way round? Backwards and forwards and backwards? She couldn't remember; and, anyhow, nothing mattered now. She could only set her teeth firmly as her animal started to unfold itself in snarling sections. How she stuck on as it rocked and heaved beneath her she never knew. Fortunately, she was unaware that Jeremy had taken a cinema of the proceedings. Anyhow, here she was at last, incredibly high up in the air, clinging like grim death to the inadequate little brass tube that stuck up in front of the saddle, her hat tilted over her nose, her cheeks flushed with emotion and exertion; shaken, agitated, terrified, but still alive.

If he sneezes, I am lost, she decided, and the next moment the animal had twisted round its long neck, that was so like Alice's when she grew, and pushed its disagreeable face close to Eve's frightened one.

I'm sure I've heard, she told herself, that an animal won't do anything to you if you look it straight in the eyes, and she leant back as far as she dared and fixed the camel with what she fondly hoped was a steady and compelling glance. The camel returned it with a look of contemptuous dislike. Then it hiked up its long upper lip and snarled violently at her. Eve still stared back like a frightened rabbit hypnotised by a cobra.

Tugged at by the boy, the camel started to walk forward, its head still turned inland, so that with every lurch its face and Eve's came closer together. Just as Eve thought her last hour had come, with a final snarl of scorn the animal turned eyes front again, and bit the behind of Moussa's camel as a relief to its feelings.

"How . . . are . . . you?" Eve managed to gasp out to Serena, who was lurching along beside her.

Serena only groaned.

"I . . . hope . . . we don't . . . look . . . as . . . frightened . . . as . . . we . . . feel," gasped Eve again.

Serena's only answer was another groan.

"How are you getting on?" inquired Jeremy cheerfully, trotting up on Eve's other side.

"I'm . . . not . . . getting . . . on . . . at all. . . . I'm . . . falling . . . off."

"Nonsense! Have a cigarette; that'll do you good." He held his case out to her.

"Idiot! I . . . can't . . . let . . . go . . . this . . . rotten . . . little . . . brass . . . thing."

"You'd get on much better if you did. As long as you make yourself rigid and hang on like that you're bound to be uncomfortable. Try sitting easy. Let yourself go with the camel."

"Oh, that's . . . just . . . what . . . I'm . . . trying . . . not . . . to . . . do . . . let . . . myself . . . go."

"Try crossing your feet on one side of its neck; you'll find that better. Put your right leg over."

"*Don't* be so silly! As if I could!"

"Will you like a trot, now, Mam'selle?" called out Moussa.

"No!"

The camel-boy called out something that sounded even ruder than before. The camel started to trot, and Eve gave herself up for lost. Then somehow—she never quite knew how it came about—she realised that at all events she was still on its back, and that she didn't feel quite so helplessly insecure as she had a few minutes ago. At the end of another two or three hundred yards she actually began to think that perhaps one day, say in a few years' time, she might even like riding a camel. Not as much, of course, as she had thought she would in the days of her innocence when she was eagerly and ignorantly looking forward to it on board the *Isis*.

"You're getting on splendidly," said Jeremy encouragingly.

"Am I really?"

"Rather! Now try putting your right leg over and crossing your feet against its neck."

" Well . . . I—I don't think I'll try *just* yet, if you don't mind."

But lo and behold, a few minutes later she was actually doing it, and finding it quite comfortable. Soon she was beginning to look about her once more, and to notice that Serena was gradually losing her look of settled agony, while Moussa was loud in his praise of them both.

I wonder, thought Eve, how soon I shall be able to put my hand in my coat pocket and get out my powder puff ? I'm sure I must look like a boiled lobster, with all the agitation and emotion I've been through.

They reached the granite quarries beyond the town before she felt herself quite equal to this feat, and here they were to dismount. Now came the experience of sitting a camel while it folded itself up like a stand camera.

" At any rate," Eve decided, as she lurched helplessly backwards and forwards, " the lower we get the less far there is to fall."

At last she stood once more on her own feet. She now knew the worst that could happen to her. The second time could never, never be as bad as the first.

It was with comparative calm that she mounted again after they had been to look at the great granite obelisk that lay full length on the ground, unfinished and abandoned, still bearing the marks of the workmen's tools of a thousand years ago.

" It will be a long time," she told Jeremy, " before I shall be able to accommodate myself with any degree of security to a camel's down-sittings and up-risings. Once you're safely up in the air, though, I don't think it's so bad."

Before long she really began to enjoy it, and soon she was trotting along quite fast, her feet negligently crossed in the most professional manner on the animal's neck and guiding it herself with its single rein; her camel-boy left far behind.

" I always knew I should love it," she cried triumphantly. " To think I'm really riding on a real, live camel
in a real desert, exactly like one reads about. This is a
real desert, isn't it ? It's a much better one than any
we've seen before. Instead of being pale-coloured, as
all the sand was below Assuan, this is really golden, like
' Afric's sunny fountains.' And how black the rocks
are ! It *is* quite a real desert, isn't it, Jeremy ? "

" Very much so."

" I mean the kind you could die of thirst in if you
lost your way ? "

" Yes, quite that kind."

" How thrilling ! Not that I want anything so
dreadful to happen, of course, but I'm awfully glad I've
seen the kind of place where you could do it."

" It would be very easy here. You've only to ride
due east. You've got between one and two hundred
miles of desert between you and the Red Sea, and many
miles more to the south."

" I wish we could go for a long, long journey over
it," said Eve—" on camels, of course. That's really the
only way to travel in the desert."

Jeremy, thinking of the change the last hour had
wrought in Eve's opinions, chuckled quietly to himself.

" I should like to travel all day," she continued
enthusiastically, " and to camp every night in a dear
little oasis. Fancy going on and on with nothing but
golden sand as far as you could see, and this blue sky
overhead."

Jeremy looked at his wrist-watch. " It's only ten
o'clock now, and it's getting hotter every minute.
You'll find you'll be quite glad to turn back before
very long."

" Oh, I'm sure I shan't ! I could go on like this for
ever."

She chattered on, and as Jeremy watched her sitting
loosely on her saddle, giving lightly to every movement
of her camel, he decided she looked the healthiest girl

he had ever seen, with her boyish slenderness and her fair skin. The heat that had taken the colour out of Serena's cheeks only made Eve more alive. They reached the spot where they were to dismount and walk a little way up the sandy hill for the view of the Nile and the glimpse of distant Philae, and here Hugh decided Serena must have a rest. They stretched themselves out comfortably in the shade of a rock and looked across the golden desert strewn with black boulders. A long string of camels passed along the caravan route below them, a route marked every now and then by an ominous heap of the bleached bones of their predecessors. Eve would have liked to stay there much longer, but by now the sun was high in the heavens and it was time to be off, Moussa said. He was a wonderful sight on a camel, and, to his great delight, Eve snapped him before they started home. He sat proudly astride his steed in his crushed-strawberry sateen, his fat legs bare nearly to the knees, save for his velvet Boston grips. The fact that one of his yellow elastic-sided boots had burst in the back seam lent him a slightly rakish air.

They rode home a different way, and reached the *Isis* hot, exhausted and triumphant, but sore—ignominiously sore—in sundry tender parts of their anatomy.

In the evening Moussa made arrangements with the owner of a tug, the *Amada*, to tow them up to Wadi Halfa if they were becalmed. The tug would not be starting for a few days, but the chances were it would catch them up before they reached Abu Simbel.

CHAPTER XXIII

THE DAM TO ABU SIMBEL

EVE was up on deck very early the next morning, for she was anxious to miss nothing of the approach to the dam. The day was fresh and lovely, though it promised to grow very hot later on. There was no wind, and the *Isis* had to be towed.

" What do you think about the dam ? " Eve inquired of Jeremy. " First I read a book which says it's the most awful thing even the English have ever done; drowning Philae and a lot of other temples just to be utilitarian and have a good water supply. Then I read somewhere else that it hasn't done any harm at all, and has been the making of Egypt. Which is right ? "

" I plump for the dam every time. It's delivered Egypt from the horrors of famine and turned a bankrupt country into one of the richest in the world."

" Heavens ! How ? "

" By never allowing the Nile to drop below a certain level. The water is stored up behind the dam during the winter months, and in the dry season its outlet is very carefully regulated, so that there's enough for everybody. It's controlled by British officials, and no amount of bribery will secure any landowner more than his fair share."

" Still it *is* awfully prosaic and utilitarian to destroy a temple thousands of years old just for the sake of food, isn't it ? "

" Food is prosaic, but it's the chief necessity of life. It may be romantic to starve, but it's not at all pleasant. It's a case of the old conundrum about the house on fire."

" What's that ? "

" Which would it be your duty to save—a priceless Old Master or the baby ? "

" The baby, of course."

" It's not so easy. The baby might grow up of no value to the community, or even a thief or a murderer who had better have died in infancy."

" Then do you think," asked Eve rather puzzled, " that it's the picture that ought to be saved ? "

" No. Not even if the baby were known to be an idiot. The point is that humanity has had to make certain rules and stick to them. Rules are no good unless they are to be kept in moments of extreme emotion. All life would be in danger unless a sufficient value were placed even on apparently insignificant lives. You have a perfect right to decide that a painting or a temple is worth more than your own life, but not that of anyone else. The fellaheen of Egypt are more important than the temple of Philae, in spite of Monsieur Pierre Loti."

" I see. It's a pity about Philae, all the same. Couldn't the dam have been made somewhere else ? "

" The experts said not, and they tried their utmost to save Philae. At one time there was an idea of surrounding it with concrete walls to keep the water out. It wouldn't have been any good, though, because it was its setting that made half the beauty of Philae. It stood on an island in a grove of palm trees."

" I can't help it, fellaheen or no fellaheen, I think it's dreadful."

" Well," said Jeremy philosophically, " you can't have an omelette without breaking eggs, and in this case the eggs were Philae. But all possible care is taken of the actual structure. Every summer, directly the river has fallen below the level of the temple, experts go up and examine every inch of its walls for traces of damage, and any necessary repairs are carried out immediately."

" All the same, I can't help feeling prejudiced against the ugly old dam."

" Ugly ! You wait till you've seen it."

" Isn't it ugly ? "

" I suppose some people might say so, but I'm pretty sure you won't."

When the *Isis* entered the first of the five locks, Eve and the others landed and left the dahabeah to her slow progress, while they walked up to look at the dam itself. A mile and a quarter long and more than one hundred and forty feet high, the stone barrage stretched across the Nile from bank to bank ; and then and there Eve threw Philae to the winds, and gave her whole heart to the dam. Standing below it, she watched the huge spouts of water rushing through the iron doors in a mass of white foam, crashing on to wide stone aprons and leaping up and crashing down again, looking like vast white ostrich feathers curving through the air. The force of the water and the roar of sound filled her with a delicious terror. She felt on her face the spray that hung about her like a cloud, and as Jeremy watched her, he knew that in its own way the power of the dam impressed her as much as the power of Karnak had done.

Presently a middle-aged man in grey flannels came up to them and introduced himself as the chief mechanical engineer. Needless to say, he was a Scotsman. For an hour they wandered with him from one point to another. He had served under all Egypt's notable men, from Cromer onwards ; had been at Omdurman with Kitchener and known Lord Beatty when he was a Second Lieutenant ; and he could talk well into the bargain. He called up a splendid-looking old native and presented him to them. This man's family, said the engineer, had been the Sheiks of the Cataract for generations, responsible in the old days for the safe conduct of all vessels through the rapids. The British, when they built the dam, made their descendant hereditary reis of the locks, and at the present moment he was superintending the passage of the *Isis* through the deepest lock in the world—four inches deeper than the famous Gatun lock in the Panama Canal, as the Scotsman proudly told them.

At last, when the dahabeah lay safely in the calm water above the dam, they said good-bye to the engineer, who promised to look out for them on their return journey, and went on board again.

"And now," sighed Eve rapturously, "we're actually in Nubia. Doesn't it sound wonderful, Serena? Much stranger and farther off than Egypt, somehow."

"Oh, much," agreed Serena; "and everything looks quite different too—wild and savage instead of cultivated like the country below."

"Are we going to see Philae now?" asked Eve.

"No, we're leaving that for the return journey," said Jeremy; "the north wind has started to blow."

"Of course. It always does directly we get anywhere near a temple. I don't mind, though. I've fallen so passionately in love with the dam that I feel a sight like that is enough for one day. I do think it's wonderful for the Moderns to have made a thing as magnificent and colossal in its own way as the most magnificent and colossal wonder of ancient Egypt. Especially as it's so different. If we'd put up a temple to compete with one of theirs, we should have come very poorly out of it. But the dam is a modern miracle. It stands on its own and doesn't suffer from comparisons."

Gradually the roar of the water faded away in the distance, and the *Isis* sailed on for hour after hour through savagely beautiful scenery. The Nile was enormously wide here, and instead of the highly cultivated strips of land, the groves of palms and the thickly populated villages of lower Egypt, it flowed through barren country. Tall, black rocks rose on either hand, utterly unlike the sandstone cliffs to which Eve had grown accustomed. Here and there the ramparts of rocks were broken, and stretches of dry golden sand spread down to the water's edge. The Libyan

desert was a very different colour from the pale sands of
lower Egypt. It glowed almost orange against the black
boulders and beneath the deep blue of the sky. The
very river flowed a steely blue instead of pale grey-
green. Here, in Nubia, quite suddenly it was as though
the whole of Nature had been painted with a richer,
more barbaric palette. Every now and then the dahabeah
passed groves of drowned palm trees whose plumey
heads stood out of the water. At the end of the
summer, Jeremy told Eve, they would be growing on
dry land again. The little huts of the villagers were
made of mud, crudely and effectively painted in patterns
of blue, white, green or red, rather like the work done
by a child in a kindergarten. Another favourite form
of decoration was a row of white enamel plates let into
the walls, and in many cases a simple design of mud
lattice-work ran round the top of a little house. All
the villages looked neat and trim and well built, in
striking contrast to the tumble-down affairs of lower
Egypt; for these had been built by the British Government above the reach of the water, when the building
of the dam had flooded the old hamlets. The people
too were quite different; they were Ethiopian in type,
and most of the women wore large nose-rings. Eve
could not imagine what they found to live on in this
savage country of desert and frowning rocks; but
Moussa explained to her that only the old men, the
women and the children lived up here the greater part
of the year. The younger men went to Cairo and
Alexandria as sailors or servants, and sent their wages
home from time to time. Life for a Nubian woman,
Eve thought, sounded a little dull.

The *Isis* sailed sixty miles that day, and the wind still
held on the day following. It blew them along past the
half-Roman temple of Dakkeh, whose exquisite pylons
alone stood above the water, surrounded by the feathery
tops of palm trees. In the afternoon the village of
Wady Saboa was reached, and, to Eve's astonishment,

she was actually allowed to land and walk to the little temple, through the soft golden sand which had covered it up until a few years ago.

She exclaimed with delight over its avenue of miniature Rameses and sphinxes and, as usual, she ran on ahead in spite of Moussa's efforts to keep her safely attached to the rest of his party.   She was back again in a minute or two with the news that she had actually found a picture of St. Peter.

" Yes, Mam'selle," said Moussa, " and he hold in his hand the Paradise Key."

He showed her, above the figure of the saint, the remains of Amon Ra, for the Christians had painted their pictures over those of the old Egyptians, and with the passing of the centuries the old had emerged again here and there; so that to-day you would often find a saint or a Byzantine angel cheek by jowl with Horus or Osiris; both parties apparently quite reconciled to the strange companionship.

It was a dear little temple, standing there in the golden sand, its walls soaked in the golden sunshine, and enfolded in the brooding peace of the centuries.

.   .   .   .   .

When Eve realised she was in the zone of the Tropic of Cancer, she was so pleased that she sat down and scribbled off a letter apiece to Harold and Hubert.   It must be admitted that she had shamefully neglected them beyond an occasional picture post-card, but "Nubia, Tropic of Cancer," looked so well at the top of the note-paper that this was an occasion not to be missed.

The day after the stop at Wady Saboa a head wind blew and progress was slow.   Towing was a more complicated affair than it had been in Egypt, for the long rope kept getting itself tangled up with the tops of the drowned palm trees, and then there was a great deal of shouting and running about among the sailors until they got it clear again.   The *Isis* passed Korosko, the place from which Gordon started on his last march to Khartoum,

DEKKAH.

WADY SABOA.

[*To face page* 176.

and later on, when she stopped for the sailors to have their midday meal, Eve and Jeremy went for a walk in spite of the heat. They strolled through a village and photographed some of the children, because Eve liked the large tin " plaques " they wore round their necks on a piece of string, stamped with a rather pleasing design and a phrase from the Koran.

" To save their lives," explained Moussa.

Nubian women, Eve decided, were of a quite astonishing ugliness.

" They have nice expressions," she remarked to Jeremy, " but their features are extraordinarily like my camel's."

She shuddered when he told her that the hair hanging in dozens of little plaits over their ears and foreheads was plaited with oil and butter, and left in this state for months on end.

Jeremy wanted to photograph a woman carrying her baby astride on her hip, but as Eve was not sure that such an attention would be well received, Moussa came to the rescue and distracted the lady's attention with a flow of arch conversation while the deed was done.

The following day was hotter, with no breath of wind, but the *Isis* struggled along to Derr, the capital of Lower Nubia, and while the cook-boy went off to buy fresh vegetables, the others went for a stroll with Moussa. Before they had gone far along the sandy lanes, between the little open shops where the pro-prietors squatted among their goods, they were met by what appeared to be the local Lord Mayor and a civic escort. The " Lord Mayor," a dusky individual in brown cotton, conducted the party through the town, while the turbaned officials kept the inhabitants at a respectable distance with a couple of long staves. The inevitable Singer sewing-machines whirred to right and left of them. The butcher's shops, laid out with curious lumps of meat, thick and black with flies, made the girls shudder.

N

Back on the river front again a smiling schoolmaster appeared, and begged, in excellent English, to be permitted to show the visitors over his school. To Eve's distress, it was, as usual, for boys only. These were of all shades from ivory to ebony, for the three races of Egypt were there: from the pale Egyptians to the bronze; from the dark brown Nubians to the black Sudanese, the descendants of the old slaves.

From the school the "Lord Mayor" conducted them to the Law Courts near by, where a trial was in progress.

Eve begged to go in and hear it, but a court official in a tête-de-nègre turban with a striped badge in front announced that everyone, including the judge, was taking a five minutes' rest.

"And that," said Jeremy, "may mean anything from half an hour upwards."

Eve spent most of that night leaning out of her window looking unsuccessfully for the Southern Cross, and the following morning found her cross and sleepy.

"The sky was full of crosses," she declared peevishly. "I counted at least six, and there was nothing to tell me which was the right one."

A climb to the ruins of a Roman fort at the top of a brown, crumbling cliff restored her temper. The thought of Cæsar's legionaries camped on those heights stirred her imagination. She could picture their bronze greaves flashing in the sun, and their horse-hair plumes blowing back against the blue sky.

That day and the next there was no wind, and the reis kept a good look-out for the tug that was to catch them up and tow them. Eve amused herself by watching the antics of a strange pair of insects about the size of grasshoppers which she had found on deck and brought down to the saloon at luncheon and placed on the flowers in the centre of the table. The larger was green, the smaller brown. Their three-cornered faces were sharply pointed, their legs were like lobsters', their tails, which they lifted up and down, were like long leaves, and they had the features of a giraffe. They were antediluvian monsters seen through a diminishing glass.

" I suppose they're husband and wife," said Eve.

" Talking of husbands and wives," said Serena, " I dreamt of a husband for you last night."

" How exciting ! What was he like ? "

" Awfully attractive. As a matter of fact I was a little annoyed when I found it was you he was interested in instead of me. Hugh didn't seem to be there, somehow. I hope you don't mind, darling ? It was only a dream, you know."

" Dreams show the way the wind blows," observed Jeremy.

" Nothing really happened," replied Serena naïvely. " Dreams are such funny things."

" Yours are," agreed Hugh. " However, don't mind me. Tell us what Eve's husband was like."

" Charming ! He had rather light hair, Eve dear, and blue eyes. He was tall and slender with the loveliest long legs. You'd have liked him awfully if you'd been there."

" Wasn't I there ? " asked Eve disappointedly.

" N—no. I think he and I were quite alone."

" Really, Serena, I wish you'd arrange your dreams more carefully. Especially as you say it was me he was in love with."

" Yes, I'm quite sure of that. As I told you, I was a little disappointed about it."

" What was he called ? " asked Hugh; " it would be interesting to know Eve's future name."

" That was the drawback. His name was the least satisfactory part about him."

" You can't have everything," observed Jeremy. " With legs like that there's bound to be a hitch somewhere."

" I'm afraid his Christian name was Percy," admitted Serena.

" Darling ! I couldn't marry a Percy ! It's worse than Harold or Hubert. But I've never been lucky with names, have I ? You remember Wilfred and Cuthbert ? And the man with the red hair who came just before them ? He was worse still, because it was his surname that was wrong. What was this man's surname."

" Garbage."

"How perfectly splendid!" exclaimed Jeremy. "Mrs. Percy Garbage ! Eve, I congratulate you. It's a rare, distinguished, delightful kind of name. I'll design you a ' going-away ' dress modelled on the uniform of the street scavengers of London. You'd look very well in one of those hats turned up at the side. Your crest, of course, will be a dust-bin."

" It's very careless to have dreamt such a horrible name for me," cried Eve indignantly. " Thank goodness you didn't tell us before breakfast, Serena. Fancy changing Wentworth for Garbage ! Nothing would induce me to."

" I don't think you'd mind so much if you'd met him," urged Serena. " He really was terribly attractive."

" Hugh, you must do something about your wife," said Jeremy, " she's an abandoned female. But what a relief to think we're going to get Eve off our hands at last. Eve Garbage," he repeated thoughtfully, " I rather like the name myself."

" I shall refuse him, of course," said Eve decidedly. " You may dream of the longest, slenderest, loveliest legs in the world, Serena. I don't care. Moussa is the only man I ever loved, and his are bandy."

.   .   .   .   .

After lunch Eve placed the insects carefully into a little box with holes in the lid ready to be taken on shore and placed lovingly on some leaf when the *Isis* tied up for the night.

This Boy Scout action duly arranged, she and Jeremy settled themselves in their deck chairs after lunch, while Hugh and Serena frankly retired to sleep below.

" It's so convenient," said Eve. " I've reached just
the same place in Amelia B. that we've reached on the
Nile. Do listen to this. Isn't it sweet? She's talking
about the Roman fort we saw this morning, and she
says, ' There are also some sculptured and painted
grottoes to be seen in the face of the mountain. They
are, however, too difficult of access to be attempted by
ladies.' Isn't that nice and Victorian? Would you
call me a lady, Jeremy? "

" Not often. But you're terribly female."

" Good gracious! What does that mean? "

" It means that you're the usual mass of contradictions
—soft-hearted and cruel, generous and acquisitive, honest
one moment and quite unscrupulous the next, and so
on."

Eve gasped. " My goodness! Of all the sudden
unprovoked attacks! "

Jeremy grinned at her.

" It wasn't an attack, it was a plain statement of fact.
You asked me a question and I've answered it, that's
all."

" It isn't all, by a long way. I like the soft-hearted
and generous bits, but I'd like to know what you mean
by calling me cruel and unscrupulous, and whatever the
other thing was."

" Acquisitive? "

" Yes. That means grasping, doesn't it? What do
I grasp? "

" Scalps, my dear child, scalps."

" Pooh! I don't do that more than any other
woman."

" I didn't say you did. I only put it forward as a
particularly female trait."

" I suppose you were thinking of that when you said
I was cruel, too? "

" Yes."

" Jeremy, you do exaggerate. Honestly, nine cases
out of ten it isn't our fault. We can't help it if men

are so terribly weak in the knees that they collapse the moment we look at them.   Now can we ? "   Eve turned her most innocent, wide-eyed gaze upon Jeremy as she spoke.   " Honestly, it's their own fault.   We treat them simply and straightforwardly, and they go and mis-understand us."

" It's simple and straightforward enough, I grant you. The female spider is simple when she devours the male. Beautifully simple.   So are you when you're really out for blood.   As I said before, you're intensely female."

" Do you think it's a very bad thing to be ? " she asked curiously.

" Not at all.   Do you ? "

" Well, I didn't like the sound of it when you began; but now you've explained it a bit, I don't mind so much.   I'd far rather be a woman than a man, anyway. I've known heaps of girls who said they'd rather be men, but I think it must be awfully dull.   Do you like being a man, Jeremy ? "

" Yes, thanks."

" I suppose you'd rather be one ? "

" Good Lord, yes ! "

" I don't think you need be so emphatic about it. It's not polite.   Still, I'm glad you're a man, too.   Men are so useful about the place."

" Thanks ! "

" You know what I mean ? "

" Perfectly.   I feel I shall be a great help to Percy Garbage, at all events."

" How ? "

" I can give the poor devil a few hints.   Naturally, I take a great interest in him.   I feel I'm going to like him too.   I think he'll turn out to be one of those strong, silent chaps that women always fall for."

" That's all you know about it.   As a matter of fact we don't like them at all.   They're only silent because they've nothing to say.   Besides," she added airily, " there's no such thing as a strong man.   I've tried them again and again; they simply don't exist. For instance, you may stick your chin out as much as you like, and people who don't know you may mistake you for one. But oh "—Eve shook her head with a wise air—" how very, very wrong they would be. No, there's no such thing as a strong man, and if there were, he would be so unpleasant that no woman would have anything to do with him."

" You're perfectly right. All the same, I shall make it my duty to tell Garbage a thing or two before you're married. From Serena's description, I fancy he's the kind of fellow who won't stand much nonsense. Take your behaviour the other day," continued Jeremy, " your disgraceful flirtation with Tony Page. You'll find Garbage won't stand for anything of that sort after you're married."

" *My* disgraceful flirtation ! I like that ! How about your own behaviour that day ? I suppose you'll say next that you didn't devote yourself in the most blatant fashion to Isobel ? *She* doesn't flirt, I suppose."

" Not with me, at all events. She wouldn't dream of such a thing."

" Wouldn't she ? That's all you know about women."

" I may not know much about women, but I do know a good deal about Isobel."

" Really ? You seem to make a habit of knowing a good deal about young girls, don't you ? "

" Don't say things like that, Eve. It isn't true, and it sounds rather common."

To her intense humiliation, Eve felt her eyes filling with unexpected tears.

" I don't pretend to be perfect like Isobel Page," she said a little shakily.

" Silly child ! Who said she was perfect ? "

" Nobody, but I'm sure she is."

Jeremy frowned.

" I hope you haven't taken a dislike to Isobel ? " he said.

" I ? Certainly not. Why should I ? I've hardly spoken to her."

" No, you were too occupied with her brother."

" Not more than you were with her."

" But, my dear child, I told you I knew her very well before. The two cases are quite different. You and Tony had met for the first time. Seriously, Eve, it'll make things rather awkward when they catch us up at Wadi Halfa if you encourage him to fall in love with you. His parents won't be pleased if you lead him on and then turn him down, as you must admit you're fond of doing."

" Perhaps I shan't turn him down. He's very good-looking and an only son, and it's obvious they've got lots of money."

" Of course, if your intentions are honourable for the first time in your life, there's nothing more to be said. But to my certain knowledge you've refused other men as eligible as Tony. These people happen to be my friends, and as his father and mother are both devoted to their only son, you'll really oblige me very much by not breaking his heart for him."

" A man's heart," scoffed Eve.

" Oh ! I know you think they haven't got them, but, believe me, you're wrong again."

Neither spoke for a minute or two, then Jeremy began :

" Why have you taken such a dislike to Isobel ? "

" I told you before that I hadn't. Why should I ? "

" I can't imagine. As it happens, she took a particular fancy to you. She admires you very much indeed. She told me so."

" I'm sure she did," said Eve sweetly.

" I've a particular reason for wishing you and Isobel to be friends," continued Jeremy.

" Why ? "

" I can't tell you just at present, but you'll know before long."

Without a word of warning Eve's heart began to do

things. Such odd things that she thought she had better escape to her cabin before anything further happened to it.

"It isn't like you to be so ungenerous, Eve," said Jeremy as she got up to go.

But Eve turned away without answering, leaving Jeremy, who had thought up till to-day that he could read her like an open book, puzzled and annoyed.

Alone in her cabin, Eve sat down hurriedly on the edge of her bed, because she had such a strange hollow feeling in her middle and such absurdly shaky legs. Jeremy was in love with Isobel Page! There could be no doubt about it, she told herself, and it would put an end to all the friendship and intimacy between herself and Jeremy; for obviously Jeremy single and Jeremy married would be two different people. Was the marriage of one's best friend always such a blow? Poor Eve supposed it was. To have to lose Jeremy! Jeremy, who had always been there whenever she wanted him; who nearly always laughed at her, but who never failed to pull her out of every scrape, or to prop her up and comfort her when things went wrong. Eve had always taken for granted, as youth is apt to do, that the existing state of things would never alter. She might marry, probably she would, but that wouldn't make any difference to her relations with Jeremy. In fact that relationship was always the more clearly defined of the two. And now Isobel Page had blown the fabric of Eve's building to the winds, and what was she to do? Nothing, she told herself, for nothing was possible. At all costs neither Jeremy nor Isobel must ever know the blow they had dealt her.

She sighed, pulled herself together, powdered her nose and changed to a more becoming hat. Thus fortified, she prepared to face a lonely future—one where she would no longer be spoilt and scolded and comforted as she had been ever since she was ten years old. In a word, to face a future without Jeremy.

. . . . .

Hugh and Serena were on deck when Eve reappeared.
A swift glance assured Jeremy that she was herself
again.

"Our tug has just turned the corner behind us," he
told her, making room for her on the seat beside him.

In a few minutes the *Amada* puffed up.   Two heavily
laden barges, as big as herself, were fastened on to her
sides.   The *Isis* threw out a tow rope and they started
off.

An hour later they came in sight of Abu Simbel.
The river here was not particularly interesting, neither
was the country through which it flowed.   But this
very lack of anything eventful in the scenery made the
four colossi on the western bank all the more startling.
Yet at this first view they gave Eve no impression of
size.   They were dwarfed by the sandstone cliff behind
them, of which they were part.   They fell naturally into
the deserted landscape.   Yet they were so alien to it
that they struck the beholder with amazement.   They
suggested Man, and the mind of Man, in surroundings
that seemed empty of all humanity.

Their backs to the cliff, their faces to the Nile, their
hands flat upon their knees, they sat in majestic solitude.
Scornful, pitying and benevolent, they gazed for ever
down the river at the puny men passing to and fro in
their little boats.

On their left a great gap in the cliff was filled in by
a curtain of golden sand, a curtain so high, so steep and
so golden that in itself it was a thing of beauty.

Beyond that, again, was the richly carved front of
the little temple of Hathor, hollowed out of the rock
like its greater neighbour.

"Now I can forgive Rameses for spoiling the reliefs
at Abydos," said Eve.   "I don't mind how often he
rubbed out other people's names and put his own over
them, or how many of their exploits he claimed for
himself.   The man who made Abu Simbel deserves to
be called the Great."

" Where are we going to land ? " asked Serena.

" We're not going to," said Hugh, " we're going on."

Eve turned to her brother-in-law with a glance of utter incredulity. " I can't believe it ! Even we couldn't do such a thing."

" My dear, we must. The tug won't stop until it reaches Halfa. Abu Simbel won't run away, you know. It will still be here when we come down the river again."

" After this," said Eve calmly, " nothing will ever surprise me again. Not even if you and Jeremy say we can't stop on the way back."

" I promise you by all the gods of Egypt that we will," said Jeremy.

" I shall believe it when it happens," was Eve's only reply.

She sat looking at the colossi as long as they remained in sight. When they disappeared, she picked up Amelia B. and marvelled anew at that gentle Victorian lady's power over words.

" ' Giants themselves,' " read Eve, " ' they summoned these giants from out of the rock, and endowed them with superhuman strength and beauty. They sought no quarried blocks of syenite or granite for their work. They fashioned no models of clay. They took a mountain, and fell upon it like Titans, and hollowed and carved it as though it were a cherry stone, and left it for the feebler men of after ages to marvel at for ever. One great hall and fifteen spacious chambers they hewed out from the heart of it, then smoothed the rugged precipice towards the river, and cut four huge statues with their faces to the sunrise, two to the right and two to the left of the doorway, there to keep watch to the end of time.' "

CHAPTER XXIV

ALL the next day the tug snorted along towards Wadi Halfa. On the eastern bank oddly shaped little mountains and great crags of fantastic shape sprang abruptly out of the sand in strange fashion. Some were like rude pyramids, one like a sphinx, and all gave the effect of having been deliberately planted there by some gigantic hand for a definite purpose, long lost in the mists of oblivion.

At dusk, the tug, the barges and the dahabeah tied up for the night, and after an early start the next morning, reached Halfa at midday. It looked a charming little place, Eve thought—like a toy town. A row of tiny painted dolls' houses, pink, blue and yellow, and a line of trees bordered what Serena insisted on calling the sea-front, and the minaret of a mosque rose up in the background.

The *Isis* had reached the farthest point of her journey, and such a great occasion demanding the sacrifice of a sheep for the crew, Jeremy arranged that the tragic deed should be performed while he and Hugh took the two girls for a walk through the bazaar.

Eve was deeply impressed by the Sudanese policemen in their khaki jerseys and shorts, with belts of jade or royal blue, puttees and sandals. Instead of the truncheon of the London Bobby, each man carried a great whip of rhinoceros hide.

The tree-shaded lanes of the bazaar were attractive, although there was nothing worth buying except the vegetables, which were excellent. Each little sandy street ended abruptly in the desert, with rather the same effect, Eve said, that you get in our coastal towns at home, where the streets all end up in the sea. Suddenly her attention was caught by a strange figure sitting outside a shabby café—that of a coal-black man attired in dirty white robes, with a tuft of green leaves apparently growing out of each wide nostril.

"What on earth is he?" she asked Jeremy, "and why does he grow his mustard and cress on his person?"

"It's not mustard and cress," said Serena, "it's spring onions."

"So it is! How perfectly awful!"

"I think it's a jolly good idea," said Hugh, "to carry a snack of your favourite food up your nose all day, especially as the best food in the world never tastes so good as it smells. Nothing can really equal the smell of coffee roasting or onions being fried."

"But what *is* he?" asked Eve again.

"I daren't tell you," said Jeremy.

"Daren't tell me? What on earth do you mean?"

"And if I did, you wouldn't believe me."

"What nonsense! Moussa, you tell me," commanded Eve.

"Mam'selle, this man is a sheik," replied Moussa innocently.

"I don't believe it!"

"It's quite true," said Jeremy.

"He live outside Halfa, Mam'selle," explained Moussa, "and he come in when he want to drink and play."

"You'd better take a snapshot of him," suggested Hugh, "and send copies to all the girls' schools in England. It'll do them a power of good."

"Let's ask him if his name is Garbage," suggested Jeremy.

"He has a sweet, gentle expression," said Serena. "But if he really is a sheik, Moussa, won't it hurt his feelings to be photographed as though he were a side show?"

Moussa spoke to the sheik in Arabic. That gentleman beamed with gratification, and immediately posed before the camera, to the envy and admiration of the crowd that had collected.

" I can't bear to believe he's a sheik," moaned Eve as she took the photograph, and she turned away with a shudder as Moussa pressed a tip into the nobleman's hand, which closed greedily upon it.

A few minutes later Jeremy ran into a man whom he knew in the Irrigation Department, walking with his wife. The latter fell to Eve's share, who soon found she had her work cut out for her. The young woman appeared to have no conversation whatever, not even the smallest of small talk, and the result was a new kind of Magnall's questions.

" Do you like being here ? " asked Eve politely.

" It's rather boring," the girl replied.

" Do you stay here all the year round ? "

" No, only six months in the winter."

" Do you play a great deal of tennis ? "

" Not a great deal."

" Golf ? "

" No."

There was a pause. Then Eve began again.

" Do you ride a lot ? "

" Not much."

" Don't you like it ? "

" Not particularly."

" Do you ride a camel ? "

" I did last month."

Come, thought Eve hopefully, anyone who has ridden a camel must have something to say about it.

" Where did you go ? "

" We went for a month's tour in the desert."

" How perfectly glorious ! Didn't you love it ? "

" It wasn't very comfortable."

" Did you go just for fun ? "

" No, my husband had to go on business."

" Well, I should think it must have been heavenly."
Another pause. Then Eve returned to the attack.
" Do you read a lot ? "
" Not much. I've read all the novels here."
" Have you a garden ? "
" Yes."
Now I've struck oil, thought Eve.
" I expect you are awfully keen on gardening ? " she
continued a little gushingly.
" Not particularly."
" Another wash-out," said Eve to herself.
This time the pause was a long one, and Eve, grown
desperate, decided the girl was probably a high-brow.
Perhaps she would respond to more intelligent con-
versation. Eve would try, and she accordingly began
by asking if Halfa were a big province.
" I don't know," replied the girl.
" How many provinces are there in the Sudan ? "
continued Eve.
" I never heard."
" I suppose Khartoum is a province too ? "
" I don't know."
" I give up," said Eve to herself. " I've done my
best, but she's cretinous. I'm not going to bother any
more."
They walked on in silence for a hundred yards or so.
Suddenly the other girl spoke. It was so unexpected
that Eve jumped.
" I'm repairing our Ford," said the girl.
" Really? How awfully clever of you ! I can drive
all right, but I'm utterly hopeless on insides. What are
you doing to it ? "
The girl began. She talked unceasingly of pistons,
carburettors, differentials and sparking plugs until Eve
was dizzy.
" Fortunately," she told Jeremy later, " the creature
talked with her mouth shut, so I missed a lot of it.
Then her husband took her away."

PHILAE.

PHILAE.

[*To face page* 193.

" Poor devil ! " said Jeremy.

" She's only here the best six months of the year,"
said Eve indignantly, " safely out of the English winter,
in a perfect climate. She has no heat or discomfort to
put up with. She's in a country with a marvellous
history, where things grow in your garden if you only
look at them, and she can't even trouble to open her
mouth when she talks. I pity her husband. She's not
worth her board and lodging except as a spare hand in
a garage."

" What do you think she wants ? " asked Jeremy.

" Oh, a suburb with trams and motor-buses and
a cinema every other night, I should think. Those
anæmic, jelly-fish kind of women make me ill," said
Eve savagely, as they entered Cook's office, where
Hugh and Jeremy made arrangements for a motor-boat
to take them to the Second Cataract on the morrow.
The agent in charge was an Egyptian, a nice fat little
man who with his nice fat elderly little dog walked back
to the dahabeah with them and confided to Eve on the
way that he and his wife were homesick for their native
town of Assyut, from which they had been exiled for
two years. It was inconceivable to Eve that anyone
should hanker after the flesh-pots of Assyut, but she
hoped sympathetically that he would find himself trans-
ferred there again before long, for which he thanked
her very politely.

Things now took a tragic turn. Either the walk had
been too short or the bargaining for the sacrificial sheep
had taken too long, for alas ! there he was still intact in
his white woolly coat, being led by the cook-boy to the
slaughter.

" Oh, dear ! oh, dear ! " wailed Serena.

" How perfectly horrible ! " cried Eve.

And in spite of all that Hugh and Jeremy could say
as they led them away again and assured them that death
would be swift and painless, they both vowed they
would never eat meat again. It was only the extra-

o

ordinarily succulent smell of the quails at dinner that night that made them change their minds.

.   .   .   .   .

At eight o'clock the next morning a smart white motor-launch, manned by three Sudanese sailors in dark blue jerseys, drew up alongside the *Isis*, and the party of four, accompanied by Moussa, Ibrahim and a large hamper containing the lunch, went on board.

Eve was bent upon getting a glimpse of a crocodile. Moussa had told her two days before that one had been seen sunning itself at the foot of one of the shining black boulders with which the river was strewn.

The sun had grown very hot by the time the boat drew in to the foot of the towering crag of Abousir, and Serena groaned when she realised she had to climb to its summit. The sand was scorching under their feet, the rocks were blistering to the touch; but once the top was reached, even Serena owned it was worth a far greater effort than they had made.

They gazed at the view and marvelled at it, though the Nile was unusually low for the time of year and the cataract little more than rather shallow rapids. Sheer below them, its olive waters hurried along in a series of curves and eddies, sleek as a seal's back, except where the yellowish foam curled round the hidden rocks or frothed over the edges of the shining, blue-black boulders. These were scattered behind Abousir, and over the pinkish-fawn desert that stretched from the opposite side of the river to the Red Sea. Here and there across the miles of boulder-strewn desert a glimpse could be caught of the windings of the river. Far away to the south rose the two bluish, conical mountains of Dongola.

There was no colour except the olive of the water, the golden and fawn sands, and the blue-black boulders, save for a few clumps of neutral-hued palms, greyish-green. The whole world was drenched in light, so fierce that colour almost ceased to exist. Even the blue of the brassy sky overhead almost ceased to be a positive colour because of its brazen quality; and the glare beat upon the eyeballs; the bleached land, scattered with dark and tumbled boulders, reached away to the white and quivering horizon. Light—fierce, unshaded, glaring light—was in itself much the strongest thing in all the world at the rock of Abousir.

Down by the river, looking no bigger than ants, half a dozen men threw themselves into the water and rushed down it on inflated goatskins. It was not a very interesting performance, but the pace at which they shinned up the rock afterwards more than deserved the baksheesh they demanded, and Moussa dispensed it with his usual magnificent air. The swimmers were splendid-looking creatures, with lithe figures of deep bronze, nude except for their loin-cloths.

Eve was sorry when the moment came to leave the rock. It was the turning point of their journey, and in a curious way it seemed also to mark a turning point in her own life. Till a few days ago she had been content to take things as they came; now, for some reason, she felt herself growing more serious, more responsible, both to herself and others. With a little sigh she cast a backward glance at the yellow desert and the distant mysterious peaks of Dongola before she followed the others down the side of the cliff.

They were all grateful for the shade of the awning as they sat down to the lunch that Ibrahim had spread out in the boat. During the meal a group of men and boys sat in a circle on the shore and sang and played to them on their native instruments.

The minor melody rose and fell to the accompaniment of the noisy river. The bright blue of the men's robes looked startling against the orange sand; on a little island opposite, a black-haired boy in white was working in a small garden; a cormorant flew clumsily by with water-logged wings; in the shallows a pair of herons were fishing; a little bird with a yellow crest perched

on a thorn tree; a semi-circle of cranes passed overhead, and everything—sand, rocks, men and birds—
quivered in the shimmering haze of heat.

Eve sighed when it was time to leave.

" I can hardly bear to go," she said.   " This is the
turning point of our whole journey.   At this very
moment we are really starting on our way back to
England.   I wish heavenly things didn't always come
to an end."

It was a sad blow, when they reached Halfa again,
to find that the great yard of the *Isis* had been taken
down and laid away for the return journey.   The big
sail, Moussa explained, could never be used going down-
stream with the powerful current, for if the dahabeah
crashed on a sand-bank with all the force of the river
behind it, there might be a serious accident.

That evening the *Ophir* drew up beside the *Isis*, and
Tony Page leant over the stern and invited everyone
to dinner.

.   .   .   .   .

Moussa was always delighted at any suggestion of a
party.   This was as it should be, he told Eve, as he
fussily escorted them down their own gang-plank and
up the *Ophir's*, lantern in hand.   Eve, who had not the
smallest wish to go, could only agree.   Tony came at
once to her side, openly overjoyed at seeing her again,
and under cover of his eager welcome Eve was able to
watch, out of the corner of her eye, the meeting between
Jeremy and Isobel; to notice the warmth of his hand-
shake and the intimate quality of her smile.   Isobel
greeted Eve with a charming warmth and that young
lady took very good care that her own manner was one
of innocent friendliness, for she felt that Jeremy's eyes
were upon her.   The annoying thing was that she really
felt she would like Isobel very much indeed as anything
but Jeremy's wife.   For one thing, Eve was always
attracted by good looks, and there was no doubt Isobel
was very pretty.   She was looking delightful to-night

in scarlet chiffon. Her mouth was as red as her frock, and her sleek black hair grew attractively away from her forehead.

Before the evening came to an end Jeremy decided that however Eve behaved to Tony in the future, the harm was already done. It was obvious to the meanest intelligence that Tony was head over ears in love.

Jeremy broached the subject to Serena in a quiet corner of the deck after dinner, but Serena only smiled enigmatically, and her answers were vague and unsatisfactory.

" Do you think Eve means business at last ? " asked Jeremy.

Serena looked thoughtful and said that Eve hadn't confided her plans to her, up to date.

" You must have formed your own opinion, though," suggested Jeremy.

" Yes," murmured Serena, " I have."

" Well ? "

" I like the whole family."

" They're all right," agreed Jeremy impatiently.

" Well ? " queried Serena in her turn.

" If Eve marries the wrong man, there'll be the devil to pay," declared Jeremy.

Serena said nothing. Jeremy chose another cigarette and shut his case up again with a snap.

" She's changed," he remarked, " changed since this trip began."

" Yes."

" She's more thoughtful, quieter."

" Yes."

" Particularly since we met the Pages."

" Yes."

" Tony's too young for her," said Jeremy decidedly.

Serena pointed out that he was three years older than Eve.

" But in some ways Eve's old for her age," argued

Jeremy, " and Tony's young for his. Eve's always been accustomed to older people."

" Yes."

" Naturally, a girl like her is bound to marry sooner or later," said Jeremy thoughtfully.

" Naturally," agreed Serena.

" What does Hugh think of this affair with Tony ? " asked Jeremy.

" He doesn't think. He's so used to Eve's young men."

" Do you want her to marry him ? " asked Jeremy point blank.

" I like him very much," replied Serena evasively.

" That's hardly an answer," objected Jeremy.

" And I agree with you that there would be the devil to pay if Eve married the wrong man."

" Well ? "

" But personally I'm not afraid of its happening. Eve is very clear-sighted—once she knows what she wants."

" She is," agreed Jeremy dryly.

" At present," continued Serena, " she doesn't know—not quite, that is to say."

" Do you know ? "

" Yes," replied Serena placidly. " I know."

Jeremy threw the end of his cigarette overboard, and it struck the water with a little hiss.

" You are talking in riddles to-night, Serena," he said impatiently; " but I gather that on the whole you are satisfied with the way Eve's affairs are shaping ? "

" Yes," agreed Serena, " on the whole."

" And you think she's going to marry the right man ? "

" Yes," said Serena, " I do."

CHAPTER XXV

THE Page family had left for the Second Cataract before Eve appeared on deck the next morning.

" And if Isobel sees a crocodile when I haven't," said Eve to herself, " I hope it eats her."

The *Isis* and her tug were scheduled to start at twelve o'clock, and while Moussa went off to collect a last supply of stores, Eve and the others dawdled about Halfa. They went to the railway station and looked at the white train for Khartoum, and Eve wished they could spare the time to go there and see where that tiresome but heroic Gordon had perished. Eve and Serena were much intrigued by the violet glass in the carriage windows, which they felt would have a trying effect on the complexion.

" I really believe," declared Hugh, " that you two would rather get sunstroke than sit in an unbecoming light for a couple of days."

" Oh, much, much rather ! " said Eve earnestly. " You and Jeremy wouldn't like to look at us for hours on end with mauve faces, either."

" It wouldn't worry us in the least. That's where women are so foolish. We know your faces aren't really mauve, so why on earth should it matter ? We should be equally mauve. Would that worry you ? "

" Don't be silly ! That's quite different. Your faces don't matter."

" Women aren't as easily upset by externals as men," explained Serena.

" Aren't they ? " questioned Jeremy. " Everything you and Eve say is proving the contrary."

" It doesn't really," said Eve. " You and Hugh are thinking the wrong way round.   You would stop loving us at once if we wore our noses shiny, or if we began to go a little thin on the temples, like Hugh's doing.   And all Serena thinks is that it makes him look more interesting and intellectual."

" Don't argue with them, darling," said Serena placidly.   " It's much too hot, and there are certain things men will never understand."

" I don't mind their not understanding," cried Eve, " if only they wouldn't talk such a lot of nonsense. There are certain things we know they do better than us. Looking up trains in Bradshaw, for instance, or reading a newspaper and keeping the pages tidy.   And even the stupidest man can mend electric bells and do ridiculous things like that."

" Yes, isn't it odd ? "

" Which is mad, Hugh," asked Jeremy, " we or they ? "

" Oh, you're not mad ! " replied Serena—" only just a little stupid sometimes.   Here is that dear little man from Cook's coming to tell us our tug is ready."

Half an hour later Eve leant on the rail and looked her last at Halfa and the little pink and blue dolls' houses along the top of the tree-bordered dyke.   She could see the tall, black figure of the muezzin pacing round the gallery at the top of the white minaret.   His voice floated across to her over the widening stretch of water, summoning the faithful to prayer.   As the last notes faded into the air, Eve turned away with a regretful feeling at her heart, for the homeward journey had begun.

" I'm afraid," said Jeremy, " there's no chance of our getting to Abu Simbel to-night, as our infernal tug was so late getting off.   That means you won't see it at sunrise."

" Were we going to ? " asked Serena, opening her eyes very wide.

" We were indeed," said Jeremy. " I strongly suspect you bribed the tug's reis to start late, Serena."

" Why this sudden desire for a sunrise, Jeremy ? " asked Hugh.

" It's not a desire exactly, but you do get a wonderful effect then at Abu Simbel. The rising sun strikes through the doorway straight on to the figure of Osiris at the far end of the temple. It really is well worth seeing, but I'm afraid there's no chance of our managing it now."

" Isn't that a pity ? " murmured Serena, with a sigh of relief.

" Hypocrite ! " scoffed Eve. " I think it's a tragedy."

Moussa thought so too, for sunrise at Abu Simbel was one of those dramatic moments so dear to his heart; but there was no help for it, the tug stopped for the night, and the *Isis*, willy-nilly, had to stop too. She started again at dawn, and reached Abu Simbel a little before ten o'clock.

It was blazing hot when the dinghy landed Moussa and his little party on the yellow sand among the sweet-scented bean flowers. Eve was surprised, when she stood at the foot of the colossi, to find how mutilated they were—that one had lost his head and shoulders, another his beard and his arms, and that not one of them was perfect. From only a little way off her mind had received the impression of four complete figures. She had grown to know the boyish face of Rameses well by this time and to love the dimples at the corners of his mouth that gave such charm to his rounded features.

And in spite of their immense size she realised that these giants were not merely gigantic blocks of stone roughly hewn to convey the idea of a man, but actual portraits of one man in particular. Their proportions were so perfect that she could hardly believe Moussa when he told her that the nose was three and a half feet in length and the nostrils more than eight inches. The bold modelling of the leg muscles and the bones in the knees were fascinating.   After looking up at them from below, everyone climbed up the slope of golden sand on the right and looked at them again from a higher level. Then, feeling like pigmies, they walked through the immense doorway of the temple into the outer chamber, where the pillars were carved in the form of Osiris, although Rameses, with his superb egoism, had added his own face instead of the god's.   On the walls, too, were superb portraits of the Pharaoh in battle, striding, like St. Michael down the sky.   At the far end of the innermost chamber sat Pthah, Amon Ra, Ra and Rameses, so placed that at the time of the equinox the sun shed its first rays on their stone figures.   Larger than life, they sat, eternally motionless, for ever looking down the dim length of the temple to the blue and gold strips of sky and sand beyond.

" They give you the feeling of that line in the Bible," said Jeremy :   " ' The same yesterday, to-day, and for ever.' "

All the splendour and horror of war were carved on the walls.   The Pharaoh charged his enemies at full gallop with his host of chariots; there was infantry on the march, and captives were led in chains.

On either side of the entrance were more strings of prisoners—portraits, evidently, for the Egyptian, Nubian and Jewish types were all distinct one from another.

A leisurely stroll across the hot sand led to the lovely temple of Hathor, and Jeremy translated for Eve the hieroglyphics on its face : " Rameses, the Strong in Truth, the Beloved of Amon, made this divine abode for his royal wife, Nefertari, whom he loves."

" How confusing of her to be called Nefertari ! " complained Eve; " it's so like Nefertiti.   But how wonderful to have your name carved in the rock so that all these thousands of years later the whole world shall know how much loved you were ! "

" Would that appeal to you ? " asked Jeremy curiously.

Eve gave a wise little nod. "Yes, it would to any woman."

"Nowadays, when they've so many more interests than they ever had before ? "

"Yes, every bit as much," declared Eve as she followed the others into the temple.

Serena and Jeremy were right : Eve had changed.

Inside the temple over and over again the names of Rameses and Nefertari were coupled together, so that no one should forget it was a monument to their love.

"I think Nefertari must have had a big say in the designs for her temple," said Serena. "It would never have been quite like this if Rameses had done it all by himself."

"It has the same feminine touch as Hatshepsut's," remarked Jeremy, "and yet it's a different kind of loveliness from hers. I'm hanged if I know what the difference is, though."

"I know," said Eve. "There was no love in Hatshepsut's temple—love between a man and a woman, I mean. Hers was full of the love of life; it had a joyousness that made you feel you wanted to dance and sing. This is full of the love of Love, and that makes it more tender in feeling."

Eve would never have worked that out for herself three weeks ago, thought Jeremy. The next minute she was laughing with Serena over some figures they had found on a pillar at the end of the first hall—three exquisite, graceful girls looking exactly like a couple of modern young women trying a new hat on the head of a third; all as fresh as if they had been carved the day before yesterday.

Then Eve suggested they should all walk back for a last look at the colossi, but only Jeremy would go with her. When they had gazed their fill, they wandered round the corner, and there, at the foot of the towering cliff, was the grave of an English officer who had died in the Expedition of 1884. A lump rose in Eve's throat as she looked at it. It was so typically English—that solitary grave with its familiar lettering in this alien land, under this tropical sun. The grey island from which this soldier came had been nothing but forest and marshland, inhabited by wild beasts and naked savages when Abu Simbel was built by a Pharaoh of Egypt. Yet what a splendid insensitive English gesture—this calm thrusting of an unæsthetic Victorian tombstone amidst the glorification in stone of the most famous of the Pharaohs ! Eve did not know whether to laugh or cry, till she realised she loved the very " Englishness " of it, apart from any other considerations.

Back once more on the *Isis*, the tug pulled them slowly down the river.

So an endless stream of people pass up and down the Nile, coming and going from the ends of the earth. And the four majestic figures, guardians of this solitary stretch of river, gaze on over their heads for ever.

CHAPTER XXVI

THE dam made it safe to sail at night in that part of the world, so Eve woke the next morning to find herself once more among the drowned palm trees of Lower Nubia. At midday the tug stopped for half an hour to make some repairs opposite Dekkah. A mirage hung over the little half-drowned temple, a lovely phantom land of trees and water in the middle of the desert.

Moussa ordered the dinghy and rowed his passengers up to the charming little pylons which stood half out of the water, and Hugh and Jeremy, who had got into their bathing suits, dived overboard and swam through into the courtyard.

The pigeons perched along the carved ledge above the pillars flew up in alarm and whirled in a white cloud over the dinghy.

In the heat of the afternoon the *Isis* re-entered the region of barren cliffs that had seemed so strange after the cultivated shores of Egypt. At first sight these stony slopes seemed destitute of life; but if you looked hard enough, Eve found, you could pick out a tiny figure here and there, hurrying to and fro between the miniature garden plots that were so diligently cultivated the moment the sinking of the Nile made it possible.

At 3 a.m. the dahabeah came to rest above the great dam, and Eve was wakened by hearing her name softly called from the next cabin. She jumped out of bed and leant out of her window, to find Jeremy doing the same at his.

"Look," he said, "the Southern Cross."

"Oh, how gorgeous!" cried Eve.   The great con-
stellation blazed across the dark sky, the pointers, that
gave it such a beautiful flying effect, hanging so low on
the horizon that they scarcely topped the dam.   Eve and
Jeremy waited, the roar of the water in their ears, until
the two brilliant stars dipped out of sight.

.   .   .   .   .

The mechanical engineer took them across the dam in
two funny little four-wheeled trolleys drawn by barefooted Nubians.   Halfway across, the boys stopped for
their passengers to look over the parapet at the torrent
of water rushing out below.   The sun, shining through
the mass of spray and foam, formed a rainbow that
floated, fairy-like, in the misty air.

"There are now," the engineer told them, "ten
million tons of water coming through per second,
although only a few of the sluices are open at this time of
year, for Egypt isn't thirsty yet.   This spot is Egypt's
heart, and we keep our finger on her pulse."

They said good-bye to him on the far side of the
river, where a little wooden boat, white, scarlet and
royal blue, waited to take them to Philae.   At this time
of the year only the upper halves of the pylons and of
the fine groups of pillars known as 'Pharaoh's Bed'
could be seen.   The effect of these, thrusting their heads
above the waste of waters, backed by the savage mountains, was desolate enough.

"Poor, dear Amelia B.!" sighed Eve.   "What
would she say if she could see 'the pearl of Egypt'
now?   She said the island with its colonnaded temples
and its palm trees was one of the most famous beauty
spots in the world.   How awful it would be for us if
we had to choose between saving the lives of thousands
of people and losing Westminster Abbey!"

"But the people would have to come first, of course,"
said Serena.

"Of course," agreed Eve.

Yet as the sailors rowed them back to the quay, singing as they went, she was conscious of an uncomfortable emotion in her breast. Was she really glad, in her heart of hearts, that a few million fellaheen had enough to eat? Or did she wish that Philae still rose above the palm groves on her sacred island, in all her lost, exquisite loveliness?

. . . . .

The *Isis* was back in Egypt again. The noisy, dirty tug had been left at Shellal to unload its barges and to take a fresh cargo on board. In two or three days' time it was to catch up the dahabeah and tow her to Cairo. Meanwhile, with a faint breeze that barely filled the mizzen, the only sail left to her, she dawdled in her old peaceful fashion down to Assuan, and came to rest opposite the Cataract Hotel.

Jeremy suggested a walk through the bazaar after dinner, where he and Hugh bargained with the shopkeepers for their beautiful woven mats, and beat them down cruelly, in Serena's opinion, though she had to own that the merchants seemed quite pleased with themselves when the bargains were struck, and their cries of protest changed to a contented purr. The night was warm, and the little party of four strolled slowly along the narrow lanes in the warm darkness. An occasional lantern before a shop door cast a pool of light that made the shadows dimmer and more mysterious. Glimpses of the night sky, strewn with stars, showed through the slits in the roof of mats overhead. Long-robed men and boys walked by, hand in hand, in Eastern fashion, or sat cross-legged on their thresholds, their wares piled up in the background. In an open booth a group of men were playing at draughts and dominoes in a circle of lamplight. Once or twice a veiled woman hurried past on some belated errand. Now and again everyone had to press closely against the wall to let a couple of laden donkeys or a tall, swaying camel pad silently by.

Eve was sorry to leave Assuan the next morning, with its trees, its islands, its shining black rocks and its air of cheerfulness; but Hugh and Jeremy wanted to get on as far as possible before the tug caught them up again. The breeze, faint to begin with, soon failed completely.

"Now," said Moussa, "Mam'selle will see how a dahabeah is rowed."

Ten hatches were removed from the lower deck, leaving ten large square holes, each about four feet deep. From the bottom of each hole a narrow plank, like a duck-run, led forward up on to the deck, and ten sailors with bare feet stood in front of them. Each man had one long oar apiece, deader, Hugh said, than any oar he had ever seen. These awful weapons were dropped into the water, and the men pulled on them in four separate jerks, taking, with every jerk, a backward step down his own duck-run, till the fourth jerk landed him in a sitting position on the plank of the deck behind him. There they sat and sang a chorus while the dahabeah lost any little way it might have made; then re-mounted their duck-runs and began all over again.

No power on earth would make them change their laborious method of rowing, the Scotch engineer had told Jeremy, or induce them to use good English oars. Men had rowed after this method in Egypt for more than four thousand years. It would take another four thousand to break them of it.

. . . . .

Eve was trying to take an interest in the Ptolemies.

"For, I suppose," she remarked to Jeremy, "I must know something about them now we are going to see their temples. It's dreadful, though, to think of Egypt being conquered by Libyans and Ethiopians and those awful people with curly beards."

"Assyrians?"

"Yes, and Persians and Greeks and Romans. A lot of miserable nobodies."

MEN WHO SWAM THE CATARACT ON GOATSKINS.

NUBIAN WOMEN.

[To face page 208.

"Should you call Cambyses and Alexander nobodies?" protested Jeremy.

"I should," declared Eve firmly, "compared with the old Pharaohs. It was a great shock to me to find that the Ptolemies were Greeks and that Cleopatra probably hadn't a drop of Egyptian blood in her veins. I shan't like any of the Ptolemaic temples," she added scornfully.

"Yes, you will," said Jeremy; and when the *Isis* landed her passengers at the foot of the temple of Komombo the following afternoon, Eve agreed with him. The scraps of colour still lingering on the temple walls, its fine position above the bend of the river, and the view of the Nile from the far end of its avenue of pillars, were lovely enough to please anyone. She wished Horus had not to share the honours with Sobkh, the crocodile god, but she was sorry when Moussa showed her the collection of sacred crocodile mummies, little fellows heaped in higgledy-piggledy fashion on the floor of one of the store chambers, so sadly fallen from their high estate.

The next day, alternately rowing and drifting, the dahabeah dawdled peacefully along between banks grown so high with the falling Nile that in many places it took four shadoofs, working one above the other, to carry the water up to the plain.

The day following she reached Edfu. An Anglo-American steamer had already landed its crowd of tourists, and the result was a scarcity of donkeys; but Moussa managed to collect five for his party, and they set off for the temple, the best preserved in Egypt, whose tall pylons could be seen across the fields, and arrived just as the mob from the steamer was leaving.

"Where on earth do they come from?" asked Serena, bewildered. "We never see people like that in England, and I'm sure you don't in America, Jeremy. Yet here they are in Egypt, and they must have come from somewhere."

" They're like people in a French farce," said Jeremy.
" Eve, what on earth are you doing ? You can't go
about taking photographs of complete strangers like
that."

" I must," declared Eve. " An elderly female
shouldn't go about in grass-green plus fours, white
canvas shoes and a pink cotton blouse unless she wants
to be photographed."

" You mustn't do it, all the same; you'll get into
trouble."

" Mayn't I just take the young man in the white cloth
cap and the pale mauve jersey ? " begged Eve.

" You may not."

" But, Jeremy, he's got tweed plus fours and leather
gaiters on his lower part ! "

" I see he has. You may pray for him, but you
mustn't photograph him; nor the woman in the brick-
coloured jersey and the divided skirt," and Jeremy laid
a restraining hand on Eve's Kodak until the last tourist
had safely vanished from view.

The splendid pylons towered above Eve and the
others as they passed between them into the great open
court flooded with light. At the far end two superb
statues of Horus, each twice as high as a man, strangely
modern in the simplicity of their modelling, stood on
guard at either side of the doorway leading into the temple
itself. Eve decided that the marvellous state of preserva-
tion of Edfu did compensate for its being a mere two
thousand years old. Built on a definite plan, instead of
having grown up in a confused mass like Karnak, the
halls, raised one step above another, were dim and
mysterious after the glare of the courtyard, but still
light enough for the wall pictures to be seen. Serena
found a particularly beautiful bas-relief on the right
of the doorway leading into the second hall : a group of
men carrying the bark of Amon, the tallest of them
smiling like Mona Lisa.

In the last hall, the Holy of Holies, stood the canopied

throne of Horus, carved out of a block of black granite. To-day, a throne without a god.

Eve looked back down the dim halls to the blaze of sunshine beyond. It gave her a strange feeling to be led on, step by step, only to find an empty throne.

" It's a shock," she told Jeremy, " but I don't know why."

" Perhaps it's because it makes you realise how very long ago it is since the gods lived in Egypt."

" Perhaps it is. Yet I feel in an odd sort of way that Horus hasn't gone very far from his temple. As though he comes back at night, when there's nobody here to see, and takes his old place again, and the ghosts of the priests and people come and worship him."

" Heavens ! " cried Serena, clutching Hugh by the coat sleeve. " Whatever's that horrible noise ? It's up there somewhere."

They looked up at the dim roof, and there were bats, hundreds of them, hanging in squirming clusters high above their heads. Eve and Serena shuddered with horror and fled out into the sunshine again, away from the juicy, sucking noise that sounded so curiously obscene.

" I have always liked an odd bat by day," said Eve; " but I've never seen them in a mass before. Besides, these look so different from English ones. Instead of being soft and mousey, they look all pinky and naked and nasty. And what a horrid squelchy noise they make ! Ugh, how revolting ! Where are you taking us now, Moussa ? I won't go where there are any more bats just yet, thank you."

" No, no, Mam'selle. We go now to the roof of the temple."

" Up a lot of steps ? " asked Serena. " It's such a very hot morning, Moussa."

" Everyone he go up to the roof at Edfu, Ma'am; it is important ! we must go to the roof."

Before the firmness of Moussa everyone was helpless,

but the climb up the many shallow stone steps proved well worth the effort. They looked down into the heart of the town, on to the flat roofs of the little mud houses where so much of the family life was passed.

" How can people live in such dirt and litter ? " wondered Serena, watching a blue-robed woman on the roof immediately below them, hanging out strange bits of washing in the middle of a crowd of naked children, hens and mangey dogs.

" It's not so bad as our slums at home," said Hugh. " Here at least they have the sun all day and every day; that's the best disinfectant you can have."

" Amelia B. climbed to the top of the pylons," said Eve; " they're twice as high as we are, I should think."

" They may be as high as Mont Blanc as far as I'm concerned," observed Hugh calmly.

" Mam'selle wants to go to the top of the pylon ? " asked Moussa hopefully.

" No, no, Moussa," said Eve hastily, " this will do quite well."

She looked round at the pale, tawny mass of the temple behind her. How grand it must have been in the days of its ancient splendour ! Now it was empty of god and priests and worshippers.

Suddenly a falcon, all soft tones of brown against the deep blue of the sky, appeared from nowhere and began to swoop silently backwards and forwards overhead, with no perceptible quiver of his outspread wings.

" Horus," said Jeremy. " Eve, you were right. He does guard his temple. He hovers over its roof by day and sits on his canopied throne at night."

And Eve felt, as she watched the big, beautiful bird, that far stranger things were possible.

    .   .   .   .   .

It amused Eve to notice the different behaviour of the English and the Americans on the private steam daha-beahs. The Americans always waved in the friendliest manner, and then the *Isis* waved back. But a boat full of other English people just stared unemotionally at the *Isis*, and the *Isis* stared unemotionally back at them.

" Yet we are nice friendly people, really," said Eve— " only shy. What is this place we are coming to, Jeremy ? "

" Esna."

" I don't think much of the look of it. What an awful crowd on the beach ! What are they all doing ? "

" Waiting for us, I'm afraid," said Jeremy, " with something to sell."

The moment they landed they were surrounded by a throng of water-carriers, their goat skins dripping and shining with wet, and men with beautiful woven baskets and other shoddier wares ; but Eve and Serena could not look beyond the rag dolls that were thrust at them from all sides.

" We must buy one for Jill," said Serena, in love with their painted faces and their gilt cardboard hats with a fringe of green and gold beads dangling round them.

" Wait till we've seen the temple," urged Hugh. " We can buy all we want when we come back."

So they walked on through the town, where the weavers were working on their hand looms in the street.

" Is this a good temple, Moussa ? " inquired Serena.

" Very good temple, Ma'am, but nearly all buried. Only Hypostyle hall can be seen."

" It sounds just my size temple," said Hugh.

" Lazy thing ! " said Eve with affectionate scorn. " Why haven't they dug it up, though, Moussa ? "

" It would cost much money," he explained. " The old Egyptians they build their houses of the mud from the Nile, and they build them all round the temple, quite close and on top of the temple too, when he was not used any more. Then their mud houses tumble down, but they did not dig away the mud—they build new houses on top of the old ones, Mam'selle. Many, many times all over the temple, and they live on top."

" It's a mercy it's only Ptolemaic," observed Eve, as they went into the Hypostyle hall. " It would be dreadful if it were really old."

" Eve sounds like a whole county family discussing a nouveau riche who has come into the neighbourhood," said Jeremy, amused.

" Well, one does feel different about the Ptolemies compared with the real Pharaohs, doesn't one? But, all the same, I loved Edfu and Komombo and Philae, and I think these great, dark pillars and that dim painted roof are fine too."

" I can't bear it," exclaimed Serena, shuddering. " There are those horrid bats again, squeaking and squelching up in that corner."

" I suppose in time they'll clear away these hovels, and find something pretty good when they do," said Hugh.

" I wish they'd build a nicer town on the top of it, if they're going to build one at all," grumbled Eve as they walked back through the shoddy bazaar where the tinsmiths were at work.

They bought one of the bead-covered dolls for Jill on the beach, but refused the coloured handkerchiefs of cheap silk from Birmingham and the ostrich eggs cut in halves and decorated with coloured beads and shells, that were offered to them. Eve made Moussa bargain for a cocoanut for her, and Serena lost her heart to a large basket, beautifully woven in various colours, which she was not allowed to have, because Moussa and Jeremy insisted that its owner was asking too much for it. The dinghy was pushed off, and a crowd of barelegged children pursued it into the water, clamouring loudly for baksheesh.

" What an awful mob ! " cried Eve.

" But I *do* want that basket," wailed Serena.

" Nonsense," said Hugh, " you've got dozens of baskets at home."

" But I want *this* one," cried Serena, and she continued

to want it at intervals all through lunch, which they ate while the *Isis* was being rowed down to the barrage, three-quarters of a mile or so below the town. Just as Mahomed had handed round the sweet, a sound of great shouting was heard outside. The *Isis* was now deep down in a lock whose stone walls rose some twenty feet above her. Through the open doorway at the end of the saloon, Moussa could be seen standing on the lower deck, his hands dramatically outspread, engaged in a loud and wordy warfare with some invisible opponent above.

" I must see what it is," cried Eve, running out, and the others followed her, napkins in hand.

Along the top of the wall, on the landward side, was a long row of crouching figures, their swarthy faces and coloured turbans sharply outlined against the blue sky, all intent upon Moussa and his adversary; an ancient man in a black robe and a white turban, who sat on the top of the wall quivering with rage and shaking his fists alternately down at Moussa and up to the heavens.

" What on earth is it all about ? " asked Eve.

" Your cocoanut," said Jeremy, laughing. " The old boy swears the two-piastre piece Moussa gave him for it was bad, and Moussa is calling him a thief and a liar."

" As though Moussa would give anyone bad money," cried Eve, indignant at the slur cast upon their Dear One.

Moussa, however, was enjoying himself to the top of his bent. Even the party in the saloon had come out to watch him. His fat hands waved more dramatically, his tongue wagged more wildly, and beads of moisture broke out on his large, upturned face as his arguments grew in intensity; the shrieks of the old man grew louder and louder until they became actual howls and sobs. This was too much for the soft heart of Serena.

" What is a two-piastre piece, after all ? " she cried. " Give the poor old man another one, Moussa, please."

" Your poor old man probably makes a very good living out of this trick," said Jeremy. " I'm pretty sure

I've met him before myself.   He changes your perfectly
good coin for a bad one and then shows it to you, and if
he's lucky, and you're weak, he gets paid twice over."

"But he's such a very old man, Jeremy, and the
two piastres won't hurt us, and suppose it really was a
bad coin ?   Perhaps he has a lot of little children who
will go without food just for want of it.   Please give
him another, Moussa."

Moussa tossed his arms out in a gesture of delighted
resignation, produced his purse, and extracted a coin
with his most lordly air.   In an instant all was peace.
A long rope with a small handkerchief fastened to the
end of it was let down quickly from the top of the wall.
The two-piastre piece was safely knotted into it and
drawn up, and the old man called down blessings upon
the head of Moussa as voluminous as the curses he had
rained upon it a moment before, while Moussa beamed
with smiles and mopped his brow.   The next moment
the rope was let down again, and there, swinging about
on the end of it, was the basket Serena had not been
allowed to buy at Esna.   Such persistence had to be
rewarded, and Hugh bought it on the spot.   In an
instant the whole wall was alive with rapidly descending
objects, each dangling from the end of a rope.   Dolls,
baskets, ostrich eggs, the handkerchiefs and scarves of
cheap papery silk—all came wriggling down.

"Just like Rahab and the spies," declared Eve.

Fortunately, at this critical juncture the lock gates
opened and the *Isis* escaped with all speed.

That afternoon Hugh announced his intention of
photographing the crew.   As soon as Moussa explained
it to them they started running about the dahabeah like
excited children getting ready for a party.   Tiny trunks
of tin or painted wood were dragged out and opened and
every man dressed himself up in his best.   As usual
Ibrahim won the beauty prize, for he appeared in a
jibbah of wine-coloured cloth and chic sandals of open-
work leather.   The fluttered hen had hysterics and got

in everyone's way in his enthusiasm, falling over his own feet and his precious feather brush more often than Eve would have thought possible. Moussa threw himself with his usual zest into the game, and insisted on dressing Hugh and Jeremy up in the most festive garments from his own extensive wardrobe. Hugh, in a robe and turban of a sweet shade of saxe, looked more British than ever, but Jeremy, in a brown jibbah and scarlet fez, looked astonishingly oriental, with his sunburnt face and hands and his dark eyes.

" Really," exclaimed Eve, tilting her head on one side as she looked him over, " I never saw such an extraordinary thing. Of course you look quite nice and all that in your ordinary clothes, but in these things you look actually handsome. You'd cause an awful commotion in a Mahommedan dovecote."

" Thanks," said Jeremy. " But I think I want a couple of spring onions up my nose to be a real ladykiller."

" Oh, do let's see if the cook has any on board," cried Eve, " and then I'll take your photograph and hang it side by side with the real sheik's."

" Thank you, no. If you won't love me for myself alone I'm too proud to tempt you with onions," declared Jeremy firmly, and Eve, to her regret, had to be content with photographing him as he was.

Soon after the dahabeah was restored to its usual calm the tug snorted round the bend of the river behind them. Instantly the lower deck burst into such a frenzy of activity that the cook boy fell overboard. When he had clambered in again, wet but still smiling, the tug and the *Isis*, once more in double harness, set off for Luxor.

Half an hour later the *Ophir* steamed up alongside.

" Just what they would do," thought Eve with disgust—" turn up when we're being degradingly towed." To add to her annoyance, Isobel Page, looking more charming than ever in pale shell-pink, took a snapshot of the dahabeah and her clumsy escort.

" See you in Luxor," the two parties called out to one another, and when the *Isis* arrived at the landing-stage at five o'clock Jeremy went, as Serena's envoy, to bring the Page family back to tea.

There was no need to invite Tony. He was waiting on the bank, and stepped on board the moment the gangway was let down.

"Isn't it great to be back in Luxor?" he exclaimed delightedly.

"Is it?" asked Eve. "I'm rather sorry."

Tony's face fell.

"One might as well be on the Riviera, it's so sophisticated," continued Eve. "Besides, it's so crowded with tourists, and the Egyptians stare at one in the streets here."

Tony's American jaw stiffened.

"Brutes! How dare they! I say, Miss Wentworth, will you let me walk with you when you go out here? I'd love to take care of you."

"Thank you very much," replied Eve sweetly; "it's very kind of you."

"Kind?" ejaculated the besotted young man. "It would be the greatest pleasure."

"He has got it badly," thought Eve.

Jeremy thought so too as he watched the pair of them set off for the book-shop after tea, and noted the reverent expression on the young man's face as he helped Eve on and off the gangway, and the air of devotion with which he opened her parasol.

CHAPTER XXVII

" IT's going to be hot," said Jeremy.

The two parties from the *Isis* and the *Ophir* had landed on the sandy western bank and were strolling towards the waiting donkeys.

" It's divine at present," said Isobel. " I do love the Egyptian mornings ! They go to one's head like wine."

" Liar ! " thought Eve. " I don't believe anything ever went to her head—she's far too calm and collected. At all events, if anything does it isn't the morning," and Eve slaughtered a fly on one of her riding-boots with a vicious swipe.

" Here is your donkey, Mam'selle," cried the already perspiring Moussa, leading up a natty-looking little animal with magenta trappings.

Jeremy came forward to mount her, as he always did, but apparently Eve did not see him, for she turned an angelic smile upon Tony and held out her foot for his eager hand. Jeremy mounted Isobel instead.

Tony and Eve led the way across the plain to the Ramesseum—the " Thinking Place " of Rameses the Great—the refuge for the man whose every action from dawn to dusk was regulated by ritual.

" I like the idea of his coming here all by himself," said Eve " and leaving his Court and his servants and everybody behind him on the other bank."

What did he think about, she wondered, in this cheerful, sunlit temple, that was so different from Karnak with its crowded pillars, or Edfu with its dim, mysterious shadows. Was his mind always busy with new battles, drafting laws, or poring over the designs for a new temple? Or did Nefertari's face sometimes come between his eyes and the parchment, to remind him that she was far more important to him than any of these things? Remembering the little temple of Hathor, Eve thought it quite likely. She stood beside his fallen colossus and marvelled at it. How incredible it would have seemed to his subjects—or to himself, for the matter of that—that such greatness could lie so low. Yet, in spite of his abasement, she felt his strength of personality as much in the Ramesseum as she had done at Abu Simbel; that personality which had kept his name more alive in Egypt than the names of all those other Pharaohs who had been far mightier warriors and far greater statesmen than he.

.   .   .   .   .

A ride over sandy hillocks and waste lands dotted with mud huts brought them to the tiny tomb of Nakht, which Eve found utterly delightful.

" It's so small and so sweet," she cried as she and Tony stood alone together in the single oblong chamber before the arrival of the rest. " And how bright all the colours are still—the brightest we've seen anywhere. Look at these fruits, and see the geese hanging up in the shop, and the one being plucked and drawn by the cook; and oh! do look at the cat eating the fish under its mistress's chair! "

She passed eagerly from one to the other of the enchanting little pictures that showed all the busy life of the countryside. There were men plucking and treading grapes, ploughmen turning the soil, sowers scattering the seeds. All the husbandry of Egypt was set out before her eyes.

" How lucky Nakht was! I should like a cheerful tomb like this when I'm dead."

" Don't talk of death," said Tony quickly. The thought of death for Eve was unbearable to him.

" I won't if you don't like it," she said airily; " but I

couldn't feel depressed about anything here—these pictures are so cheerful. They're so full of sunshine and laughter and the fun of being out of doors. They make these people on the walls, who've been dead thousands of years, seem quite real and alive to me to-day. Quite near, too; as though I might meet them and talk to them at any minute if I wanted to."

Jeremy, coming in at that moment, noted her glowing face and her bright eyes. It seemed to take Tony to make her look like that.

While the others were looking at the tombs, Eve wandered out and photographed one of the low, round, fat little towers built of mud with the lattice-work parapets round the top, where Moussa told her the babies were put in the summer to play out of reach of snakes and scorpions.

Then the whole party trotted off again on their donkeys to the tomb of Ramose, the Vizier of Akhnaton, which Jeremy said was important because it marked the transition between the old conventional art of Egypt and the natural art of Akhnaton.

The two could be seen side by side on the walls in exquisite shallow reliefs.

" Look at those women following the funeral procession of Ramose," said Eve. " How beautifully slim they are ! I wonder if they bothered about their figures as much as we do."

" Why are they waving their arms over their heads ? " asked Serena.

" It's a sign of grief," said Jeremy. " There's a strange story about that. You remember Maspero and the pit of Der-el-Bahri ? "

" Let me see," stammered Serena, a little nervously, " what pit was that exactly ? "

" Angel ! " cried Eve, laughing as she passed her arm through her sister's. " What a shame to ask you ! It's the great pit where Maspero discovered all the royal mummies, you know. They had been hidden there thousands of years before to save them from the robbers who had broken into the tombs. What on earth have they to do with these women, though, Jeremy?"

"Nothing, actually. But when the mummies were discovered in '81, the Government sent a steam-boat up to fetch them down to Cairo, and all the length of the Nile, from Luxor to Cairo, the women came down from the villages and stood on the banks, wailing and waving their arms and tearing their hair as the royal mummies passed by; just as the women of Egypt had mourned their dead five thousand years before."

"By Jove! It's rather fine—the Pharaohs having that last tribute paid to them," exclaimed Hugh.

"I *am* glad they did," cried Eve, "after all the glory and honour they had been used to in their lives."

"So am I," agreed Isobel, turning back to the wall pictures again. "Some of these women have the loveliest dresses and girdles," she pointed out.

"Here is one with a fichu exactly like Marie Antoinette's," said Mrs. Page.

"It's foolish to say that modern fashions come from Ancient Greece," said Isobel. "Here are any number of simple sleeveless frocks just like those we are wearing to-day."

"The Egyptians were like us," said Eve—"they put comfort first."

"I like that," scoffed Hugh. "Comfort, indeed! Women would wear hair shirts if they came into fashion again."

"Hugh, why will you be so Victorian! We won't look at anything nowadays unless it's comfortable. Paris has tried to bring in tight waists and long skirts over and over again, and we simply turn a deaf ear to them."

"Of course we do," agreed Isobel. "Look at the old photographs of tourists who came to Egypt thirty years ago, Sir Hugh. They're all wearing long skirts and high collars instead of soft shirts and riding breeches like us. And talking of riding suits," said Isobel as she turned to Eve, " I do think, Miss Wentworth, yours is just the sweetest I ever saw."

" It is rather nice, isn't it ? " Eve dropped a complacent eye down her person. " I have a wonderful little tailor in South Molton Street. I'll give you his address, if you like."

" Will you ? That's sweet of you."

" But I don't think mine's any nicer than yours, all the same. In fact, I think I like your short coat rather better."

" Well, what I feel about a short coat is this . . ." and without a backward glance at the carven draperies they had been admiring a moment before, the two girls strolled out into the sunshine, still talking.

" Good Lord ! " exclaimed Hugh. " Fancy discussing clothes in a tomb four thousand years old ! "

" I bet those girls on the walls discussed their clothes with each other when their parents were trying to improve their minds with a visit to the Great Pyramid," chuckled Mr. Page.

" Oh, dear, how hot it's getting ! " sighed Serena. " Have we much more to see, Moussa ? "

" We go to the tombs of Rameses's son and Queen Nefertari and the temple of Medinet Abou, Ma'am."

" Three more ? Good gracious ! " exclaimed Mrs. Page.

" Moussa would have taken us to another half-dozen if I'd let him," declared Jeremy, " but I drew the line at those. Didn't I, Moussa ? "

" Yes, sir," sighed Moussa, wagging his head regretfully, and he sighed again when he wasn't allowed more than a few minutes for the tomb of the young son of Rameses, although everyone liked the pictures of the boy wearing the side-lock of youth.

In spite of the scorching heat in the barren Valley of the Queens, they had to stop at the tomb of Nefertari, with the delicious Hathor cows and their attendant bull painted in many colours. Eve declared the spotted cows were exactly like the pair in the old Noah's Ark she and Serena had had in the days of their youth.

"I shall come out in spots, too, if I'm made to do much more sight-seeing in this heat," declared Serena. "Haven't we nearly done, Moussa?"

"Nearly done, Ma'am. We go now to the temple of Medinet Abou. The temple of Rameses III."

Eve supposed that it was because the last of the great Pharaohs had fought so hard to save the crumbling empire that his temple looked so like a fortress. The towering sand-coloured walls of colossal thickness, the lofty pylons and magnificent gateways, told of war as plainly as the Ramesseum had told its tale of peace. She strolled through one great square court after another, where a few lovely patches of colour still glowed upon the walls.

"It's the strongest thing we've seen in Egypt," she said. "I shall never forget Rameses III after this."

"I like the jolly way he holds a bundle of captives by their hair in one hand and brandishes the sword he's going to behead them with in the other," said Hugh. "Have you seen the harem pictures? The one of Rameses playing chess with a naked concubine is particularly pleasing; and the one where he's chucking her under the chin."

"You have a low mind," said Serena calmly.

"I love the pair of pale blue pigeons up there," cried Eve. "How beautifully the Egyptians drew birds! Those two are actually flying." The pigeons were the one tender note, she felt, in this majestic fortress, guarded by the two sinister statues of Sekmet. She liked it all.

Hatshepsut's temple had been full of the joy of life; at Abu Simbel the temple of Hathor had told of a warmer, closer love; Karnak was peopled with the ghosts of priests, and the Ramesseum was a place of peace. But Medinet Abou was full of soldiers, and of the spirit of war and courage. There was something terrifying in its fine, impregnable air. Standing with her

ABU SIMBEL.

TEMPLE OF HATHOR AT ABU SIMBEL.

[To face page 225.

back to the pylons, looking across the Theban plain,
Eve saw the backs of the Colossi, dignified and majestic,
against the burning blue of the sky.

. . . . .

Hugh was getting nervous about his figure, and
before the *Isis* left Luxor, late in the afternoon, he
decided that everyone must go to the chemist's and be
weighed.

"You'll be awfully silly if you do," declared Serena.
"I know I've got fatter, but as long as I don't weigh, I
can pretend it's only a trifle. When the chemist hands
you one of those horrible little cards with all the stones
and pounds put down in black and white, you can't
pretend any more. I do hate those little cards."

In a quarter of an hour the others were back again, a
wiser and sadder party.

"Well?" inquired Serena.

"Jeremy and I are eight pounds up," muttered Hugh
gloomily, "and Eve four."

"Perhaps the machine was incorrect, darling," suggested Serena.

"It's no good trying to be a sympathetic wife,"
declared Eve. "We tried two shops and two machines.
Hugh's told you the better one. The other made us
half a pound more."

Jeremy said nothing, but stalked off to find Moussa
and command him to cut down the food supplies.

A few minutes later the tug set off with the *Isis* in
tow. The *Ophir* waved farewell. The two parties
were to meet again in Cairo.

No one seemed inclined to talk, and Eve settled down
in her deck chair with a sigh, in rather melancholy mood.

"I hate leaving Thebes, and the Colossi and the
Valley of the Kings for good," she thought, gazing
wistfully across the plain at the pillars of Hatshepsut's
temple. From this distance they looked no bigger than
tiny pinkish fingers at the foot of the tawny hills.

How she had flirted with Tony there on the first day!

Q

It had been Jeremy's fault, really. He had driven her into it by neglecting her for Isobel Page. "And I ask you," said Eve to herself, "could any self-respecting girl be expected to put up with that? Of course she couldn't; one had to keep one's end up."

Unfortunately for poor Tony, he had been ready to hand, so to say. Honestly, after that one day she had been perfectly natural and friendly with him—nothing more. Except perhaps just once or twice when she knew Jeremy was looking on. The nuisance was that so often just being natural and friendly seemed to do more harm than anything else! What a pity men were so terribly susceptible! The least little thing, and they seemed to be thrown off their balance. No stamina, Eve supposed. It was a great pity in this particular case, because Tony was such a dear and she really liked him ever so much.

Then there were Harold and Hubert, still waiting in England while Eve " thought about it " in Egypt. And then—and then there was Jeremy.

She glanced at him under her eyelashes. He lay back, his face hidden by his panama, his hands resting on the arms of his deck chair. Isobel had remarked one day that Jeremy's hands were his one beauty. Isobel and Jeremy! Eve's heart missed a beat, as it had done the other day in Nubia when she and Jeremy had nearly quarrelled.

Why did it give her such a funny sharp pain to say those names together? For an instant everything in her mind and body seemed held up in a breathless pause. Then, like a flash, she knew what had happened. She was in love with Jeremy.

Her heart—she supposed it was her heart—began to knock so loudly that she felt everyone must be able to hear it. What a little fool she'd been! All the time she had thought it was Jeremy's friendship she minded losing—and it was really Jeremy himself. While she had played with the idea of marrying Harold or Hubert or

Tony, or half a dozen others, she had really been falling in love with him. And love was a real and terrible thing, not just a kind of temporary madness and inconvenience. It was something that hurt you so much that you didn't know how you were going to bear it.

If only Isobel Page were empty-headed, or bad-tempered, or fickle, there might still be a chance that Jeremy would find her out and get tired of her before it was too late.

But, with her usual honesty, Eve admitted to herself that Isobel was as charming and as intelligent as she looked. There was no hope of failure there, and if there were, it wouldn't do Eve any good. A man didn't fall in love with a girl he had known from childhood up. Why, Jeremy had had as much share as anyone else in forming what she was pleased to call her mind. The very fact that she held such a firm and, in a sense, a unique place in his affections was against her now. If she had met him for the first time grown-up, as Isobel had done, they would at least have started level.

As it was, Isobel would marry Jeremy, and Eve would break her heart over it. But, whatever happened, no one—least of all Jeremy—should ever know.

.   .   .   .   .

In spite of the sun, everybody on board the *Isis* complained of the cold on the journey back to Cairo. The north wind, which had so basely failed on the way up, now blew in their faces with maddening persistence.

"It's like bicycling," grumbled Hugh. "You start out with the wind against you, and console yourself by thinking that you'll have it behind you on the way back. Then directly you turn round you find the infernal wind has changed, too, and is blowing against you as hard as ever."

"I want to go back to the Sudan and the heat," wailed Serena, turning up her coat collar.

"We shall probably stick on sandbanks all the way down," said Jeremy gloomily.

"We must push on to Cairo," said Hugh, "and see about our passage home. We ought to sail before the end of the week."

"And to-day's Monday," exclaimed Serena. "I never realised our trip was so nearly over, did you, Eve?"

"No. And when we started off it seemed to me it was going to be so long. I couldn't realise it would ever come to an end. I think," Eve added thoughtfully, "that Egypt has aged me."

"Poor darling!" murmured Serena sympathetically. "I know what it is. You are worrying about Harold and Hubert. Of course they'll want to know what you've decided directly you get back."

"I'd forgotten all about them," declared Eve with obvious candour—"or almost, anyway. I suppose they were at the back of my mind somewhere. Oh, dear! Life is full of worries, isn't it?"

"You wouldn't be the least bit happy with either of them," said Serena. "I used to think you and Hubert would get on well together at one time. But I don't now. He's very kind and nice, poor thing, but he's just a little dull. It's so depressing when husbands and wives just do what's called ' getting on with one another,' isn't it, Jeremy?"

"Whatever is the good of asking him?" put in Eve quickly. "He doesn't know a thing about it. I shall write to both Harold and Hubert to-day and explain everything to them, quite simply."

"What is everything?" asked Hugh blandly.

Serena flashed him a warning glance.

"You'd better write at once, darling," she said, before Eve could reply. "You'll be ever so much happier when it's off your mind."

"I will," agreed Eve, and went off to her cabin for her fountain-pen.

"Dear Eve is a little prickly nowadays," explained Serena when her sister had left the saloon. "It isn't a bit like her. She's so very sweet-tempered as a rule."

"What do you think's the matter with her?" asked Hugh. "Or don't you know?"

Serena smiled mysteriously.

"Oh, yes, I know."

"Do you mean young Page?"

"I shan't say what I mean," replied his wife; "but I know what I know, all the same."

"Hadn't we better go up on deck and talk to Moussa and the reis?" asked Jeremy abruptly. "They must push on as quickly as they can. We shall have to skip Denderah; we've no time for it."

"Right," agreed Hugh, and they left the saloon together as Eve came back to it.

She spent the morning in frowning concentration over her blotting-pad. Serena said nothing, but every now and then she glanced sympathetically across at her sister. Both drew a sigh of relief when at last Eve licked two stamps and firmly affixed them. Unfortunately, as it turned out later, she put the letters into the wrong envelopes.

. . . . .

Every hour of the homeward journey brought back to Eve only too clearly some happy memory of the journey up. There was the spot where the *Isis* had run into the bank for the fourth time in one morning. While the sailors pushed it off, she and Jeremy had walked up to look at the sakieh worked by steam, and the kind little Greek engineer had picked Eve a lovely bunch of roses out of his garden.

There were the pigeon-cotes of Prince Yousef who refused to marry, and later, the *Isis* tied up for the night at the little model town of Nag-Hamada, where she and Jeremy and Moussa had gone for a walk together and talked about Jeremy's future wife.

Baliana, the starting place for Abydos, was passed during lunch on the next day, and in the afternoon the

north wind blew stronger and colder, and did not drop
until the fourth morning after leaving Luxor. Then
everyone basked in heavenly warmth all that day and
the next, when they passed Tel el Amarna, with its half
moon of hills curving down to the river and its memories
of the heretic king, his dream and his failure.

At noon on the sixth morning the *Isis* hailed an up-
coming steamer and collected two mail-bags full of
letters. At one o'clock the tug stuck on a sandbank.
At five minutes past one it was off again, and at a quarter
past it had stuck on another. This time it looked like
being a long affair, so Hugh, Jeremy and Eve played a
game of golf on the sandbank, which Serena said was
adding insult to injury.

The north wind blew coldly again when the tug started
at five o'clock the next morning and stuck on its first
sandbank of the day at seven. But when Jeremy and
Eve went for a walk before breakfast, it seemed nothing
more than a cool, refreshing breeze, and the world shone
blue and green and gold in the sunshine.

At ten o'clock the tug set off once more and the cool
breeze became an icy head-wind again. For another
forty-eight hours the dahabeah went on her way, waiting
every hour or so for her tug to struggle off a sandbank,
until the moment came when tug and barges stuck once
and for all, and firmly refused to budge. The *Isis*
washed her hands of them, shook them off as a bad job,
and meandered along in her old familiar fashion, rowing
and drifting for two days more.

Then Hugh and Jeremy came to an end of their
patience. Moussa was put ashore and sent by train
from Heliopolis to Cairo that he might clamour loudly
in the ear of Mr. Johnson for a new tug. He was also
to inquire if they could get suitable steamer accommo-
dation to Marseilles in four or five days' time.

All that morning and afternoon the dahabeah lay
tethered against the western bank, and to Eve it was a
day of intense irritation. They played golf, but in the

absence of their " Dear One " the game fell flat. Serena
wrote letters; Hugh had got hold of a new detective
story and didn't answer if you spoke to him; and Jeremy
only spoke in monosyllables. Moussa and the tug
arrived just as they had sat down to dinner, and by that
time Eve felt as though she could have screamed. The
tug towed them through the darkness to Cairo.

CHAPTER XXVIII

BULLS, MAMELUKES, AND TREASURE TROVE

WHEN Eve woke the next morning she found the *Isis* moored in her old berth at the foot of the gardens where they had first seen her. At breakfast Jeremy told her that Moussa had secured a car for the expedition to Sakkara.

" What is there to see there ? " asked Serena.

" Tombs and pyramids—not *the* pyramids—older ones."

" We're starting in twenty minutes," Hugh warned Eve, " so you'd better get a move on, or you'll never be ready."

" I'm quite ready now," she replied coldly.

" Aren't you going to wear a hat or coat, then ? "

" Of course, but they won't take me a second to put on."

" I know your seconds, my child. It's a long way, so don't entirely undress and dress all over again in something different if you can help it."

" It will be funny to go in a motor again," said Eve, who thought it was time to change the conversation.

" It seems terribly fast after a dahabeah," gasped Serena, half an hour later, as they swerved violently to avoid a camel who was taking up an unfair share of the highway. The road was thick with livestock of one sort and another all the way to Memphis.

Palm trees, a charming little sphinx lying in a pool of water, and two colossal statues of Rameses, were all that remained of the birthplace of Egypt's history. An atmosphere of gentle melancholy enveloped it—a sort of resigned mourning for a long dead past.

The car drove on across a waste of pallid sand to the pyramids. As Eve looked at them, so battered and so incredibly old, she felt she was looking upon Age for the first time. Everything she had seen before appeared young in comparison with these brown, uncouth shapes. Snefru's lumpy pyramid was older than anything at Gíza, she knew, and the Step pyramid of Zozer had been there more than two thousand years when Abraham was born. Their crudeness and their clumsy strength impressed Eve hardly less than their age.

The wall reliefs in the tombs, though they, too, were the oldest in Egypt, looked fresh and youthful, for no work of the later dynasties was more beautiful or more delicate. Here were boats being built or sailing before the wind. Hunting scenes. Men sowing, reaping and tilling the land. There was an orchestra playing on strange instruments, and a corps de ballet. There were flocks and herds. Tradesmen, and artisans working at their different crafts, and, as usual, there were birds everywhere—the loveliest thing, to Eve's mind, in all the art of Egypt. Herons, cranes and homely domestic fowl, geese, chickens and ducks. Everything in this resting-place of death told of the love of life and the joy of work, of hunting, fighting and dancing—all that life had been so full of to those Egyptians who had left it, thousands and thousands of years ago.

Beautiful as these tombs were, it was the Serapeum, the burial-place of the sacred bulls of Apis, that fascinated everyone the most.

They rode there on camels after lunch at the rest-house.

The air grew hot and close as they followed the guide down the wide, dark corridors, and the vastness of the place struck awe into Eve's soul as she stood in the long gallery and looked down into the big, sunken chambers on either hand. In the centre of each lay a stupendous sarcophagus of black granite. But what sarcophagi! All exactly alike, severely plain, and shining with a black gleam in the dimness. Looking at the one nearest her, Eve saw that the sides and the lid, which had been pushed back, were about two feet thick. These rows of black monsters filled her with a sense of oppression, brute force and giant strength. The gloom of the mausoleum was profound and the hot closeness shut them in.

Awed and silent, Eve followed the others down the corridor, and there, right across their pathway, lay one more of the great black coffins. There was something sinister about the huge, sombre thing that had failed to reach its allotted chamber. Failed, perhaps, to receive its huge, gorgeous mummy encased in gold?

"Why is it here?" Eve asked Jeremy in an undertone.

"No one can say. Perhaps the bull worship came to an end suddenly, just while the workmen were dragging it in. Who knows?"

"How could they move it at all?" wondered Eve. "How they must have groaned and struggled and strained and sweated over each of these monsters! Hundreds of workmen!"

"One left his mark behind him," said Jeremy. "Marietti, the French archæologist, who discovered this place, must have got a good thrill out of it."

"How?" asked Eve eagerly.

"There, on the sandy floor were the naked footprints of the last Egyptian to leave the mausoleum, more than three thousand years ago."

"O-o-oh," sighed Eve, on a long-drawn-out breath of rapture.

.   .   .   .   .

"Where are we going to?" asked Serena, as she settled herself comfortably in one of her favourite little carriages soon after breakfast the next morning.

"To Cook's first," replied Hugh, arranging his long legs with care, "to fix up our berths for the day after to-morrow. Then to the Citadel."

" Eve will despise that terribly," said Jeremy.   " It's a mere mediæval affair.   Let's hope the fact that it was partly built by the romantic Saladin may console her a little."

Eve knitted her brows and nibbled her finger thoughtfully.

" Saladin," she murmured doubtfully.   " I know ! He was a Crusader."

" When I think of the money spent on your education ! " groaned Hugh.

" I'm sure he was.   It all comes back to me.   Godfrey de Bouillon, and Richard Cœur de Lion and all that lot."

" Unfortunately, you've put him on the wrong side, though.   Saladin fought for the Crescent, not for the Cross."

" Oh, well, it's much of a muchness.   He fought *in* the Crusades, anyway, whichever side he was on."

" He had all the virtues we modestly describe as Christian," remarked Jeremy—" loyalty, courage and wisdom.   I expect that's what's confusing Eve."

" I thought he was someone in the ' Arabian Nights,' " said Serena—" a sultan or something."

" Sultan will do," said Jeremy.   " His father was a Kurdish Governor.   Saladin was made Grand Vizier of the Calif, and he then made himself Sultan of Egypt and Syria."

" The ' Arabian Nights ' is full of sultans," said Serena.   " How many years ago was Saladin one ? "

" Seven or eight hundred years, I should think.   He was a great soldier and a fine civil administrator.   Also he was a very chivalrous opponent, which the Crusaders appreciated."

" Richard Cœur de Lion downed him in the end," said Hugh.   " I suppose they were about the two most romantic figures in the Crusades.   It's years since I read ' The Talisman,' and I don't suppose you've ever read it, Eve."

"It's a gorgeous position for a citadel," said Eve, by way of turning the conversation, as the horses climbed the hill.

"Look, Hugh," cried Serena when they clattered through the archway a moment later. "There are real Highlanders on sentry duty. The lambs!"

"I think they heard you," said Hugh.

"I hope they did," said Eve, leaning out for another look at the 'lambs.' "I expect they're glad to hear she loves them, so far from home as they are. Do you think a kilt is a cool or warm thing in this climate, Hugh? And is it true that they don't wear—— ?"

"That will do, Eve," said Hugh firmly. "I know exactly where this discussion leads to; and it's not true, anyway."

"Really? Oh, well, I've always wondered. You do hear such contradictory stories, don't you? What is this place?"

"The mosque of Mahomet Ali, the Sultan, Mam'-selle," cried Moussa, clambering down from the box-seat with a generous display of Boston velvet grips. "You will come this way, please, and the man he will tie shoes over your feets."

"What delicious things! They're miles too big for us," exclaimed Eve, as the attendant at the door lashed a pair of flat, canary-coloured slippers firmly on to her little white shoes. "I like this big courtyard. How exciting to be going into a mosque! I didn't know they allowed Christian women inside."

"They don't everywhere," said Jeremy. "This is a commonplace affair, though. The interior, as you see, is like a war profiteer's drawing-room, swollen out of all proportion. There are two or three lovely mosques in Cairo which I want you to see, but Moussa would have burst into tears if I hadn't allowed him to bring you here first."

"Look, there are men praying," whispered Eve. "Aren't these carpets wonderful—though they do make

it look awfully like a drawing-room ?   So do the chan- *
deliers.   But it's thrilling in spite of them."

"Mam'selle, he is the biggest mosque in the world,"
announced Moussa with triumph. "He is copied,
Mam'selle, from a mosque in Constantinople.   Napoleon, Mam'selle, he give that big chandelier."

"Did he ?   How nice of him !   It must have been
terribly expensive."

"This, ladies and gentlemen," explained Moussa with
a wave of his hand, " is the shrine of the Saint."

"Oh, yes," said Serena, bowing a little nervously to
the gaudy tomb on the left of the door as they passed
out again into the courtyard.

They went into the little palace, and laughed at the
delicious imitation clocks painted on the wall, and the
naïve ship frescoes.   Then stood for a long while at the
open windows, looking out over the city.

"What a lucky man Mahomet Ali was ! " said Serena
enviously.   "I hope he appreciated having this always
in front of him."

"It didn't have a particularly good effect on his
character," grunted Jeremy.

"Perhaps he wasn't a nice man to begin with," put
in Eve.

"He carried out the prettiest bit of treachery against
the Mamelukes."

"Who were they, Jeremy ? "

"The Emirs—governors of provinces—descendants
of Circassian slaves.   Mahomet Ali wanted to raise a
big sum of money one day, so he invited all the Mameluke
nobles to attend a banquet in the citadel.   Five hundred
of them accepted the invitation, and rode up the hill in
their most splendid clothes, all magnificently mounted
and attended by their followers.   When the festivities
came to an end they were escorted down the narrow
road from the citadel with Mahomet's bodyguard in
front and a squadron of Turkish soldiers behind.   At a
given signal the gates were closed, the bodyguard turned

round on the Mamelukes, who were unsuspicious and unprepared, the Turkish soldiers fired on them from the rear, and the Mameluke Emirs were wiped out for ever. Brutally murdered."

" All of them ? " asked Eve in horrified tones.

" Well, there is a legend that one escaped by jumping his horse over the edge of the cliff and riding away to safety, but I'm afraid there's not much truth in it. It's a pleasant thought that Mahomet Ali died a madman."

" Of all the dirty dogs ! " snorted Hugh.

" I'd like to live in this Palace, all the same," said Serena. " I should spend all day sitting by this window."

The whole of Cairo lay spread out at their feet, with its domes and minarets, its palaces and hovels; beyond it rose the Pyramids; on all sides the desert stretched endlessly away to the horizon, and the Nile, winding its way through the sand, bound desert and Pyramids and city together with a green curving ribbon.

.   .   .   .   .

Hugh faced the museum with comparative calm, and before they had been there many minutes he, as well as Eve and Serena, realised that it was like nothing they had ever seen, as treasure after treasure met their eyes. The statue of Khafra with the noble spread of the falcon's wings shielding his head, and all the dignity and grandeur of royalty in the serene beauty of the seated Pharaoh. The short, thick-set wooden statue of the Sheik-el-Beled, a contrast in plebeian sturdiness, and the crouching scribe whose eyes of alabaster and crystal gave him such a weird touch.

They walked slowly through one big room after another, pausing every now and then to note the amazing forward thrust of a kneeling woman making bread, or a Pharaoh pushing the remains of a broken boat before him; to look at the bed of Osiris with the brooding falcons at the head and the foot, and the tent of green and red check leather that had sheltered a queen's mummy. Hugh coveted a chair with arms carved in the likeness of a pair of leopards, their slinking prowl caught with the perfection of simplicity by the artist. They saw the painted floor from Akhnaton's palace and a tablet or stela of the Pharaoh worshipping, and another stela with a charming border of yellow figures on a grey-green ground; but it was the lovely Hathor Cow from Der-el-Bahr that they loved most. Eve vowed she had never seen anything more like a cow before—not even a real one—than this living, breathing creature whom the Egyptian sculptors had endowed with god-like attributes as well as life. The longer Eve gazed upon it the more she felt the charm of the gentle dignity and peace which enveloped this strange goddess of love, fidelity and maternity.

Presently they wandered upstairs to the hall of the mummies. There lay the coffins, row upon row, each with its brown shrivelled occupant, all so alike and yet so different, for each mummy retained in marvellous fashion the personality that had been his during life. With a curious sense of chill, Eve looked down at them—at their thin arms and the claw-like hands on which the nails had continued to grow after death. How strange to read those gorgeous names—names before which all their world had trembled—and then to look at their owners, helplessly exposed to the vulgar laughter or the pity of anybody who paid a small sum to stare at them. There was something tremendously impressive in those shrivelled corpses. In death, as in life, they seemed conscious of their high rank and their superb destiny.

Suddenly Eve's heart missed a beat. For an instant it seemed to her that some ghostly hand had stayed her steps. But it was a real hand—if a hand that has ceased to be flesh and blood for more than three thousand years can be called real—the shrivelled hand of Rameses the Great, lifted above the rim of the coffin, and pointing a menacing finger. He was the most wonderful of them all, she thought, although it was difficult to reconcile the rounded, boyish face she had learnt to know so well

EDFOR.

HORUS AT EDFOR.

at Thebes and Abu Simbel with the withered features,
arrogant, hooked nose and insignificant chin, of the man
who had been a god as well as a king; who had seen and
done everything, and who had lived to be so old that
he was wearied and surfeited because he had learnt that
there was nothing new under the sun. He looked more
asleep than dead, she decided, and she shuddered once
again as she turned back for a last look at that threaten-
ing, uplifted hand that still seemed to hold such power
in its shrunken fingers.

It was a relief to pass on to the gallery of Tutankhamen,
where everything glowed with colours as fresh and
beautiful as on the day they were painted. Never before
can so much beauty have been found in one place.
There was the king's throne of carved wood covered
with gold leaf and precious stones, that Jeremy showed
them must have been fashioned before the young
Pharaoh had thrown off the last traces of heresy, for the
solar disc of Tel el Amarna still decorated its back.
There were the two life-size statues of the king covered
with black resin, each with a staff in his extended hand,
and the lids and eyebrows, the sandals, staffs, necklaces
and other ornaments all of gold leaf. It was easy to
imagine how these striding figures had struck terror
into the thieves as they saw them guarding the inner
doorway.

Jeremy led them on from one treasure to another:
from the chairs and the chariots richly decorated with
gold leaf and inlay, and exquisitely painted, to the
canopic jars, the little chests so beautifully gilded, the
sticks whose handles were finely carved with the heads
of captives, the alabaster drinking-cup in the shape of a
lotus, and the couches, chairs, chests, beds and stools
inlaid with precious stones, blue and green, yellow and
white and red, or painted in the same vivid colours.
There was gold everywhere, laid on with the lavishness
of unbounded wealth and yet with the restraint of perfect
taste. Only on the mummy case of Tutankhamen did

R

the precious metal seem almost too new, too shining. The face of the king, round and plump with youth, the whole figure, the sacred serpent and Horus, who reared their heads upon his forehead—all were of pure gold inlaid with coloured enamels.

" All these things are supposed to be rather after the best period, to be too elaborate, and a little debased," remarked Jeremy. " But I call that hyper-criticism. Personally, I think they're as near perfection as makes no matter. Anyway, it's the greatest treasure trove of our life-time."

" I don't know when I've enjoyed myself so much," sighed Eve rapturously. " Oh, Jeremy, it's been the loveliest afternoon we've ever spent."

Jeremy looked pleased.

" If you and I could squeeze in another visit to-morrow, would you care to come again ? " he asked.

" I'd adore to," cried Eve; and all sorts of foolish ideas and hopes rushed into her head.

And then they turned round a corner and walked straight into the arms of Tony and Isobel Page.

CHAPTER XXIX

THE SPHINX

Eve wanted nothing less than to visit the Sphinx and the Pyramids with the Pages. However, as Jeremy and Tony had fixed it all up at the museum, there was nothing left but to submit as cheerfully as she could, or invent the world's worst headache and stay at home alone. Eve told herself as she dressed for the dinner at Mena House that disaster was imminent. Jeremy and Isobel would wander off by themselves; and she would be left with Tony. It was hard enough to avoid getting engaged with a full moon at home. It must be next door to impossible with a desert and a sphinx thrown in. She should stick like a leech to Serena. Even the most determined American couldn't propose in front of a third person. But why, oh why, couldn't she have fallen in love with Tony instead of with Jeremy? She was sure he was a great deal nicer. He never laughed at her or treated her like a silly child, as Jeremy often did.

At dinner, seated between Mr. Page and Tony, she cheered up a little. Both father and son appeared to entertain a flattering opinion of her knowledge of Egyptian matters, and as Jeremy was at the far end of the table, she was able to prattle of Cheops and Khafra without fear of meeting his amused glance.

"Why, you know as much as the guide-books," exclaimed Mr. Page admiringly; "and I'm sure you put it very much more plainly."

"Oh, no!" replied Eve, a picture of charming modesty. "It's really Jeremy who explains everything to us."

"Ah! he's a clever fellow."

"We took so long sailing up the Nile, too, that we had weeks and weeks with nothing to do but read; our dahabeah got so full of books there was hardly room to move. At one time we thought no people could have read so much about Egypt and seen so little—that was when we had seen nothing but the tombs of Beni Hassan. I really began to be afraid we should have to leave Egypt without seeing the Sphinx or the Pyramids at all. As it is, we shall only see them by moonlight. I should have liked to have seen them in the daytime as well."

"Won't you come again to-morrow?" asked Tony eagerly. "I can get a car and take you out there any time you like."

"It's very kind of you, but I don't think I shall be able to manage it," replied Eve, determined that if she escaped being proposed to to-night, she was certainly not going to run the risk again to-morrow. "It will be our last whole day in Cairo, you know, and we are supposed to be going to the Azhar mosque."

"Is that something extra special?" inquired Mr. Page.

"Yes, though Jeremy says it's nothing particular in the way of architecture. But it's the university, and you see thousands of students, from quite tiny boys to old men with grey beards, all squatting in groups round the courtyard, chanting the Koran. Then I want to go to the mosques of Sultan Hassan and Ibn Tulun, and the Coptic churches, Abu Seyfen, and Abu Sergeh where Jeremy says the Holy Family are supposed to have lived on the flight into Egypt.

"Now I think the way you get the hang of these names is wonderful," exclaimed Mr. Page. "If I try and get my tongue round them no one can even guess which of them I'm after. They are as great a puzzle to me as the Sphinx herself."

"Jeremy says there isn't any riddle about the Sphinx at all. He actually has the impertinence to pretend she's a man! Did you ever hear anything so absurd?"

" It's a pretty revolutionary idea to anyone of my generation," Mr. Page admitted, " but Tony here sprung it on me the first time we saw her."

" Do you believe it, too, then ? " asked Eve reproachfully.

Tony collapsed instantly.

" Well, no," he stammered, while he decided for the hundredth time that hazel eyes with green in them were the most beautiful in the world. " I'm not at all sure that I do. After all, Egyptologists can make mistakes like everybody else, can't they ? She certainly looks like a woman. I believe she is," he concluded, gaining in firmness as he went on.

" Who did you tell me it was supposed to be ? " asked his father tactlessly.

" Oh, they fixed on one of the Pharaohs that happened to be on the spot at the time," said Tony hurriedly. " But those old fellows were always boning each other's monuments and pretending they were their own. I don't believe a word of it."

" It's supposed to be Khafra," said Eve, " who had the rock carved into the shape of a lion and put his own head on it. But if all the historians in the world said it was true, I wouldn't listen to them. The Sphinx has been a woman for thousands of years, and it's ridiculous to try and change her now. Besides, who is going to take any interest in a statue of a Pharaoh ? Especially as Khafra didn't even build the biggest pyramid—only the middle one."

After dinner they sat on the terrace in front of the hotel and drank their coffee and liqueurs while they waited for the moon to rise. It was still fairly dark when Moussa came for them. Eve insisted on riding a camel, so Tony chose to ride one too. If Eve had preferred a boa-constrictor, Tony, Jeremy imagined, would have mounted one with an equal degree of cheerfulness. Mrs. Page and Serena set off in a sand-cart and the rest on donkeys.

Two Arabs, white shrouded figures, ran up to Eve, crying, " Tell fortune, lady ! Tell you very good fortune ! "

But Eve was in no mood for fortune-tellers. In the warm darkness behind her she could hear the soft drawl of Isobel Page and the deeper tones of Jeremy, and she urged her camel impatiently on. The animal's feet made no sound on the sand, and no one spoke. Suddenly the Great Pyramid loomed high above them, a dark, stupendous mass against the still dark sky, the last and the greatest of the Seven Wonders of the World, on which the tourists from ancient Greece and Rome had carved their names, after the manner of tourists from time immemorial.

Past the other pyramids, through a world of dim, giant shadows, Eve's camel bore to the left, and she dismounted in the middle of a group of waiting Arabs. It grew lighter every moment as Tony and Eve walked forward to the edge of the deep hollow where the Sphinx lay.

Alone with Tony, sitting in the warm sand, Eve gazed at the huge face with its battered features that had stirred the mind of man through the centuries. There she lay, this monster in stone, bathed in the silver light, aloof, mysterious, the most wonderful of all the wonderful things that Eve had seen in Egypt. She would like to lie between those great paws—at the foot of the pyramids—where legend said Mary had laid her little son to sleep on the flight into Egypt. Then perhaps she might learn from the Sphinx the age-old secret of her wisdom and her peace.

But Tony was close beside her and the others not more than twenty yards away. And now Tony was beginning, in his warm, eager fashion, to tell her all the things she so terribly wanted not to hear.

" I want to tell you something," said Eve quickly— " something very important, that nobody else knows."

" But I want to tell you something very **important**,

too," he urged—"at least it's terribly important to me."

"Let me tell you mine first. Please, please do, because I'm so unhappy, and I want to tell you about it before things get worse still."

"Good Heavens! Of course you shall tell me, and I'll help you, whatever it is."

"You can't. Nobody can. I don't think I deserve any help either."

"You—of course you do!"

"It's not very easy to talk about, though." Eve's voice shook a little. "But there are two men at home—there are more than two really, but these two more particularly than the others," she added rather incoherently, "who want to marry me. And it's my own fault that they want to, only I didn't know then the harm I was doing. I didn't indeed."

"Of course you didn't," said Tony gently. "It wouldn't matter what you did or didn't do, you couldn't stop men falling in love with you. You're so sweet."

"Oh, I'm not," cried Eve. "That's where you're all wrong. I can see now that I've always been utterly selfish. I never thought about them—the men, I mean; I liked them all, and I liked the wonderful time they gave me. But I never knew, I never even guessed for a moment, how I must have hurt them . . . until I got hurt myself."

Tony didn't speak; he sat quite still beside her.

"There was one man," Eve continued, "who was different from the rest—who never seemed to take any interest in love and all that sort of thing. I think perhaps this annoyed me a little, for although I never consciously thought of anything happening, I can see now that I did instinctively feel it would be amusing to attract him ever so little, if only just to shake him out of his attitude of taking me for granted. I don't know if I can make you see what I mean? I didn't flirt with him. You might as well try to flirt with the Sphinx, I should think." Eve gave a bitter little laugh. "But I tried to make him realise I was there, and a real person, not just the child he always made me feel. Well, I didn't succeed. What happened was that I found I was in love with him, and he didn't care two straws about me; and I shall never, even if I live to be a thousand, be able to love anyone else. So you see I'm not sweet at all, I'm horrid—and I deserve everything I've got."

Tony was silent for so long that Eve began to wonder if he had understood anything of what she had told him.

"I think it's wonderful of you to have told me this," he said at last. "It must have been horribly difficult for you, and I know why you did it. It was because you knew I was going to ask you to marry me, and you wanted to save me the pain of being turned down. And you call yourself selfish! Why, you're thinking of me at this moment instead of yourself. I can't imagine how any man in his senses can fail to love you, especially if he knows he's so stupendously fortunate as to be loved by you."

"Oh, but he doesn't know," cried Eve. "It's the very last thing in the world that would ever enter his head—and he never will know, either. I should die of shame if he ever found out. I've never breathed a word to a soul except you."

Tony laid his hand on hers for a moment.

"It's quite safe with me. But Eve, dear, I can't bear that you should be unhappy."

"Oh, I've made you unhappy too; and now I know how terrible it feels, I can't bear that either. Before, I never used to mind hurting other people, especially men. It always seemed to me they fell in love so easily that it couldn't hurt them very much. Now I know, I shall spend all my life trying never to let anyone love me again."

"You won't be able to help it."

"Oh yes, I shall," said Eve wisely. "Men always know when a woman isn't interested in that sort of thing.

They feel it somehow, without exactly knowing what it is."

"Look here, can't I do anything to help you? With this other fellow, I mean."

"Oh, Tony, you are good! You make me feel worse than ever. Please don't."

He gave her hand a little squeeze.

"I'm not pretending it doesn't hurt. It does. But far the worse thing is seeing you unhappy. I should like to go and take hold of that man and knock his stupid head against a wall and say: 'You infernal idiot, don't you know Eve loves you?'"

"There's nothing to be done," said Eve, who couldn't quite picture Jeremy allowing Tony to take liberties with his head—or his heart either. "But thank you ever so much, Tony dear, for wanting to try. I suppose this has happened to lots of other girls, and I shall get over it in time, like all the rest. You will too, won't you, Tony? After all, you've only known me a few weeks."

"I loved you the first moment I saw you. Time has nothing to do with it," declared Tony, convinced that this was the solitary passion of a life-time. Nor had Eve's announcement that she would recover carried any conviction to either of them. They were too young, both of them, to believe such a thing possible. Indeed, the mere idea of recovery was slightly revolting. They preferred to go through life bravely concealing their broken hearts.

"Perhaps," suggested Tony eventually, "years and years hence you may decide that you can bring yourself to marry a man who loves you, even if you can never care for him."

"But I should be middle-aged," objected Eve, "and quite plain."

"That's impossible. And, anyway, I should only love you all the more."

Eve felt a little doubtful about this, though she

reminded him that as friends they could support and comfort one another through the dreary waste of years that stretched before them.

The next instant a burst of jazz music from some Italian tourists shattered the peace of the moonlight scene, and Mr. Page called out that it was time to leave. Hugh and Serena sauntered up, and Eve recognised, from the look on Serena's face, that she and Hugh had been saying the sort of things to one another that people were supposed to have finished saying on their honeymoon.

"Where are Mr. Vaughan and Isobel?" inquired Mrs. Page.

"Here," replied Jeremy.

Eve cast a swift glance at Isobel. No, she didn't look in the least like Serena. She looked rather sphinx-like. Eve looked past her at Jeremy, and met his gaze directed full on herself. Far from looking happy, he appeared unusually grim. Could it be possible he had proposed to Isobel and been refused? No! No woman in her senses could refuse Jeremy!

To such ignominious depths had Eve descended!

Turning sadly away to find her camel, she looked back for a last, wistful glance at the Sphinx. There she lay on her couch of sand, unheeding and untouched by the joys or sufferings of the human pigmies who came and gazed upon her and went away again, without ever learning the secret that lay hidden behind her stony brow.

CHAPTER XXX

HATHOR

It was fitting, Eve thought, that the rain should come down in torrents on their last day in Egypt, when everything was so hopeless and miserable. Only one incident had cheered her. On going to her cabin to wash her hands before lunch, she had found on her pillow a strange and ghastly bracelet, composed of coloured pebbles set in silver. Beside it lay a type-written letter.

MLLE. WENTWORTH,
    Dahabeah *Isis*,
      CAIRO.
        LADY,
            I beg you kindly to pardon me addressing you this letter. I am a poor man, my hand is quite short to offer you any valuable present, but this very, very poor thing, which I am enclosing with this letter, trusting that you will kindly accept it.

I ask God the Almighty to keep you from evil and grant you a long, long life.

Your Obedient Servant,
AHMED MOUSSA.

Serena found a similar piece of jewellery and a similar equally touching epistle on her bed. Moussa could only read and write Arabic letters, so he must have sought the help of a public letter-writer. Dear, dear Moussa!

In spite of this, lunch was a depressing affair.   Jeremy
and Hugh talked business all the time, Serena was gently
reminiscent and Eve herself almost completely silent.
She did suggest that the rain needn't prevent their going
to the Coptic churches and mosques that she wanted to
see, but nobody even took the trouble to answer her.
The moment lunch was over, Hugh and Jeremy went
off for a final settling-up with Mr. Johnson.   They
were also to get the cash needed for the lavish tips that
everybody on board was to receive, from the reis down
to the pariah filterman.   Moussa's reward was to be so
handsome as to soar into the grander regions of a
cheque.

Serena went to lie down in her cabin, and was soon
fast asleep under the eiderdown.   Eve looked out of
the saloon window at the rain and wondered how on
earth she was to get through the dreary afternoon.

If only it had been fine, Jeremy might have taken her
to the Zoo.   He knew her passion for Zoos, and he
had told her that this was one of the prettiest.   What a
lot of jolly mornings they had spent together at the
London Zoo !   Years hence she might meet Jeremy
and Isobel there, by accident, on a Sunday afternoon.
All the best fathers took their children to see the lions
fed on Sunday afternoons, and Jeremy would make a
" best father," Eve knew.   " But I mightn't exist now,
for all he cares," she thought sadly.   " He's hardly
spoken a word to me since last night."

Suddenly she felt she couldn't bear to stop indoors a
moment longer.   Since nobody loved her or cared two
straws what happened to her, she would give them all
the slip and go out alone.   Jeremy had half-promised
to take her to the museum again for a last look round ;
but it was obvious that he hadn't the smallest intention
of doing it, so she would go without him.   There were
lots of things she wanted to see again.   Hathor the
Cow—goddess of love, for one, whom hundreds and
thousands of women must have visited when she was in

Hatshepsut's temple at Der-el-Bahri, all those centuries ago. Perhaps she still had some strange power of comfort left? After all, quite a lot of people at home half believed in wishing-wells and things.

Eve hurriedly pulled on a hat and coat, picked up a little bag with money and the other necessities of life inside it, and was ready to start. Then she hesitated. " Perhaps I'd better leave a note for them," she thought, " though it's more than they deserve, after neglecting me like this. Still, they might make a fuss if they came home and found I'd vanished." So she tore a sheet of notepaper off the writing pad and scribbled in pencil: " I have been carried off by a sheik. Expect me back when you see me.—EVE."

Mahomed seemed a trifle startled when she appeared on the lower deck, and tried to suggest, in his limited English, that she should take two of the men with her.

" But I'm only going to the Museum, Mahomed," she explained, waving him aside, " and I will take a carriage there and back; so nothing can possibly happen to me."

The rain had stopped at last, and the grey sky was growing lighter as Eve walked briskly along the gangway and up the garden path.

By the time she reached the Museum the sun was actually shining, and two sweepers were collecting the rain-water out of one of the large puddles in their cupped hands, and dropping it into a bucket.

The big Museum was very empty, doubtless because no steamer load of tourists had arrived in Cairo that day, and Eve wandered about for a long time without meeting more than two or three people. She stood for several minutes by the dark statue of Khafra with his brooding falcon. What real individuals those great Pharaohs were to her now, whose names she had hardly heard before she came to Egypt! The shadowy Menes; Zozer, the first great builder in stone; the hero of the Egyptian legends, Snefru; Cheops, who had built one of the Seven Wonders of the World; the fighter,

Sesostris; Amenemhet III, wisest of kings; the gallant Queen Hatshepsut; the third Amenhotep, the Napoleon of Egypt; Akhnaton, the heretic and idealist; the strong Horemheb; the stately Seti, the Good Shepherd; Rameses the Great, the builder of Abu Simbel, and the third Rameses, the warrior of Medinet Abou, with whose death the splendour of Egypt had passed away forever. The personalities of each and all of them were now as distinct to Eve as the Henrys and Edwards and Charleses of her own country.

She wandered upstairs for a last look at the mummies. She gazed for a long while at the regal dignity of Seti, and again the menacing finger of Rameses stirred her strangely. When she passed on to the Tutankhamen room her troubles began. A party of young Egyptian students had come noisily in, and Eve soon realised that a girl of her type could not wander about in an Eastern city as comfortably as she could at home. At first she pretended to be too absorbed to notice them, but when they began to comment on her looks in fluent English she grew so uncomfortable and so angry that she asked an apathetic custodian the way to the main entrance, hoping by this subtle device to give the objectionable young men the slip. She walked away so quickly that the two who had followed her to the top of the stairs decided to give up the chase, and with burning cheeks and fury in her heart, Eve took shelter in the small, empty room of Hathor.

" It's a beastly world," she told the gentle cow, " and Jeremy would only say it served me right for coming here alone. Not that I shall tell him about it. For one thing, he doesn't care; I don't suppose he'd mind if every horrid young student in Egypt was rude to me."

The quiet goddess looked straight in front of her with serene, gentle dignity. " She looks so kind and good," thought Eve, " I wonder if she ever helped any of the poor women who came and prayed to her all those centuries ago ? I'm sure she did. But she can't help me now. Nobody loves me except poor Tony— not counting my family, of course—and I don't love him; at least not in that sort of way. I love Jeremy, and Jeremy loves Isobel Page."

Eve's eyes grew suspiciously moist as she turned these sentences round and round in her poor little head.

Suddenly a well-known footstep startled her, and before she had time to find the minute handkerchief that had hidden itself away under the powder-puff, lip-stick and all the other trifles in her handbag, Jeremy was standing beside her.

" Hallo ! " said Eve in a small voice, " what are you doing here ? "

Jeremy took one swift glance at her face and then gazed hard at the cow.

" That's exactly what I was going to ask you. I found your note when we got back from Cook's. You shouldn't have come here alone. Not that anything could happen to you, of course, but somebody might have annoyed you. Have they ? " he added sharply as he saw her blush.

" Only just the last two minutes. Some students. But I pretended I was going out, and that seemed to stop them."

" Why didn't you bring Mahomed or a couple of the men with you ? " asked Jeremy irritably. " They wouldn't have been in your way."

" I wanted to be alone. I'm so tired of never being able to walk about without somebody following me. It's as bad as being royalty. I know now how sick they must get of it, poor dears."

" Well, I'm sorry, but I'm going to follow you about now. That is, unless you've had enough of this stupid place and are ready to come home ? "

" I haven't had enough of it, and I shan't come home until I want to, and it's quite unnecessary for you to sacrifice yourself and stay here too. I'm perfectly capable of looking after myself, thank you."

" Don't be childish ! "

" How dare you call me childish ! I'm not ! I'm every bit as sensible as your precious Isobel Page."

Jeremy raised his eyebrows. " Is there any need to bring Isobel into this charming discussion ? "

" That means you don't think me as sensible."

" I do not."

" Then why do you bother about me ? "

" Will you stop being silly and come home at once ? "

" No, I won't."

Jeremy shrugged his shoulders. "My dear child, what is the matter with you ? " he asked, longing to give her a good shaking.

Eve didn't answer. Apparently she was absorbed in the beauties of the Hathor cow. Jeremy swore under his breath. Suddenly something pulled him up with a jerk. He saw two large tears fall from beneath Eve's hat and splash down on to the floor.

" Eve, look at me," he commanded.

" Shan't," muttered Eve.

Jeremy put out his hand, took hold of her chin and gently but firmly turned her face up to his. Her eyelashes lay on her cheeks in a long curve, and one after another the large tears ran down her poor, pale little face, and fell on to his hand.

" Eve, dear, for God's sake tell me what's the matter. Eve, has that young blighter Page treated you badly ? He can't have. If he isn't head over ears in love with you, I'll never believe my own eyes again. Eve, do stop crying, for the Lord's sake."

" Can't stop now I've started," sobbed Eve as the tears came faster and faster.

" Eve, I've never seen you cry before, and I simply can't bear it. Can't you tell me what's the matter ? We've always been such friends. You know whatever you say will be perfectly safe with me." He drew her into a corner where she might escape notice if anyone came in, and he caught something like " The one person I can't tell."

" Then tell Serena. Only do stop crying and dry your eyes."

But it was no use, and Jeremy grew desperate. Here he was, alone in a museum with a girl who appeared capable of crying for a thousand years. He looked at Eve's down-bent face, her quivering mouth and her alarmingly increasing stream of tears, and he knew that at last he must face what he had been trying to ignore for the last two months. He drew her to him and held her close, and Eve laid her wet cheek against his coat and continued sobbing.

" Eve "—Jeremy bent his head down to the little green hat—" Eve darling, do stop. I can't bear it, I love you so much."

There was a sudden silence, except for the little involuntary gasps that came from Eve. Jeremy felt her heart beating quickly against him. Then she lifted her head and looked up at him, and he held her a little closer, as though he were afraid she might run away.

" What did you say ? " she asked in a shaky voice.

" I said I loved you. I know it's perfectly hopeless. You are going to marry Tony Page, of course. I meant never to let you know. I shouldn't have if you hadn't broken me down like this." His mouth turned up at one corner a little wryly. " I am only another scalp to add to your collection, but such as it is, it's yours, my dear."

" Oh, Jeremy ! " Eve was gazing up at him as though she couldn't believe her ears. " I thought you were in love with Isobel. Serena and I were both quite sure you were. At least, now I come to think of it, perhaps Serena didn't think so. Perhaps it was only me."

" In love with Isobel ? What on earth made you think of such a thing ? The idea never entered my

s

head, nor hers either, for the good reason that my brother Dan is in love with her."

" *Dan?* "

" Yes. She turned him down once, but she's made up her mind to marry him since she's been here."

" But, Jeremy, why didn't you tell me? I've been so horribly jealous. I've hated every moment since she first came because I thought you loved her more than me. You always seemed so pleased to see her, and you had such a lot to say to each other all the time."

" Of course we had. I think a lot of Isobel, and I was doing my best for Dan. The poor boy adores her, and they'd suit each other down to the ground. She wanted to talk to me of Dan, and she did. We hardly ever talked of anything else."

" Oh, dear," sighed Eve, dropping her head down again to the wet patch she had made on Jeremy's shoulder. " Oh, dear! What a little fool I've been! "

Jeremy looked at her with a peculiar expression on his face, half-undecided and half-determined.

" Eve," he said after a little pause, " let's get the thing straight while we're at it. You made a mistake about Isobel. Will you tell me the truth about Tony? He has proposed to you, hasn't he? "

Eve twisted one of Jeremy's coat buttons nervously round and round. " Well—in a sort of a way. But honestly, Jeremy "—she looked up at him earnestly— " I did try and stop him. I told him . . ."

" Well," questioned Jeremy rather shortly, " what did you tell him? "

" I told him," murmured Eve in a voice so low that he could hardly hear it, " I told him I was in love with somebody else."

There was a silence.

" Go on! " ordered Jeremy.

" And I told him," sniffed Eve, for the tears were beginning again, " that the man "—sniff—" didn't care two straws about me "—sniff.

" And whom were you talking about ? " asked Jeremy in a curiously level tone.

" You, of course, you silly idiot ! " cried Eve, digging her fist vigorously into his hard chest. " You might have known it, if you weren't so horribly proud and superior."

Jeremy held her firmly in front of him.

" Eve, is it true ? " he asked. " If you're playing the fool with me, I'll . . ."

" Can't you see it's true ? " she cried, looking him straight in the face, although she knew that her eyes were heavy with crying and that her nose wanted blowing. " And I do think it's hard," she thought, " that one's eyes can't cry without one's nose joining in." But Jeremy only saw the truth that looked at him out of her wet eyes, and he took her in his arms again and kissed her as she had never been kissed before.

" We've both been fools," he said, " but I've been far the bigger one."

" You have," agreed Eve, instinctively beginning to establish their new relationship on the proper footing. " But, oh dear, where is my hanky ? " And she started frantically hunting in her bag as well as she could in her cramped position.

" Here's mine," said Jeremy, pushing a large, clean, silk handkerchief into her hands.

" But I want more than that. I want my powder puff and my mirror."

" Good God ! "

" Well, of course I do. This is the first time I've ever been proposed to looking like this. I don't mind. It gives you such a feeling of security. If you can bear me like this, I feel you can put up with anything."

" Don't you make any such mistake."

" Of course I don't mean that I should ever let you see me with cold cream on my face or with my hair in curling-pins—not that I ever use them, but I've often read warnings to young wives about them. Oh,

Jeremy ! ''—Eve paused a moment in the work of repairs—" what an extraordinary thought ! Have you really asked me to marry you ? ''

" Not in so many words," admitted Jeremy, " but that's my intention."

" How funny ! " Eve gave a little giggle, " but how lovely too," she added enthusiastically. " And how nice to think that now I can be fond of Isobel Page ! You know, I've always wanted to like her, only I hated her so. Why, we shall be kind of sisters, shan't we ? Are you sure she's going to marry Dan ? "

" Quite sure."

" I must say, I don't think she has treated him at all well," observed Eve, with a slight primness that tickled Jeremy enormously.

" That—from you—Eve ! "

" Jeremy, I have never treated you badly. I have hardly even flirted with you—in the ordinary sense, anyway. But Isobel seems to have kept poor Dan dangling at the end of a string for months and months."

" There are always two ways of looking at a thing. She told me she had come to Egypt to think it over. That has been done before, hasn't it ? "

Eve had the grace to blush. " Poor Harold and Hubert," she said a little hurriedly. " But I'm quite sure, poor things, that they've forgotten all about me now. Of course if *that* was what Isobel was doing it's quite understandable."

Jeremy laughed. " Oh, Eve, what fun you're going to be and what fun we're going to have ! "

" Yes, that's a nice way of looking at it, isn't it ? I expect we shall fight like mad, but everything will be so amusing, and that's what really matters."

She drew her lip-stick carefully across her mouth and looked at the result with her head on one side.

" Jeremy," she said, suddenly transferring her glance to his face, " did you mean to propose to me when you came here this afternoon ? "

" No."

" Oh ! Did you want to propose to me ? "

" No."

" Oh ! How disgraceful ! How perfectly disgusting of you ! " Eve put away her lip-stick mechanically, her eyes growing larger and larger as she thought the matter out. " Then why have you ? "

" Because when the irresistible force meets the immovable object, something has to happen."

" Good gracious ! Which am I ? "

" The irresistible force, of course."

" But why didn't you want to propose to me ? I can't understand it," exclaimed Eve with engaging candour. " Lots of people have wanted to—most people, in fact. I mean, all the kind of men that do propose."

" That's just the kind I don't belong to."

" Do you mean to tell me, really and truly, that I'm the first girl you've ever asked to marry you ? "

" You are, and you'll be the last."

" I don't quite like the emphasis you put on that . . . but it's all very thrilling ! " She looked up at him a little wistfully, " Are you glad you've done it, or are you "—she caught her breath a moment—" are you sorry ? "

He gave her a little reassuring squeeze.

" I'm damn glad. Do you remember, Eve, our first walk in Egypt, before breakfast, that morning in Cairo ? "

" Yes, very well."

" Do you remember my telling you I hoped you always got what you wanted, and you asked me if there was anything I wanted very particularly ? "

" Yes. And you were most mysterious. You said there was something you had that you wanted to keep, and you wouldn't tell me what it was. And you said you hoped you never would have to tell me. I was devoured with curiosity, but after a bit I forgot about it till now. What was it, Jeremy ? "

Jeremy looked at her as she stood in the circle of his arm, her lovely, eager face turned up to his.

" My freedom," he said.

" Oh, Jeremy, and do you feel that you've lost it now ? How awful ! But you haven't, my dear— indeed, indeed you haven't. I know I often talk a lot of rubbish, and pretend I shall be a difficult person to be married to, but I shan't, really."

Jeremy bent his head and kissed her mouth.

" Damn ! " he said a moment later. " All your beastly lip-stick's come off."

" Bother ! " exclaimed Eve. " Now I shall have to put it on all over again."

They went out of the Museum together into the pale shining of the sunlight that had followed the rain. And as she went down the steps, Eve gave a thought to the very different emotion with which she had ascended them a brief hour before. Again, but now mighty and blurred as in a too rapid film, the familiar gods of Egypt and their loves flitted through her imagination.

Poor Hatshepsut, such a marvel, so valorous and so rich in state-craft ! Had she known how to make a man love her ? Nefertiti, the lovely and enigmatic, whose end no one knew. The luminous, foolish, inspired Akhnaton, that splendid failure. And Rameses the Great, whose uplifted finger had seemed, such a short while ago, still to carry power and menace.

Poor things ! Poor, dear things !

All dead; and not walking with Jeremy down into a sunlit afternoon with all of life before them.